Forever You

By

Sandi Lynn

Acknowledgments

Thank you to my husband for all the endless and countless hours I spent writing this book. I want to thank you for doing the laundry, cleaning up the house, and never complaining when I stopped cooking dinner. It's been a tough road trying to get this book finished with working full-time and you stuck by me and helped out. Now that I work part-time, I promise I'll cook more! Thank you for your love and support. I love you!

To my 3 beautiful teenage girls who never thought their mom would become a USA Today Best Selling Author. There's nothing you can't do! Follow your dreams and make them happen! I'll be with you every step of the way. I love you girls!

To my editor Lucy! A huge thank you for all your help and hard work in making this book possible for release. I never could have done it without you! Big hugs and kisses! I look forward to working with you on Forever Us and all my future books. You rock girlfriend!

To a few of my author friends who have been there for me and have given me help and great advice along my journey of becoming an author: Beth Rinyu, Dawn Martens, Aleatha Romig, Saoching Molly Moose, and Adriane Leigh. Thank you again for all your help! It's a pleasure knowing each and every one of you!

I dedicate this book to my Mom

Table Of Contents

Prologue

I met Amanda through a friend. I was 18 years old, and she had just turned 17. She was a cute girl with long brown hair, a nice curvy body, and tits that were to die for. I could tell she liked me right from the start. We were at a party the night we met, and we sat near the bonfire. Amanda and I bonded that night, and I had also learned of her twin sister named Ashlyn. We talked for what seemed like hours about our families, goals, and dreams. I took her home, and we exchanged phone numbers. Little did I know, this new relationship would change my life forever.

We went out at least three times a week, usually on Fridays, Saturdays, and Sundays. When I wasn't busy working with my father over at Black Enterprises, I would occasionally stop by Amanda's house during the week and spend a couple of hours with her. Things started out great for us. I really liked Amanda. The sex was great and there was a lot of it. Everything was good until I started talking about going away to college. She would freak out and make me promise her to call her every day and that I wouldn't look at other girls. Every time I would try to go out with my friends, she would get upset and start to cry. She accused me of not wanting to spend time with her and that I put others before her. I tried to explain that I wanted to see my friends every once in a while and that it's not healthy spending every waking moment together. Amanda disagreed and frequently accused me of cheating on her if I didn't answer her calls right away.

I felt as though I was being suffocated. I couldn't have any time to myself, and her behavior was erratic. She told me every day how much she loved me and that she could never live without me. She said we'd be together forever and that nothing would ever separate us. I didn't love Amanda. I liked her, but I wasn't in love with her. I wasn't even sure what love was. The day I tried to end the relationship, Amanda told me that she might be pregnant. A million horrible thoughts ran through my mind, and I couldn't see myself being tied to this girl for the rest of my life. Luckily, the pregnancy turned out to be a lie. I had a long talk with her sister Ashlyn; she told me that Amanda was fine and that I just needed to be patient with her.

I finally reached the breaking point one day when I went to dinner with a group of friends. Amanda found me and caused a scene in the middle of the restaurant. I took her outside to try and calm her down, but nothing worked. I didn't have feelings for her anymore, and I could barely stand to look at her. I broke up with her. I had told her that I'd had enough, that it was over between us, and to never call me again. I left her standing on the street crying. I had no choice; she was crazy, and she needed help.

I received a call from Amanda two days later; she wanted me to come over to talk. As far as I was concerned, there was nothing to talk about. I broke up with her, and I didn't want to discuss it anymore. She cried and begged me to come over. She said that she had one last thing to talk to me about, and then she would accept that we were over. She told me to wait about an hour because she wasn't home yet. An hour had passed when I pulled up in her driveway. I knocked on the door, but there was no answer. I knew she was home because her car was in the driveway. Noticing the door was unlocked, I pushed it opened, walked in, and looked around. I called her name, but didn't get a response. I slowly walked up the stairs and stopped in front of her closed bedroom door. I put my hand on the knob and slowly turned it as I pushed the door open. I gasped at the sight that was before me, Amanda lying on the floor in a pool of blood, and a razor blade lying next to her. I ran over and put my arms under her. "Why did you do it

Amanda? Why?" I sobbed as I held her lifeless body in my arms, covered in blood and shaking, as the tears wouldn't stop pouring from my eyes. My heart was racing, and my body went numb. Suddenly, I saw a shadow in the doorway. I looked up as Ashlyn knelt down beside me and stared at her twin sister.

"Amanda, how could you do this to me?!" she screamed at her. "We had so many plans. We were going to backpack in Europe together," Ashlyn cried as she hovered over Amanda's body and shook her by her shoulders. I pushed her away and yelled at her to stop.

Ashlyn slowly got up from the floor and walked over to the dresser where she found a letter from Amanda. She picked up the piece of paper and looked at me with uneasiness in her eyes. I slowly released Amanda, stood up, and walked over to Ashlyn where I took the piece of paper from her.

Connor,

You are the love of my life. I've never felt this way before about someone. You gave me hope. A hope I needed to get through life. When we're apart, I'm empty inside and lonely. I thought you were the one who was going to save me from myself. I love you more than life itself, but if I can't have you, and we can't be together, then I no longer want to live this life. I'm sorry it has to be this way, but you have no one to blame but yourself. I couldn't go on without you in my life. Please tell Ashlyn I love her and that I'm sorry.

Amanda

I stood there with the note in my hand while Ashlyn sobbed. I walked over to comfort her as she held up her finger and spoke to me in a harsh tone.

"It's all your fault that my sister's dead. All you had to do was love her and she'd still be here!"

That day changed my life forever.

Chapter 1

My eyes flew open. My heart was rapidly beating with fear. My bed sheets were soaked as I was drenched in sweat from the nightmare that constantly plagued my nights. I looked over at the clock sitting on the nightstand, and it was exactly 3:00 am. I got out of bed and walked to the bathroom. I had a hard time catching my breath as I leaned over the sink and then looked at myself in the mirror. I turned on the cold water and splashed my face, taking in a deep breath and closing my eyes.

I never told anyone why Amanda killed herself. I've kept this secret buried within me for the past twelve years. The only other person who knew was her sister, Ashlyn. She promised that she wouldn't speak of it because she didn't want people to think her sister would harm herself over a guy. I rubbed my face as I walked over and sat on the edge of the bed. I picked up my cell phone from the night stand and saw a text message from Ashlyn.

"Connor, thank you for tonight. As usual, you completely satisfied me. I look forward to seeing you again for another round of tantalizing sex!"

I sighed and placed the phone back on the nightstand. I got up, put on my running clothes, and headed out the door for a run. Running always cleared my head, especially after having the nightmares. I ended up running four miles in Central Park. Once my head was clear and I could think straight, I made a mental note to call Dr. Peters. It's been a while since I've seen him, and I think it's time that I start going back for some therapy sessions. I took out my cell phone, thumbed through my contacts, and decided to text Sarah.

"I need a stress release. Are you up for it?"

"Hi to you too, Connor. Do you realize its 5:15 am? Sure, I'm game."

"Good, meet me at the penthouse in 30 minutes."

"I can be there in 10."

"No, I said 30. I need to shower first."

"Yum, Connor, can I join you?"

"No thanks, I'd rather shower alone. 30 minutes, and don't be late."

I met Sarah through a business associate. Being newly divorced, she was more than willing to have casual sex with no strings attached.

I ran back to the penthouse and hopped in the shower to wash the sweat from my body before I fucked her. I stepped out of the shower with a towel wrapped around my waist. I walked into the bedroom, and she was already lying on the bed ready and waiting for me.

"Drop that towel and get over here before I change my mind," she smiled.

I dropped the towel on the floor and walked towards the bed. "I promise you aren't going anywhere until I've fucked you every which way, Sarah."

"Now that's one promise that I know you can keep," she grinned.

Rough sex is all I know. It's all these women want, and who am I to complain? Keeping it quick and rough is the best stress relief for me, especially after a long hard day at the office or whenever the occasion arises.

"Thanks, you may leave now," I told her.

"Connor, it's 6:30 am, so how about some coffee together before I go?"

I walked over to her as she was lying on the bed with only the sheet covering her naked body. I looked into her brown eyes.

"You know the rules, Sarah, now get dressed and go. I have to take a quick shower and head to the office."

She got up from the bed. "Whatever, Connor, it's just coffee for fuck sake. Oh, and another thing, I'm going out of town for a couple of weeks, so don't bother calling me for another stress relief."

***

Some people often say that I'm too young to be the CEO of Black Enterprises and that the pressures and demands will ultimately destroy me. As far as I'm concerned, I've already been destroyed emotionally.

Black Enterprises is my company and my sole purpose in life. It's all I have, and it's all I want. Sure, I date a lot of women. What millionaire CEO wouldn't? The only relationships I believe in are the sexual ones with no strings attached. The last thing I need in my life is some woman tying me down and suffocating me. With that being said, I've composed a list of rules for the women I see.

No sleepovers. Once our sexual encounter is over, you must get dressed and leave immediately. There are no exceptions.

No strings attached. There will never be anything more than just physical sex.

No calling or texting. If I want to see you again, I will contact you.

When in my presence, you will act and behave like a woman. I don't tolerate childish behavior.

No threesomes. I like my women one at a time. No exceptions.

No condoms. I get checked once a month, and I've had a vasectomy. I expect the women I'm with to be clean as well. Proof may be required.

Date night will only consist of dinner and sex; nothing more, nothing less. There will be no hand holding, walks, carriage rides, or movies. No exceptions.

I give this list out to women before dinner to ensure that they are fully aware of my expectations. If a woman has a problem with any one of the rules, they are free to leave. Women are nothing but sexual creatures to me. I've never been in love, and I never will be. The person who decided my fate to become this way had killed herself because I couldn't love her, and I can never let that happen again. I have a group of women that I see on a regular basis. Ashlyn is one of those women. I started seeing her about a year ago when she showed up at my office, broke and with nowhere to go. I sat at my desk and stared at the door, remembering that day.

"Mr. Black, there's someone here to see you," Valerie spoke over the intercom. "She says it's important and that you know her."

I sighed. I didn't have time for unannounced visitors who think they can just come to my office and demand to see me.

"I'm very busy, Valerie. Tell whomever it is that they'll need to make an appointment. I don't have time right now."

Suddenly, the door flew open as I looked up from my computer and nearly stopped breathing.

"I'm sorry, Mr. Black. I tried to stop her," Valerie spoke.

"It's alright, Valerie. Please shut the door."

"Hello, Connor. It's good to see you again; it's been way too long," the tall woman spoke.

"Ashlyn, what the hell are you doing here?" my voice angered.

She walked further into my office and made herself comfortable in the plush chair that sat across from my desk.

"Is that any way to talk to a friend that you haven't seen in ten years?"

"Cut the bullshit, Ashlyn, and answer the fucking question."

She cleared her throat and shifted in her chair. "I'm in a bit of a situation, Connor, and I was wondering if you could help me?"

I sat down in my chair and glared at her. She really hadn't changed too much in the past ten years. Her black, straight hair was the same, and her dark brown eyes still displayed the same sadness as they did all those years ago. I folded my hands in front of me.

"What do you want, Ashlyn?"

"I'm completely broke. I was kicked out of my apartment, and I don't know what else to do. I guess you can consider me homeless," she said as she took in a deep breath.

"What about your parents? Why aren't you going to them?"

"They told me that I'm a disgrace to the family and that I need to get my act together. They've helped me countless times, and they refuse to do it again."

I got up from my seat, walked over to where Ashlyn was sitting, and leaned up against the desk, trying to figure out why she came to see me.

"Why me, Ashlyn? We haven't seen or spoken to each other in ten years."

At that moment, before she could answer, Valerie buzzed in and told me my meeting was about to start.

"I'm sorry, Ashlyn. I have a meeting, and I'm afraid I won't be able to help you. So, if you'll excuse me, I have to leave."

She got up from her chair in a huff, grabbed her purse, and started towards the door. She abruptly turned around.

"You owe me, Connor Black. My life is a clusterfuck because of you. My sister committed suicide because of you, and it ruined my life. I miss Amanda so much, and she would still be here if it wasn't for you!" she yelled.

I stood there, unable to speak, as everything Ashlyn just said was true. She turned away and walked to the door.

"Wait," I said. "I'll take you to dinner tonight where we can discuss this further. Maybe I can help you. I'll have my driver pick you up at 7:00 pm. Where are you staying?"

"I'm not staying anywhere. I just told you I was broke, and I sure as hell don't have enough money for a hotel."

I walked to the door and opened it, motioning for Ashlyn to

16

step out.

"Valerie, please book a room at the Marriott Downtown for Miss Johnson and have it billed to the company." Valerie nodded and picked up the phone.

"Thank you, Connor, I knew I could count on you," she smiled.

"My driver will pick you up at 7:00 pm sharp."

I turned away and shook my head. Why the hell would she just show up here after all these years and then throw Amanda's death in my face?

***

I sat at my desk, pondering why she was still in my life a year later, and why I haven't done anything about it.

I was startled by a knock at the door as Valerie came in and set a cup of coffee on my desk.

"Good morning, Mr. Black."

"Good morning, Valerie. Do me a favor and clear my schedule for this afternoon. I have something that I need to do."

"Yes, Mr. Black, I'll get on that immediately."

"Thank you, Valerie," I said as she left my office.

I pulled out my cell phone, dialed Dr. Peters, and made an appointment for later this afternoon. With the return of the nightmares, I figured it was about time. I finished up some paperwork, made a few business calls, and alerted Denny that I was leaving the office early and to come pick me up.

I stepped into the Limo and instructed Denny to take me to the penthouse, so I could pick up the Range Rover and drive myself to Dr. Peter's office. I didn't want him knowing where I was going. I consider Denny one of my best friends. He's been with Black Enterprises for the past ten years. He drove for my father and now he drives for me.

Denny is in his early fifty's, and he's seen a lot from me in the past ten years. He's always been there for me and even bailed me out of trouble a few times without ever telling my father. He's like a second father to me as well as my confidant. I could always count on him to help me out if I needed it. In return, I make sure that he and his family are well taken care of.

Chapter 2

"Long time no see, Connor," Dr. Peters said as he sat in the blue chair across from me. "I thought you'd given up coming here."

"I haven't given up, Dr. Peters; I've just been too busy to make an appointment," I sighed.

I've been seeing Dr. Peters for a few years, and he's the only other person who knows about Amanda apart from Ashlyn. He's an older gentleman, with salt and pepper hair and a medium build. I found him very easy to open up to. I suppose that's why I continued seeing him for so long. I've tried other therapists, including women, but it became too complicated when they wanted to sleep with me instead of trying to help me.

"Tell me, Connor, have you made any progress since our last visit?"

I leaned back and rested my elbow on the arm of the chair. "No, I haven't, but like I told you before, I'm not interested in being in a relationship. I like my life just the way it is."

He narrowed his eyes at me. "So, why are you here today?"

"I've been having the nightmares again," I answered as I took in a deep breath.

Dr. Peters looked intently at me and cocked his head, "When did they resume?"

"They came back about a month ago," I said.

"What do you think triggered them this time?" he asked as if I would really know the answer.

"I don't know, Dr. Peters, that's why I'm here."

"Are you still seeing Ashlyn?"

I looked to the side as I answered his question, "Yes, I am."

"Are you starting to have feelings for her?" he asked in a serious manner.

"Fuck no, I'm not starting to have feelings for her," I snapped as I got up from the chair, put my hands in my pocket, and walked over to the window.

"She's a good lay, that's it. There's nothing more to her than that!"

"Why did you get so upset when I asked you that question? It seems to me that you're angry because you might want something more with someone. Maybe not with Ashlyn or with the other woman you see on a regular basis, but I think you're starting to feel lonely."

I turned around and looked at him. Anger began settling in my eyes. "I don't want anything more with any woman. How many times do I have to tell you that?"

"Calm down, Connor, and sit back in the chair. You need to listen to yourself. It's not healthy not to want anything more in life than just work. You've let your emotions die because of Amanda, and you need to accept the fact that her death wasn't your fault. You said it yourself; the girl already had emotional problems when you met her."

I walked back and sat in the chair directly across from Dr. Peters. "She did have some emotional problems, but she clearly pointed out in the letter she left that she killed herself because I broke up with her. How the hell does someone ever get over that? How can I ever get into another relationship with someone knowing that I was the cause of someone else's death?"

Dr. Peters sat there, staring at me and taking in every word I spoke. "Doc, I don't feel anything when I'm with a woman. I don't feel any type of connection at all. There are no emotions running through me, and I could care less if they want more from me. I'm upfront with the women that I sleep with. I use them for pleasure alone, nothing else, and if it's not good, then I toss them aside and find someone else."

"Those are harsh words, Connor," he said tilting his head to one side.

"No emotions, remember, Dr. Peters?"

He sighed and got up from his chair, "I just think you haven't allowed yourself to find the right woman yet."

"There is no right woman out there for me, and even if there was, it wouldn't matter. She would find out who I really am and want nothing to do with me. My past will always stand in the way of that."

"I'm prescribing you some sleep medication," Dr. Peters said as he handed me the small piece of paper. "Take one right before bed, and hopefully you'll be able to get some rest. It won't stop the nightmares; only you can put an end to them."

I got up from the chair and sighed. "Thanks for seeing me today; I'll be in touch."

"I want to see you next week, Connor, so make sure you make the appointment."

As I walked out of the office, a text message from Ashlyn

came through.

"Let's meet up tonight at Club S for some fun."

Club S wasn't exactly my cup of tea, but I didn't mind going there to look at the beautiful women. I can't even count the number of times I've brought women home from that club. They don't call it Club S for nothing. After the session I just had with Dr. Peters, I needed to go out tonight and get drunk to take my mind off things. I replied back to Ashlyn.

"I'll meet you there around 8:30 pm."

"Wonderful, I'll be waiting, and I'll be wearing something extra sexy for you."

I arrived back at the penthouse and changed into my workout clothes. I grabbed my bag and had Denny drive me to the gym. A good workout is what I needed right now. I needed to decompress from my session with Dr. Peters. I will never allow myself to fall in love, and there will never be a Mrs. Black walking around the streets of New York, even though many women have stepped in line to try and be the first.

I ran six miles on the treadmill, lifted some weights, and fucked Stephanie in the steam room. I'd say it was a very productive workout. Stephanie is fully aware of my rules, and she's less complicated than the others. She likes it quick and rough with a lot of hair pulling, so of course I have to oblige to keep her wanting more. She's one hell of a kinky girl. Afterwards, there's no talk and no questions asked; just a smile and a wave goodbye.

I walked out of the gym with a smile on my face, and as I slipped into the back of the limo, Denny turned around and looked at me.

"Judging by the smile on your face, I assume you had an exceptional workout?"

"I sure did, Denny, I sure did," I smiled as I leaned my head back.

Upon arriving back at the penthouse, I threw my gym bag in the closet and headed upstairs for a quick shower to wash off the smell of sweat and sex from my body.

I opened the closet door and pulled out my black Armani suit and white shirt. I looked it over and decided this would be perfect to wear to the club. I fixed my sandy blonde hair, put on my suit, and headed to the kitchen where Denny and Claire were talking.

"Denny, I'll need you to drop me off at Club S tonight and then you're free to go home."

"You won't need a ride home, Connor?" he asked.

"No, I'm meeting Ashlyn there, and she can give me a ride home. You go and spend time with your family."

Denny smiled and nodded his head.

"Connor, can I get you something to eat before you go?" Claire asked.

"No, Claire, I'm good."

I looked at my watch, and it was 6:30 pm. I wanted to get to the club before Ashlyn did in case there was someone there that I needed to speak with. Plus, I needed a few drinks before she showed up.

I arrived at the club around 7:00 pm and was surprised at how crowded it was at such an early hour in the evening. I walked to the back by the bar and sat down at my usual table. Rebecca, my favorite waitress, walked over with a smile on her face.

"Good evening, Mr. Black. What can I get you?"

I looked at her and ran my tongue across my lips. She was a twenty-something sex on legs.

"Give me a scotch, and make it a double. In fact, bring two." I said.

She smiled at me with her eyes and turned away. She returned in a short amount of time and set my drinks on the table.

"Is there anything I can do for you, Mr. Black," she winked.

I smiled and tilted my head. "I know something you can do for me."

I got up from my seat and escorted her down the hallway and into a small room that is used for storage. We walked inside as I shut and locked the door. She unbuckled my belt, unbuttoned my pants, and took them down seductively. She didn't need to stroke me; I was already hard and waiting for her lips to wrap themselves around me. Her mouth was amazing as her tongue made circles around my cock. I let out a low moan as I thrust my hips back and forth while keeping my hands placed on her head. Relax; this isn't the first time I've been with her. She provides me a service occasionally when I come to the club because she's the best at it, and she knows it. In return, I provide a large tip to thank her for her services.

I left the small room first and walked back to my table with sex on legs following behind. I looked at my watch, and it was 8:00 pm. I had just enough time to down my scotch before Ashlyn showed up. I stopped dead in my tracks when I looked up and saw her sitting at the table.

"Ashlyn, you weren't supposed to be here until 8:30 pm."

"Nice to see you too, Connor," she said as she kissed me on the cheek. She cocked her head and glared at me.

"What? Why are you looking at me like that?" I asked.

"Were you just with that waitress that was following behind you?"

I picked up my glass and took a drink. I turned so I was facing her and cupped her chin in my hand.

"That is none of your business, Ashlyn. We've been over this a thousand times. What I do and with whom I do it with is none of your concern."

She looked down and then back up at me. "Connor, there's something that I need to talk to you about, but first I want to dance. I'll be back and then we're going to talk."

I sighed as she got up and made her way to the dance floor. I called over Rebecca and ordered a few more drinks. I sat there watching beautiful women stare and smile at me as they walked by. A couple of them grabbed my attention, but it was quickly diverted when Ashlyn came up behind me and wrapped her arms around my neck.

"Are you ready for that talk now?" she asked.

I took her arms and quickly removed them from me. I was feeling the effects of the alcohol, and I was in no mood for whatever it was she wanted to talk about. I raised my hand, and once again, I caught Rebecca's attention to bring over a few more drinks.

"Connor, we need to talk," Ashlyn said.

I looked over at her and sighed. "Ashlyn, what is it that you want to talk about?"

She started running her finger up and down my arm. "We've been seeing each other casually for about a year now, and I think maybe it's time to take it to the next level."

I took another drink and looked directly into her eyes. "What the hell are you talking about? What do you mean by 'the next level'? There is no next level Ashlyn; how many times do I need to tell you that?"

I saw the anger growing in her eyes with each word I spoke. She clenched her jaw and pointed her finger at me, shaking it while starting to yell.

"We've been together for a year, but you still see other women! This has to stop, Connor! I know you have some feelings for me in that dead head of yours. I can feel it!"

I took the last sip of my drink and slammed the glass down on the table. I took my finger and pointed it at her; it was my turn now. My voice was angered as I found myself yelling over the loud music that was playing throughout the club.

"I have no feelings for you, Ashlyn! I never have, and I never will! You need to stop this right now or that's it; I'm done with you for good. You're nothing but sex to me, and that's all you'll ever be!"

Anger overtook her face as she raised her hand and slapped me. The sting of her hand felt permanently etched into the side of my face.

"That's for disrespecting me, you bastard!" She yelled before turning on her heels and storming off.

I sat there and stared straight ahead. I didn't care that she left or that I hurt her feelings. She entered into this arrangement fully aware of where she stood with me, and for her to think otherwise is stupid on her part.

I finished off the last of my scotch. I was feeling good as I noticed some girl staring at me from across the bar. Her beauty was breathtaking. I was about to get up and go talk to her until she stood up suddenly and went to the dance floor. I shrugged my shoulders and stumbled to the bar for another drink.

Chapter 3

The next morning, I was awoken by the sound of someone making a lot of noise in the kitchen. Everything was blurry, and my head felt like it had been beaten with a hammer. I looked around the room, trying to remember how the hell I got home last night. The last thing I remember was Ashlyn slapping me across the face. I glanced over to the other side of the bed and noticed the comforter was messed up. Clearly, I was with someone last night. I got out of bed and walked over to the dresser. After finding a pair of black pajama bottoms, I pulled them on before heading downstairs to see who the fuck was making all that noise so early in the morning.

I reached the entrance to the kitchen and stood there with my arms crossed as I watched this girl making something in my kitchen. I stood there for a moment, staring at her from behind. Her blonde hair was long and wavy. I couldn't believe she had the nerve to stay the night. She broke my number one rule. No one has ever broken that rule, or any rule to be exact. I cleared my throat to let her know I was there and watching. I didn't want to completely scare the hell out of her.

She slowly turned around and looked at me. I gulped as my heart started to beat a little faster. It was her eyes. She had the prettiest ice blue eyes that I've ever seen. They had a clarity to them that reminded me of a beautiful aquamarine gemstone. They sparkled amongst the light that filtered through the kitchen windows. As much as they sparkled, they were also filled with fear as she looked straight at me.

"Did I not go over the rules with you last night?" I said as I cocked my head to the side.

"Huh?" she frowned.

"I don't do sleepovers. You were supposed to leave after I fucked you, so would you mind telling me why you're still here, in my kitchen, making yourself comfortable?"

My tone was harsh, but who does this girl think she is? She put a glass on the counter and slid it over to me. I reached for it before it slid off the counter and broke all over my floor. She stood there, looking at me without answering my question.

"I asked you a question, and I expect an answer."

Her beautiful ice blue eyes suddenly darkened as she raised her voice to me.

"Listen, buddy, I don't know what you think happened here last night but you didn't fuck me!"

I looked at her intently as she continued on with her rant.

"You drank yourself into oblivion at the club last night, and they kicked you out. I was walking outside when it happened, and being the good person I am, I called a cab to make sure you got home safely. You then proceeded to vomit all over yourself, so I had to get you to the bathroom and out of your clothes, because frankly, you smelled. I was on my way out the door when I decided to check on you one more time. I went back to your room, and you were lying on your back, so I rolled you on your side again in case you vomited; I wouldn't have wanted you to choke to death. I fell asleep from exhaustion after dealing with you, and when I woke up, I decided to make you a pot of coffee and a hangover cocktail. I was leaving in a few minutes, and I didn't expect you to be up for at least a few more hours."

I shifted my weight, folded my arms, and took a few steps

closer to her. "So, you're telling me that nothing happened between us?" I asked.

"No, nothing happened. I just wanted to make sure you were going to be ok. You were obnoxiously drunk," she said as she looked down at the floor.

Her voice had become soft and pained. Who is this girl, and why the hell would she help me like that? I was intrigued by her; not only by her beauty, but by her kindness. I could tell she had a gentleness to her; an innocence I've never seen in a woman before.

I picked up the glass and looked at it. "What is this?" I asked.

"Just drink it, and you should start to feel better in about 15 minutes," she said with a smile.

It was only a small smile, but it caught my attention in more places than one. She said she was going to pour me some coffee before she left. It's beyond me why this girl would even bother after the way I just spoke to her. She reached into the cupboard to grab the cup as it fell out of her hands and onto the floor. She cursed as she bent down to pick it up. I walked over to her because I didn't want her cutting herself.

"You're going to cut yourself," I said.

She didn't listen, and she wouldn't stop picking up the broken pieces.

"Stop," I commanded in a harsh voice.

She still didn't listen, so I had no choice but to grab her wrists and force her to stop. I turned over her hands to take the broken pieces from them. I took in a sharp breath when I saw the scars along her wrists. Our eyes met, and she quickly pulled away. She stood up, and I continued picking up the pieces as she grabbed her purse.

"I'm sorry for the mug; I'll replace it for you, and I hope you feel better," she said as she headed for the door.

I threw the broken pieces in the garbage and followed after her. I couldn't let her leave. I didn't want her to leave. I still had more questions.

"Wait," I said. "At least let me pay you for your trouble last night."

She turned and looked at me with her beautiful blue eyes.

"I'm not taking your money."

Shit, I had to think fast. I wasn't about to let her leave.

"Then at least have a cup of coffee before you go," I said.

I was relieved when she agreed and sat down at the island. I poured her a cup of coffee and placed it in front of her. I picked up the glass of what she called 'a hangover cocktail' and forced it down. It was disgusting, and I could tell she was trying not to laugh at me as I was drinking it. I leaned over the counter and looked at this beautiful woman sitting across from me.

"Why on earth would you help me like that? What if I was a rapist or murderer?" I seriously asked.

She threw her head back and laughed. "You couldn't rape or murder me even if you wanted to. You were so far gone last night; I could barely get you home."

I ran my hand through my hair because she wasn't taking what I was saying seriously, and she could have been in danger if it was anyone else besides me.

"You shouldn't be doing those kinds of things; it's not safe in this city for a girl to be doing shit like that," I said with agitation.

She put her elbow up on the counter and leaned her head on her hand as she stared intently at me with a smirk on her face. I got the impression she thought I was joking, so I narrowed my eyes at her.

"Are you even listening to me?" I asked.

Instead of answering my question, she lightly laughed and got up from the stool.

"Thanks for the coffee, but I need to get home. Have a lovely day, Mr. Black, and next time, don't drink so much," she said with a smile.

Damn that smile. I followed her to the elevator and asked her if she had a name.

"It's Ellery Lane!" she yelled.

I stood there and watched the elevator doors shut as the beautiful woman known as Ellery Lane disappeared from my sight. I swallowed hard as I ran my hands through my hair. I raced up the steps to my bedroom. I threw on a pair of jeans and took out a shirt from the drawer. I grabbed my shoes and raced down to where my Range Rover was parked. I climbed inside, put on my shoes, and pulled out of the garage. That's when I saw her get into a cab around the corner. I discreetly followed the cab to her apartment. I parked the Range Rover across the street and watched her as she got out and waved bye to the driver. I quickly typed her address into my phone. I sat there and watched as she walked into her apartment and shut the door. I felt like a stalker. What the hell was I doing? I asked myself as I pulled away from the curb.

I didn't want to think about Ellery Lane anymore. She was a

nice girl who made sure I got home safe. I'm still baffled as to why she thought it was a good idea to help a total stranger like that. Is she oblivious to the dangers in the world?

I had some paperwork to catch up on at the office, so I headed there instead of going back to the penthouse. Being Saturday, the building will be quiet, and I'll be able to work without any distractions. I entered Black Enterprises and pushed the button for the elevator. I heard my phone go off, and as I pulled it from my pocket, I saw a text message from Ashlyn.

"Connor, I'm sorry about last night, and I think it's important we talk."

I sighed as I put my phone back in my pocket and took the elevator up to my office. I couldn't think about Ashlyn right now. I didn't want to deal with her, but I knew at some point it was going to happen. I walked to my desk and turned the computer on. I put my hands in my pocket, turned around, and stared at New York City from my large office window. My mind was racing. I have a lot of paperwork to do and phone calls to make regarding the sale of a company that I'm interested in buying; however, that's not what my mind was racing about. The thoughts running through my head are of Ellery Lane, her beautiful eyes, and her sinfully sexy smile.

I sat down at my desk and started going through some paperwork. My phone went off again with another text message from Ashlyn.

"Don't you dare ignore me, Connor. I want to apologize, and maybe we can settle this disagreement another way."

If I didn't answer her back, she'd be messaging me all day. I sighed as I dialed her number.

"Hello, Connor. Thank you for calling."

"Ashlyn, I'm very busy, and I really don't have the time to talk or text you. Say what you have to say, so we can move on."

"I wanted to apologize for last night, and I understand that you're not ready to commit to one woman yet. I have made peace with our little arrangement for now, but I do have one stipulation."

I sighed and leaned back in the chair. "What's your stipulation, Ashlyn?"

"I want you to double what you send me monthly, and I'll forget about our little conversation last night."

"There's no way I'm doubling what I pay you. If it wasn't for me, you'd still be on the streets. Keep in mind, I'm only helping you because of Amanda." I heard her take in a deep breath as she spoke into the phone.

"I'm sorry, Connor, but I'm not happy, and I've been feeling really depressed. My self-esteem is at its lowest right now, and you made it worse last night with the cruel things you said. I don't know if there's any reason for me to go on anymore. What's left here for me, Connor?"

I got up from my chair and paced around the office. "Ashlyn, don't speak like that. You have a lot going for you. I gave you a job at my company. I pay you a monthly salary in addition to what Black Enterprises pays you, and you get to see me three times a week. You know how I am, Ashlyn, and you know my rules."

"I know, Connor, but I just feel like I don't belong in this world anymore."

I couldn't believe she was saying this. She was reminding me of Amanda, and I couldn't be sure that she wouldn't do the same thing. So, I hesitantly agreed to her demands.

"Fine, Ashlyn, I'll double your monthly salary, but I want you to promise me you're going to do something with your life with that money. Take some classes or something."

"I knew you'd understand, Connor. Thank you for everything, and I'll consider what you said."

"I have to go, Ashlyn; I'm busy, and I have a lot to do."

I hung up the phone and rubbed my face. What the hell did I get myself into? I asked myself as I sat there and stared blankly across the room. I picked up the paperwork in front of me and began looking through it. It wasn't too long before I threw my pen across my desk and leaned back in my chair, thinking about Ellery. I couldn't get that woman out of my head, and it's driving me crazy. I felt the need to really thank her for helping me last night. She wouldn't take my money, which is odd because all women do. She didn't seem to want to stay with me any longer than necessary, and she had an attitude problem. Then it hit me, I'll treat her to a nice dinner. Every woman likes to go to a fancy restaurant and have a nice meal. Carson Williams is a friend of mine and the owner of Le Sur. I called him and had him make a reservation for two for 7:30 pm that evening. I didn't want to give her the option of turning me down if I called her on the phone and asked her, so I decided to send the invitation via messenger. I quickly typed a note on my computer.

"Miss Lane, I'm going to properly thank you for your services last night. I will be waiting for you at Le Sur Restaurant. My driver will pick you up promptly at 7:00 pm ~ Connor Black"

I took the paper off the printer, neatly folded it, and placed it in an envelope. I wrote her name on the outside and headed out of the building. I called Justin and asked him to meet me at Starbucks. Justin's an intern at my company, and I occasionally have him run some personal errands for me when my secretary isn't available.

"Good afternoon, Mr. Black," he said as he sat at the table.

"Hello, Justin, I need you to do a favor for me," I said as I sat down across from him.

I slid the envelope across the table to him. "I want you to deliver this letter to Miss Ellery Lane. I have her address right here."

Justin took the envelope and smiled. "Of course, Mr. Black, I'll do it right away."

I took out my wallet and handed him a $50 bill. "Thank you, Justin, this is very important."

He smiled as he got up from the table. "Thank you, Mr. Black, I'll deliver it now."

I sat there, wondering if this was such a good idea. What if she doesn't show up? I sighed as I headed back to the penthouse.

Chapter 4

I arrived at the penthouse and walked into the kitchen for a bottle of water. Denny followed behind me.

"You wanted to see me, Connor?"

"Denny, I need you to pick up Miss Ellery Lane at this address promptly at 7:00 pm," I said as I handed him the paper with her address on it.

Denny looked at me as the corners of his mouth turned up. "Miss Lane, huh?"

"Don't get any ideas, Denny. She helped me home last night from the club, and I'm just thanking her by taking her to dinner, that's all."

"What happened to Miss Ashlyn driving you home?" he asked.

"Let's just say we didn't agree on something and then she left. Miss Lane was kind enough to get my drunken ass home safely. To be honest with you, Denny, I don't remember a thing about last night. I found her in the kitchen this morning, making me some nasty hangover drink and coffee."

He looked at me with a strange look. "So she's another one of your girls from the club?"

"No, Denny, she's not. Nothing happened between us when she brought me home."

He smiled and walked out of the kitchen. I opened the bottle of water and took a sip as I leaned up against the counter. I headed up the stairs, heading to the bathroom for a shower. I stood under the stream of hot water as it ran down my body. I was thinking about Ellery and how I can't get her smile out of my mind. My heart started to beat a little faster every time I thought about her. I stepped out of the shower and got dressed. I reached in the cabinet for my cologne. Tonight, I opted to go with Armani instead of the Dolce & Gabbana that I usually wear. I looked at my watch, noticing that Denny will be picking Ellery up in 15 minutes. When I arrived at Le Sur, Allison, the red headed hostess, led me to a private table that sat in the corner of the restaurant.

"Is there anything that I can get you or do for you, Mr. Black?" she smiled.

"No, Allison, I'm good, but thank you," I said as she frowned and walked away. She's been trying to get me in bed for a couple of years. What she doesn't understand is that she's not my type. I pulled out my phone and sent a quick text message to Denny.

"Is she with you?"

"Yes, Mr. Black, she is," he replied promptly.

I sat at the table, sipping on water because I suddenly became very hot. I took out my phone to check the stock market, and as I looked up, I saw Allison escorting Ellery to the table. I stared at her from a distance, and my stomach tied itself in knots. I got up and walked around to her side.

"Good evening, Miss Lane. I'm glad you decided to join me," I said as I pulled out the chair for her.

"Good evening, Mr. Black. Thank you for inviting me, but it really wasn't necessary. Please call me Elle."

I didn't understand why she wanted me to call her Elle. I liked Ellery. I think it's a beautiful name, and it shouldn't be shortened. I

40

looked at her intently.

"Isn't your name, Ellery?" I asked.

"Yes, but my friends call me Elle," she said as she took a sip of water.

She considered us friends? How can that be when I only met her this morning? I took my menu from the table and opened it.

"But we aren't friends, Ellery."

I think she took offense to my comment because she narrowed her eyes at me as she said, "Alright then, Mr. Black, why don't we just stick to Miss Lane?"

The way she said it was so sarcastic and with such attitude, that I couldn't help but let a small smile escape from my lips. I watched her look over the menu, and I didn't want her to feel uncomfortable, so I told her to order anything she liked. Did I mention that I told her she was too thin, and it looked like she hadn't eaten in weeks? She looked at me sternly then proceeded to tell me it was none of my concern. The attitude of this beautiful woman was starting to arouse me. I didn't mean anything by saying she was too thin. I don't even know why I said it. I can be such a bastard at times.

The waiter brought over a bottle of Pinot Grigrio and poured some in each glass. As he took Ellery's order, I couldn't help but stare at the way she presented herself and the way she smiled at him as she ordered her food. She noticed I was staring at her, and I was praying I wasn't making her feel uncomfortable. Suddenly, she threw a question at me.

"So what's your story, Mr. Black?"

She caught me off guard, and no woman has ever done that

before. I looked at her as I picked up my glass and took a sip of wine.

"My story?" I asked.

A small smile escaped her lips as she tilted her head to the side and answered my question, "Yes, your story."

"What's to tell? I'm a 30 year old CEO, I have more money than I'll ever need, I don't do relationships, I usually get everything I want, and I do whatever I want."

She was staring at me like she was trying to figure me out, so I threw her question right back at her.

"Now that we got that out of the way, what's your story, Miss Lane?"

"I don't have a story, Mr. Black. I'm 23 years old, I moved here with my boyfriend a little over a year ago, I work part-time at a small record company, I paint pictures, and I volunteer at the soup kitchen."

I pressed my lips together because all I heard was the word 'boyfriend'. It made me a little edgy, and I don't know why. I asked her the obvious question.

"What does your boyfriend think about you having dinner with me?"

Her eyes instantly left mine as she looked down at the table when she answered my question. I could sense the pain in her voice.

"He doesn't; we aren't together anymore. He moved out over three weeks ago."

I was curious to know more about her and her relationship with her ex-boyfriend. Was she the one who broke it off with him? I couldn't imagine him leaving her; she was way too beautiful to be left alone. I asked her how long they'd been together. She told me they had been together for four years and that she moved here with him from Michigan. I was caught off guard when she decided to tell me more.

"Yep, he came home from work one day and said he needed space. He packed his bags and walked out," she said as she stared directly into my eyes.

I was feeling something at that moment when she said that. I saw the sadness in her eyes, and I felt bad for her. I told her I was sorry that he did that to her and was shocked by her next words.

"Don't be; nothing lasts forever," she said as she waved her hand in front of her face.

When I heard her say that, I was elated. She believed the same thing I did. She just said it, 'nothing lasts forever'. Did I just meet a woman who shares the same views as me? I watched her as she looked around the restaurant. I could tell she was taking in the beauty and class of it. I asked her if she liked it here. She smiled at me and told me how much she did. I knew she'd like it.

I was intrigued by her and the fact she volunteered at the soup kitchen. I wanted to know more, so I asked her why she volunteered there. She lightly smiled and cocked her head.

"I like to help people in need; you should know that by now, Mr. Black."

Of course she likes to help people in need. I was in need of help last night, and she didn't think twice about getting me home safely. Although, I'm still pissed about it because what she did was very unsafe, and she could have gotten hurt. I apologized for asking such a ridiculous question. She smiled at me as she cut up her chicken and started telling me personal things about her family. I stared intently at her and listened to every word she said.

"I had a rough childhood. Let's just say there was nobody there to help me."

"What about your parents? Didn't they help you?" I asked as she looked down and away from me.

"My mother died of cancer when I was six, and my father was an alcoholic who passed away right before my 18th birthday."

Jesus Christ, what the fuck has this poor girl been through?

"Is that why you helped me last night? Because you think that I'm an alcoholic?" I asked.

"No, my father choked to death on his vomit during one of his drunken nights. I found him dead in his bed the next morning. I didn't want that same fate for you. What people don't realize is how easy it is for something like that to happen. I spent my entire life taking care of my father who absurdly drank himself into oblivion almost every night because he couldn't get over my mother's death. So, it's just second nature for me to help people."

I wanted to look away from her, but I couldn't. I wanted her to know that I was listening to every heartbreaking word she spoke. I lightly smiled at her as I held up my glass and motioned for her to do the same.

"Well, thank you for your help last night, and as mad as I was this morning to find you standing in my kitchen, I do appreciate it."

She smiled as our glasses touched one another. Damn that smile.

As we were sitting and continuing our conversation, my phone went off. I pulled it from my pocket and there was a text from Kendall, another one of my casual flings.

"Connor, I just wanted to tell you that I'm leaving the door unlocked, so just come in and head straight to the bedroom. I'll be waiting for you."

Shit, I forgot all about Kendall and tonight. We'd arranged this last week. I sighed as I looked at Ellery. She asked me if everything was alright.

"Everything's fine; it's just business," I said as I put my phone back in my pocket.

After we ate and finished our wine, we got up and headed out of the restaurant. As soon as we stepped outside, Ellery asked me if I wanted ice cream. I looked at her with a puzzling look because I thought it was odd she would just blurt that out.

"No, I don't want any ice cream. I'm taking you home and then I have somewhere I have to be," I said.

She kept insisting that we go for ice cream, and to be honest, I was beginning to get irritated because I didn't want any.

"Miss Lane, I don't want any ice cream, now get in the car so Denny can take you home." My tone was adamant, but she wasn't listening to me, and I wasn't used to that.

Before I knew it, she turned her back and started walking down the street. She put her hand up and waved.

"Thanks again for dinner, Mr. Black. I'll see you around

sometime."

I stood there and watched her walk away. What the fuck is this girl's problem? Why the hell doesn't she listen?

"Miss Lane, get back here!" I yelled.

She kept walking, so I hastened my pace to catch up to her. "Miss Lane, I will not tell you again to get in the car," I said in an adamant tone.

I think I pissed her off because she abruptly stopped in the middle of the sidewalk, turned around, and pointed her finger at me.

"I don't take orders from anybody, Mr. Black, especially people that I've only known less than 24 hours. I'm not your responsibility. You thanked me for my help with a nice dinner, and now it's time for us to part ways. I'm going to get some ice cream, and then I'll call a cab to drive me home."

Wow, this girl doesn't take shit from anyone. She continued walking away from me. I took out my phone and called Denny.

"It looks like we're getting ice cream. I'll call you when we're leaving."

She told me that I didn't have to come if I didn't like ice cream. I tried to explain to her it wasn't that I didn't like it, but I just didn't want any. It didn't matter because Ellery Lane was getting ice cream with or without me. I think that I've just met my match.

We continued walking down the street, and I tried to explain to her that it wasn't safe for a beautiful young woman to be walking the streets of New York alone at night. I noticed her smile

46

when I called her beautiful. It made my heart do something weird which I can't explain because I've never felt anything like it before.

We sat down at a small table in the ice cream shop, and she asked me when the last time I had ice cream was. I found that odd, and why was it important to her?

"I don't know; since I was a kid, I guess," I answered.

"Are you kidding me? You haven't had ice cream since you were a kid?"

"No, is that a problem?"

"No, I'm just surprised," she said.

"I think you'd find a lot of things surprising about me," I grinned.

I didn't want her to know how I live my life. She was a nice girl, and she didn't need to know about all the women I see. She didn't need to be exposed to that.

"So, where are you going later?" She asked out of the clear blue.

"Miss Lane, I don't think you really want to know the answer to that," I said as I raised my eyebrow.

As we were finishing our ice cream, I called Denny to come pick us up. I went to open the car door for her, but Denny beat me to it, and Ellery seemed very pleased he did. I slid into the seat next to her as she looked at me and lightly smiled. She seemed to be either nervous or uncomfortable as she didn't say a word the whole way to her apartment. Denny pulled up to the curb and got out to open the door for her. I leaned over to take a closer look at her apartment and simply asked about her having her own private entrance. I think she took offense to that because she responded in a sarcastic tone.

"I don't live in a fancy apartment building with a doorman and private elevator. This is it, Mr. Black; my little apartment with its own outside entry."

"I didn't mean anything by it; I just think it's unsafe, and anyone can break in," I responded with an irritated tone. She didn't need to be so sarcastic with her answer.

She thanked me for putting that thought in her head as she surprised me by giving me a light kiss on my cheek. I flinched because it caught me off guard, and I hadn't expected her to do that. She got out of the limo, winked at me, and told me to have a pleasant night. Denny pulled away and looked at me in the rearview mirror.

"She's a great girl, Connor, and I think you just met your match," he smiled.

I rolled my eyes and sighed. "She is a nice girl, Denny, and I'm going to make sure she stays that way."

I pulled out my phone and sent a text to Kendall.

"Sorry, but something's come up, and I can't meet you tonight. We'll have to reschedule for another time."

I didn't want to see Kendall tonight. I just wanted to go back to the penthouse, have a drink, and try to get Ellery off my mind.

Chapter 5

I spent the next few days burying myself in work. No matter what I did, I couldn't get Ellery off my mind. This was killing me because I needed to focus on the business acquisition that my company would be making soon. I sat in my office chair and turned so I was facing the window. I looked out onto the streets of New York, hoping that I may see her walking down the street. She got under my skin somehow, and I couldn't get her out. I picked up the phone and made an appointment to see Dr. Peters this afternoon. I needed to talk to him about the clusterfuck that was going on in my head.

I walked out of the building and hailed a cab to Dr. Peter's office. I wasn't looking forward to this session because I already knew what he was going to tell me. I walked in his office and sat down in the leather chair across from him.

"This is a pleasant surprise, Connor. I didn't expect you to be back so soon," he said.

I took in a deep breath and looked at him. "Something happened, and I can't get it out of my head."

Dr. Peters looked at me and cocked his head. "What happened, Connor?"

"I met a girl, Doc."

He let out a light laugh. "You meet girls every day, Connor; this is nothing new."

I looked at him in irritation, "You don't understand; this girl's different. She's beautiful, kind, giving, sweet, strong, stubborn, and quite a smart ass."

Dr. Peters leaned forward and rested his elbows on his thighs. "Are you telling me that you have feelings for this girl?" he asked.

I shifted in my seat and sighed. "No, I don't have feelings for her."

"Then why are you here, Connor?"

"Dr. Peters, I pay you $1,000 an hour to tell me what's going on in my head, whether I want to hear it or not."

He leaned back in his chair and removed his glasses. "You want my honest opinion? I think you like this girl and that you're starting to have feelings for her. Let me ask you a question. When was the last time you saw her?"

"I saw her a few days ago; why do you ask?"

"I want you to tell me what you've been doing and thinking since you last saw her."

I got up from my chair and walked over to the window. I put my hands in my pocket and cleared my throat.

"I've been burying myself in my work because I'm trying to acquire a company that's up for sale."

"Have you been thinking about her as well?" He asked quietly.

"I can't get her out of my mind. She's all I keep thinking about both day and night. I haven't been able to concentrate on anything else. I've cancelled all my dates because I only want to see Ellery."

"Ellery is a pretty name," He said.

"Ellery is a beautiful name, and she's a beautiful woman," I replied as I stared out the window.

Dr. Peters got up from his chair, walked over to me, and put his hand on my shoulder.

"It sounds like the right woman just walked into your life, Connor. Just don't screw it up. Become friends with her. This is the first time you've opened up since you've started coming to see me. If you start falling for Ellery, the first thing you must do is tell her about your past and the women you see. There can be no secrets, Connor."

I sighed as I looked at him. "I know, but let's not get ahead of ourselves."

He patted me on the back and asked me to make an appointment to see him in a couple of weeks. I walked out of his office and out of the building. I headed towards the Starbucks down the street and called Denny to pick me up. As I climbed in the back seat my phone rang.

"Richard, did you get it?"

"Yes, Mr. Black, I got Miss Lane's phone number."

I asked Denny to hand me a piece of paper as I took a pen from my pocket and wrote down the phone number Richard obtained for me. "Thank you, Richard; that's a job well done." I hung up the phone and looked at the numbers on the paper. Denny was looking at me and shaking his head.

"What?" I asked him.

"Don't you think it would've been better just to ask Miss Lane for her phone number?"

"Do I ever do anything the easy way, Denny?" I smiled.

Just as I got out of the limo, I see Ashlyn's name appear on my phone.

"Connor Black here?" I answered.

"Why do you always answer like that, Connor?" she said with an irritation in her voice.

"What do you want, Ashlyn? I'm very busy at the moment."

"Let's have dinner together," she said.

"Not tonight, I'm working from home."

"You've been working a lot lately, and we haven't been together in over a week," she whined.

I stepped into the elevator hoping that I'd lose service and our conversation would come to an end. I smiled when the other end went quiet, and I looked at my phone to confirm that the call was dropped. As I stepped out of the elevator, I walked over to the bar and poured myself a glass of scotch. Claire emerged from the kitchen with a smile on her face.

"Good evening, Connor, I have your dinner warming in the oven should you be staying in tonight."

"Thank you, Claire, I'll be staying in tonight. Have a good night, and I'll see you on Monday."

"Thank you, have a nice weekend," she smiled.

I nodded my head as I drank my scotch. I held my phone and stared at Ellery's number, debating whether or not to call her. I wanted to hear her voice, but it was too soon, and I'm pretty sure she wasn't thinking about me. After all, I was kind of a prick to her that night. What the fuck is wrong with me? Why can't I get this girl out of my head? I brought my laptop into the kitchen and set it on the table. I grabbed a plate and took the dish Claire had prepared out of the oven. I set it on the table and opened my laptop. I did the unthinkable; I Googled 'Ellery Lane'. There was a link to an article about her paintings that she has on display at the Sunset Art Gallery. When I clicked on the link, her picture came up, and I couldn't help but smile. She was beautiful with her long, blonde, wavy hair and ice blue eyes. Damn that smile. I started to get aroused as I studied her perfectly shaped lips. I distracted myself from her picture and read the article on her paintings. I decided that tomorrow morning, I'm going to that art gallery and looking at her work. I had a feeling they would give me more insight about her. I laid there in bed, thinking about the dinner we had together and gave thought to what Dr. Peters said in reference to having Ellery as a friend.

The next morning, after I showered and dressed, I went to the kitchen for some coffee. Denny was already sitting at the table when I walked in.

"Morning, Denny," I said. "I appreciate you getting here early on a Saturday."

"Good morning, Connor. Well, that's what you pay me for," he said with a smile.

I sat at the table across from him as I drank my coffee.

"I need to stop by the office first to pick up some papers before heading to the airport, and I want to swing by the Sunset Art Gallery."

Denny cocked his head to the side, "The art gallery? Are you in the market for some new artwork?" He asked.

"I guess you can say that," I said as I got up from the table and put my coffee cup in the dishwasher.

"Miss Lane is an artist, isn't she?" Denny asked me.

"She mentioned that she painted pictures," I replied.

"They wouldn't happen to be on display at the Sunset Art Gallery, would they?"

I sighed. "Yes, Denny, her paintings are on display there, and I want to see them."

"Are you ok, Connor?" he asked.

"I'm fine, why do you ask?"

"Ever since you met Miss Lane, you've seemed different. You hardly go out, and you've been moodier than usual. I think she's affected you in some way."

"Don't be ridiculous, Denny; Miss Lane has not affected me. I've just been really busy with work."

The way he was looking at me told me that he knew I was lying. "I need to run upstairs and grab my iPad. I'll meet you in the limo," I said.

With my iPad in hand, I slid into the back seat and checked the stock market. We were stuck in typical Saturday traffic when Denny asked me something that caught my attention.

"Isn't that Miss Lane over there?" he pointed to Central Park.

I quickly looked up and saw her entering the park. She was wearing tight skinny jeans and a cream colored, short-sleeve top. Her hair was pulled back in a ponytail that swayed from side to side as she walked. I noticed she was carrying a large pad of paper.

I opened the door amongst the traffic and told Denny to find a spot to park. I wanted to see what she was up to, but most of all, I wanted to see her. I kept a great distance behind her, so she couldn't see me if she turned around. I watched her as she entered the Conservatory Gardens. I had to think of a way to see and talk to her without appearing like a stalker. Hell, I am a stalker, but only to Ellery Lane. She had made me like this. I stopped outside the Conservatory Gardens to formulate a plan. What excuse was I going to give for being in Central Park? I pulled my phone from my pocket and looked at her number. I walked into the gardens and saw her sitting on a bench with her pad open and pencil in hand. I hit her number and watched her ignore my call. I lightly smiled because I called her again, and I was going to keep on calling her until she answered.

"Hello?" her sweet innocent voice answered.

"Hello, Miss Lane, are you enjoying Central Park?" I asked.

I watched her turn her head from side to side before looking behind her and seeing me walking towards her.

"I am, Mr. Black, and it looks like you are too," she said with a smile. Damn that smile.

I put the phone in my pocket and sat down next to her on the bench. She looked at me, frowned, and didn't say a word. She just kept staring at me until I spoke.

"What?" I asked as I tilted my head.

"How did you get my phone number? I don't remember giving it to you."

"I have my ways of finding out anything about anybody, Miss Lane," I smirked.

"So, you're a stalker then?"

I threw my head back and laughed, "No, Miss Lane, I'm not a stalker. I just wanted your number in case I needed you to help me home some night." I was even impressed at how quickly I came up with that one.

"How did you know I was here?" She curiously asked.

"Denny pointed out that he saw you walking down the street, and I asked him to stop."

"Why?"

"I don't know. I guess I just thought I'd say hi." Her questions were starting to irritate me, but turning me on at the same time.

"Then you could have just called since you have my number and all," she smirked as she waved her hand.

"Miss Lane, enough with the questions please," I sighed.

"Can I ask you one more thing?" she innocently asked.

I narrowed my eyes at her as the corners of her mouth turned up.

"What is it?" I asked quietly.

"Could you please stop calling me Miss Lane, and just call me Ellery?"

"It would be my pleasure, Ellery," I smiled as I slightly tilted my head.

I loved saying her name as it was unique. She was unique, and she made me feel different when I was around her. Hell, I haven't felt the same since I saw her in my kitchen. I looked over at her sketch pad and watched her as she drew two people. Her drawing was amazing, and I could only imagine what her paintings looked like.

"What are you drawing?" I asked her.

"The bride and groom over there," she pointed.

"Why?" I asked curiously.

"Why not? They're a cute couple, and I think it would make a good painting. I'll call it 'A Wedding in Central Park'."

"And what makes you think someone would buy that?" I'm pretty sure that came out the wrong way.

"People love weddings, and I'm sure any couple that got married here would buy it as a memory of the beginning of their life together."

"It's all a bunch of shit if you ask me," I mumbled.

"What is?" she asked as she tilted her head to the side.

"Weddings, starting a life together, relationships; all of it. You even said it yourself that nothing lasts forever."

"Well, a lot of people believe in the happily ever after and the fairy tale relationships. Let's not take that away from them," she softly spoke while drawing.

"Do you believe in any of that?" I asked her not knowing if I wanted to hear her answer.

"I don't know. I thought I once did, but I'm not so sure anymore."

I stared down at her pad and watched her draw. The scars on her wrists became more visible with each stroke of the pencil. I put my hand on hers and stopped her from drawing. She looked at me as I turned her wrist over and lightly rubbed her scar with my thumb. She froze at my touch. Her skin was soft and warm. I don't know what possessed me to do what I did, but I needed to touch her.

"Tell me about your scars," I said as I looked directly in her eyes.

I could tell she was uncomfortable so I gently laid her hand back on the drawing pad. She looked down as she spoke.

"I made a mistake. I was young and stupid, that's all."

"Everyone is young and stupid from time to time, but they don't try to kill themselves," I said in an irritated way as the memories of Amanda started to rush through my mind.

"Connor, you don't know me or anything about me. We aren't friends remember, so what happened to me in my past is none of your business," she snapped at me.

I stared straight ahead and found that I couldn't look at her. I never should have said what I did. I'm sure she probably hates me now, and I wouldn't blame her.

"I apologize," I said without looking at her.

She looked at me, and I could see a slight smile on her face out of the corner of my eye. She got up from the bench and asked me if I wanted a hot dog. I didn't want a hot dog. What I wanted was to take her to a nice restaurant for lunch because I had something that I needed to discuss with her.

58

"No, I don't want a hot dog. If you're hungry, then I'll take you to a proper restaurant for lunch," I said.

She laughed as she turned her back to me and started walking away. "Suit yourself, Mr. Black, but I'm going to get myself a hot dog from the hot dog stand."

I got up and quickly caught up to her. This girl was stubborn, and I didn't know how to handle it.

"You don't listen to anyone, do you?" I asked.

"No, I do what I want," she smiled.

"I can tell," I mumbled under my breath.

We approached the hot dog stand, and she asked me again if I was getting one. I guess I was giving in and eating a hot dog. I frowned as Ellery lightly smiled. I paid for the hot dogs and then took mine over to a small wooden table and sat down. Ellery stopped at the condiment stand and topped her hot dog with just about everything there. God, it looked disgusting. She looked happy as she walked over to the table with a smile on her face, and her ponytail was swinging from side to side.

"That's gross," I said as I took a bite of my plain hot dog.

"Gross? No way man, this is heaven," she said as she took a large bite.

"You do realize how bad that is for you, right?" I asked her.

She put her finger up, "You only live once, so we should make the best of it." I tried to hold back a smile, but she was so damn cute when she did that, so I couldn't help it. She saw me and smiled too.

"Here, take a bite," she said as she shoved her hot dog in my face.

"No, get that out of my face," I frowned.

"Not until you take a bite, Connor, then you can judge if it's gross."

Ellery kept moving the hot dog closer to my mouth. I rolled my eyes and finally took a bite. She grabbed her napkin and wiped the corner of my mouth. I put my hand on hers and stared into her eyes. She smiled and told me that I had a glob of ketchup on me, and she didn't want it to get on my shirt. She smiled as I thanked her.

It was a beautiful afternoon, and Central Park was certainly the best place to enjoy it. There was no place that I wanted to be but here with Ellery. She was a refreshing change of company, and I enjoyed every moment that I spent with her. I watched her as she took the last bite of her hot dog and gently wiped her mouth with her napkin. I was beginning to feel nervous about what I wanted to ask her. I didn't know how she was going to react, and I was fretting that she'd never want to see me again.

"If you don't mind, I want to ask you something," I spoke.

"Go ahead," she said.

"I gave some thought to our recent outing, and I was wondering if you would be interested in being..." I stopped because I didn't know how to put it.

"Being..." she motioned for me to proceed.

I cleared my throat and took in a sharp breath, "Would you be interested in being a companion?"

She narrowed her eyes at me. "What? I don't get it."

"Would you be interested in being a person who would accompany me to certain functions, no strings attached, and I would pay you of course."

She spit out the water she was drinking. "What? You mean like an escort or call girl?!" she yelled.

"NO, NO! That's not what I meant, Ellery," I tried to explain. "I mean like a friend."

"You mean go out as friends, like me and Peyton?" She asked.

I ran my hand through my hair, and she lightly touched my arm.

"Connor, if you want to be friends, then all you had to do was ask. Actually, I already considered us friends, and there will be no money involved either," she smiled at me.

Her words made me happy. Of course she already considered us friends. She's one of the nicest girls that I've ever met, and I wanted to get to know her better, as friends of course.

"There's a benefit I need to attend tomorrow night. It's a charity function, and I need to attend to represent my company. Would you like to accompany me?"

She lightly bit her lip and sweetly smiled at me. "I would love to go."

"I'll pick you up at 6:00 pm sharp," I smiled back.

As we got up from the table, I heard my phone chime. I pulled it from my pocket, and there was a text message from Denny.

"Am I to assume that you will not be going to Chicago today?"

"No, I'm not going. I lost track of time, and it's too late. Call Jerry and tell him I'm sorry, but something's come up, and I won't be flying today," I messaged back.

We started walking out of Central Park when suddenly, Ellery came to a halt, and I stopped beside her. Someone had called her name as she looked over to the side to see who it was. I could tell by the look on her face that she wasn't happy. The person who called her name was her ex-boyfriend, Kyle. She introduced us and continually smiled as she talked to him. I was amazed by this woman as she could even hold a conversation with him after he hurt her so bad. The woman standing next to him was licking her lips as she eyed me up and down. Ellery pulled Kyle over to the side and told him to tame his dog. I laughed to myself at the spunk of this woman. I stood there smiling at her.

"What?" She asked as she looked at me.

"Nothing, you're just..."

"Just what, Connor?" she asked as she looked at me.

"You're just full of life. Let's put it that way," I laughed.

She smiled and bumped my shoulder with hers. I put my hands in my pocket and smiled all the way back to the car.

Denny had the limo parked and was waiting for me. "Are you getting in?" I asked as I held the door open.

"No, I'm walking," Ellery said as she started walking down the street.

"Elle, get in the car," I demanded.

"Bye, Connor, see you tomorrow."

I stood there with the door open and watched her walk down the street. What is with this girl? I slid into the limo, and Denny turned around, looking at me with a grin on his face.

"She's quite a firecracker, Connor; you've definitely met your match."

I sighed and looked out the window. "Follow her, and don't stop until I say so."

Denny followed Ellery for about three blocks. She stopped at the corner, and I rolled down the window.

"Are you ready to get in now?" I smiled.

"You never give up, do you?" she asked.

"No, not until I get what I want," I said.

She rolled her eyes and opened the door. As she slid into the limo, she smacked me on the arm and told me to move over. Denny was watching through the rear view mirror, and he was lightly laughing. As I moved over, I couldn't help but chuckle. I was glad to have her in my limo even if it was a short drive to her place. We reached her apartment, and as she was getting out, I lightly grabbed her hand.

"Thank you for agreeing to come with me tomorrow," I said softly.

She looked at me, crinkled her nose, and smiled, "That's what friends are for."

Chapter 6

Denny and I got out of the limo and walked through the doors that led inside the art gallery. I've been to this art gallery only one time before, and it was with my sister, Cassidy, when she was looking for a painting for Camden's nursery. A gentleman walked over and asked if he could help us.

"I'm looking for some paintings that you have on display by Ellery Lane," I answered.

"Ah yes, Miss Lane's paintings are right over on this wall," he said. "She's quite a talented artist."

I stood in front of the wall that displayed her artwork and stared at each painting carefully. They were simply breathtaking. The painting that caught my attention was the one of the child sitting in a field of flowers as three angels looked down upon her from the sky. I couldn't help but think of the scars that I saw on both her wrists.

"She's a very good artist, Connor," Denny said as he looked at her paintings.

"She is indeed. I must have all of them," I replied.

Denny and I stepped out of the art gallery. I quickly pulled my cell phone from my pocket, and I called my secretary, Valerie.

"Hello, Mr. Black," she answered.

"Valerie, I know it's Saturday, but I need you to do me a favor. I need you to go to the Sunset Art Gallery and purchase three paintings from an artist named Ellery Lane. I'm calling Scott to pick you up in the SUV in about an hour. I will give him an envelope with cash in it for the paintings. I want you to tell the salesperson that you are paying triple the price of each one. Once you make the purchase, Scott will deliver the paintings to my penthouse."

"Very good, Mr. Black, I'll be ready."

"Thank you, Valerie. There will be a separate envelope with your name on it for your help."

I hung up the phone and met Denny in the limo. We started to pull out of the parking lot when I had an idea.

"Denny, drive me to Saks Fifth Avenue; we have some dresses to look at."

"You're kidding, right, Connor?" he laughed.

"No, Denny, I'm not kidding."

He shook his head and didn't say another word. Judging by the size of Ellery's apartment and her living on her own, I was thinking she didn't have much money. I wanted to buy her something to wear for the charity function tomorrow. It's a black tie affair, and I didn't want her to feel out of place. Besides, a beautiful woman like Ellery Lane deserved to wear a beautiful designer dress.

"Drop me off in front of the store and park around back. I'll let you know when I'm done," I said to Denny.

"Have fun dress shopping, Connor," he smiled at me.

I rolled my eyes as I got out of the limo. I walked into Saks and ran into a woman I know named Jillian.

"Connor Black, long time no see and no fuck," she smiled.

66

"Hello, Jillian, it's good to see you as always," I smiled as I kissed her cheek.

"Where have you been hiding? I've been waiting to hear from you," she said as she lightly put her hand on my chest.

"I've been really busy, Jillian. I've been working hard, trying to secure a business deal. Unfortunately, I don't have time for anything else."

Who was I kidding? I had time; I always made time for sex. I just haven't wanted anything to do with other women since I met Ellery. Even though she was only a friend to me, she's the only woman I want to spend time with.

"Well, give me a call when you do find time. I bought some new toys that I'd like to try with you," she winked.

I politely said goodbye and headed up the escalator to the dress department. I've never done this before, well, with the exception of my sister. I would send her dresses from time to time for certain functions. She would get mad because she said she liked to shop and that she could pick out her own dresses. However, she never failed to love the ones I picked.

"Connor Black, how are you?" Camille smiled as she gave me a light hug.

"I'm good, Camille," I replied.

"I saw your mother in here yesterday. She was buying dresses for the charity tomorrow. What brings you here today?"

"I'm looking for some dresses that I would like you to take to a friend of mine. She will be attending the charity function with me tomorrow night. She's about 5'7" and very thin."

Camille looked at me and placed her finger on her lip. "Describe her hair and eyes to me," she said.

"Her hair is long and blonde, and her eyes are an ice blue color," I answered.

She took me over to a wall with a rack of dresses that just came in. I took a seat on the couch across from the wall as Camille pulled out dresses to show me. I picked ten dresses that I thought would look stunning on Ellery. The last dress Camille showed me was a Badgley Mischka strapless lace gown in black. I envisioned it on Ellery, and out of all the dresses, it was my favorite one. I got up and handed Ellery's address to Camille.

"Pick out some shoes to go with the dress, and maybe some jewelry too," I said as I started to walk away.

"Don't worry, Connor, I'll take care of everything," she smiled.

As I walked out of Saks, my phone started ringing. I looked at the screen as Ashlyn's name appeared.

"Hello, Ashlyn," I answered.

"What the fuck is going on, Connor?!" she yelled.

"Watch yourself, Ashlyn. What's the problem?"

"Why am I not on the list for the charity event tomorrow evening?"

I heavily sighed because I was waiting for this call. "I'm sorry, Ashlyn, but I didn't make the list."

"You knew I wasn't on the list, didn't you?" she sounded angry.

"Of course I knew, but there's nothing I can do. There are only so many seats available. Anyway, I don't have time for this. I have to go."

"Wait!" she yelled. "I heard a rumor that you're taking someone to the event tomorrow night."

"That's none of your business, Ashlyn. How many times do we go over this?"

"So, it's true?" She asked.

"If you must know, then yes, I'm bringing a friend with me," I said as I slipped into the back seat. "I have to go, Ashlyn; I'm working."

I hit the end button before she could say another word. The last thing I needed was her attending the charity tomorrow night and saying something in front of Ellery. I was beginning to feel stressed out, and I needed to hit the gym for a good workout. As soon as we got back to the penthouse, I grabbed my gym bag and headed for the gym. I ran on the treadmill, lifted some weights, and did some laps around the pool. I was on my way to the locker room when Stephanie stopped me in the hallway.

"I was hoping you'd show up here today," she smiled.

"Why's that?" I smiled back.

She had a seductive look in her eye that told me she wanted sex, and she wanted it now. It felt like an eternity since I've had sex, and it was driving me crazy. She led me to a small room where towels are stored. I pushed her up against the wall and ran my hand up her shirt, feeling her large breasts and hardened nipples as she kissed my neck. I moved my hand slowly down her torso and down the front of her shorts until I felt the edge of her thong. Stephanie reached down the front of my swim shorts and abruptly stopped, pushing me away and staring at me.

"What the hell, Connor? You're not even hard," she snapped.

I couldn't believe this was happening as this has never happened to me before. I sighed and took a step back as I ran my hands through my hair and shook my head.

"I don't know what the problem is. I've been under a lot of stress at work."

She opened the door and looked at me. "Sex is the best stress reliever in life, so maybe it's something else. Call me when you figure it out," she said as she walked out.

I walked to the locker room and got dressed. Damn Ellery Lane. I just couldn't stop thinking about her. Not only did she fuck with my head, now she's messing with my sex life. I walked out of the gym and climbed into the Range Rover. I put my head on the steering wheel for a minute while I tried to figure out what I was going to do.

I drove to the penthouse and threw my bag on the bed. I stood in the shower and let the hot water run down my body. I couldn't stop thinking about Ellery and what her reaction is going to be when Camille shows up at her apartment with the dresses. I stepped out of the shower and wiped the steam from the mirror with my hand. I looked at the man in the mirror and didn't recognize what I saw anymore. My heart is flipping out, and my mind is fucked up, compliments of Ellery Lane.

I slept pretty well all night. I'm sure the amount of scotch I drank before bed had helped. The next day, I got up, showered, dressed, and headed downstairs to the kitchen where Claire was making homemade banana nut bread.

"Good morning, Connor. Did you have a nice evening?"

"Good morning, Claire. Today's Sunday, and it's your day off. What are you doing here?" I asked her as I lightly kissed her cheek.

"Remember, I'm taking tomorrow off instead to take my husband to the doctor?"

"That's right, I'm sorry, I forgot. Thank you for making banana bread, it smells delicious." I said as I took my coffee and sat at the table.

"It will be ready in about 5 minutes. You seem like you're in a great mood today. Is there any special reason why?" she smiled.

I got the impression from her smile that she knew about Ellery. I'm sure Denny told her; those two seem to tell each other everything.

"The charity function is tonight, and I'm attending it with a very beautiful woman," I answered as I opened my laptop.

"Very good, Connor; I hope you enjoy yourself tonight," Claire smiled as she set the plate of banana bread on the table.

I smiled and thanked her. I checked my emails and started to answer a few of them when a text from Ellery came through to my phone.

"Hi Connor, it's me Ellery. Thank you for the beautiful dress, but it's too much, and I don't feel right accepting it."

I smiled because I knew she loved it. I wanted to make her feel like a princess tonight, even if she's just a friend.

"You're welcome, and it's not too much, see you at 6:00 pm sharp," I replied.

I was anxious to see what dress she picked out. They were all stunning, but the strapless black lace was my favorite. I could picture that dress, hugging her small silhouette, and with her breasts uplifted, forming a sexy cleavage. I picture her hair in curls that cascade over her shoulders and her smile when I pick her up. Damn that smile. I instantly became very aroused and needed to go upstairs to take care of myself. This has become a daily habit since I haven't had sex in a while. How the hell was I going to control myself with her tonight?

I put on my tuxedo, fixed my hair, and put on my Armani cologne. Why the hell was I getting so nervous? I put my cufflinks on and headed downstairs. My phone rang. I took it from my jacket, and saw that it was my mother calling.

"Hello, mom," I answered.

"Connor, darling, we won't be attending the charity. I need you to send our apologies to everyone."

"Why? What happened?" I asked.

"Nothing to worry about darling; we're all sick with the flu."

"I'm sorry, mom, is there anything you need?"

"No, Connor, just give our apologies and have a nice time."

"Call me if you need me or anything," I made her promise.

I made my way to the garage where Denny was waiting for me. I slid into the back of the limo and took in a deep breath. Denny looked at me through the rearview mirror.

"Are you ok, Connor?" he asked.

"I'm fine, Denny. Let's go pick up Miss Lane."

72

We pulled up to the curb of her apartment building. I got out and walked up to the door, then knocked and waited for her to answer. The moment the door opened, I took in a sharp breath at the sight of Ellery standing there in my favorite dress. An intoxicated feeling came over me as she smiled. Damn that smile.

"Were you afraid that I'd get mugged between my door and your car?" she smirked.

"Very funny, Ellery," I smiled at her.

She nudged my shoulder playfully, and I nudged her back. I opened the door for her, and she gracefully slid into the seat. I climbed in and sat beside her. I grabbed a glass and handed it to her as I poured champagne into it. Once again, my heart began beating faster than normal, and my palms were sweaty. I held my glass up to her.

"You look beautiful, Ellery. What a lovely dress," I said.

"Thank you, Connor. I was hoping you'd like this one," she winked as she held up her glass to mine.

She was exquisite. The dress hugged her just like I'd pictured it would, framing her small petite body. Her soft curled hair was in an up do that featured her elongated neck as small diamond teardrop earrings hung perfectly from her ears. I subtly took in her scent as it filled the enclosed space we were in. Needless to say, it was arousing me. I could tell this was going to be a long night.

Denny pulled up to the entrance of the hotel and got out to open Ellery's door. I walked around to her side, took her hand, and helped her out of the limo. Her hand was warm and soft, and fire ignited throughout my body when I touched her.

"Do you think that you can behave yourself tonight?" I smirked as I held my arm out to her.

"I don't know, but I can't make any promises," she smiled as she wrapped her arm in mine.

We walked into the hotel and straight down the hallway to the Grand Ballroom. It was one of the most elegant ballrooms in New York. I need a drink, and I need one now.

"What can I get you from the bar?" I asked.

"I'll take a glass of white wine, please."

I told her to wait at the table as I went to the bar and got our drinks. I gave her the glass of wine while I steadily drank my scotch and admired the most beautiful woman in the ballroom standing before me. I saw a good friend and colleague of mine, Robert and his wife, standing at the other side of the room. I lightly touched Ellery's elbow and escorted her to where he and his wife were standing.

"Good evening, Connor," Robert said as we shook hands.

"Hello, Robert, Courtney, I would like you to meet a friend of mine, Ellery Lane."

"You have beautiful friends, Connor," he smiled as he lightly kissed Ellery's hand.

I gave a small smile and watched as Courtney eyed Ellery up and down. Courtney and I had a bit of a history, and it left her bitter. She fell hard and wanted more, but I had nothing to give. Robert put his arm around me and led me off to the side where the women couldn't hear us.

"Connor, Ashlyn is coming. I just thought you should know," he said.

"What? I thought I told you to make sure she wouldn't be here," I snapped.

"I did make sure, but then she went and swooned George Frankel, and he fell all over the opportunity. You know how he is with beautiful women."

"Damn it," I shook my head.

We walked back to where Ellery and Courtney were standing. I put my hand on the small of Ellery's back and escorted her back to the table. I needed to try and find Ashlyn before she saw Ellery. I pulled the chair out for her and excused myself to the restroom.

I headed down the hallway and saw Ashlyn entering the ballroom with George. She saw me coming and smiled. I was angry at her and she knew it.

"George, good to see you, buddy," I smiled as I put my arm around him. "Why don't you go to the bar and grab a drink for you and Ashlyn. She'll meet you at the table, but first, I have something that I need to discuss with her."

He nodded his head and walked down the hallway till he reached the ballroom. As soon as he was out of sight, I turn to look at Ashlyn with a burning anger in my eyes.

"What the hell are you doing here?!" I said through gritted teeth as I looked around to make sure nobody was watching.

I backed her up against the wall. "Relax, Connor, George asked me if I'd like to accompany him, and I graciously accepted. Is there is a reason that you don't want me here?"

I looked away and then back at her. I grabbed her arm and led her around the corner. "I'm here with someone, and so help me, Ashlyn, if you even say one word to her – I swear…"

"Don't worry, Connor, I won't spill our little secret to your new toy," she devilishly grinned.

I stared directly at her, and she knew I was pissed. "Are we clear, Ashlyn?"

"Don't worry, you've made yourself very clear," she whispered.

I turned around and headed back to the ballroom. As I approached the entrance, I noticed Ellery dancing with another man, and anger started to burn inside me. I walked out on the dance floor and tapped Andrew on the shoulder.

"Excuse me, Andrew, but she's here with me."

He gave me an apologetic look. "Mr. Black, I'm sorry. I didn't know she was yours."

He stepped aside as I took his place, placing my hand on her waist and taking her hand in mine. Her hand was so soft, and it felt good to hold it.

"I leave you alone for a minute, and you go off and dance with strange men? Is that what you call behaving?"

She narrowed her eyes at me. "You left me alone to disappear with the woman who slapped you at Club S."

I looked at her in confusion. "You saw that?"

She shook her head. "I think a lot of people saw that."

"So, let me get this straight, you saw me before you found me drunk outside?" I curiously asked.

"Yes, I was sitting at the bar. Why do you ask?" she cocked

her head.

"Interesting," I said as the corners of my mouth curved up.

"What's interesting?" She asked. "Oh, I get it now. You think I had my eyes set on you from the start."

I wickedly smiled at her, "Your words, Miss Lane, not mine."

She rolled her eyes and leaned closer into me, bringing her lips inches from my ear. I couldn't help but take in her alluring scent as she whispered, "You are a delusional man, Mr. Black."

I closed my eyes for her scent was mesmerizing. She smelled like lilacs. This dance needed to end quickly or else she was going to get the wrong idea, if you know what I mean. She proceeded to ask me why I chose this charity to represent. This is something that's very personal to me, and I didn't feel the need to share something so personal with her. After all, we're only friends.

"May I ask why this specific charity?" she asked.

"Why not this charity?" I vaguely asked.

"Why did you though?" she continued.

I looked straight ahead into the crowd. "It's just a charity that my company is involved with. Why is it so important that you know a specific reason?"

"Just forget I asked," she said as she refused to look at me.

"You're mad," I spoke.

"You'll know when I'm mad, Mr. Black," she responded.

The thoughts running through my head were sexual ones when she said that. I can't help it, I'm a man, and that's what we think about. Thank god the music ended when it did because there was no way of hiding my arousal any longer with our bodies pressed up against each other. I let go of her, placing my right hand in my pocket, and my other on the small of her back as we walked back to our table. I introduced her to some of my associates that were already sitting. I glanced over at the next table and saw Ashlyn glaring at Ellery. I shot her a warning look, and she turned away. We sat down and had dinner. I took the liberty of ordering Ellery the Filet since she needed to put some meat on her bones. I'm not sure if she appreciated that, but she did impress me by eating the whole piece. After dinner was over and we listened to a few speeches, Ellery excused herself to the restroom.

I got up and headed to the bar to get Ellery another glass of wine and another scotch for myself. I walked back to the table and was surprised when she wasn't back yet. I set the drinks on the table and walked to the restrooms. I leaned up against the wall opposite the ladies restroom and folded my arms. I was tempted to open the door and make sure she was in there. The thought of her being in trouble or just leaving because she was bored entered my mind. Suddenly, the door opened and Ellery looked startled when she saw me standing there.

"Uh, hi? Why are you standing there like that?"

"Because you've been gone for quite a while, and I was checking to make sure you're ok. I was giving you five more seconds before I was opening the door and coming in after you."

"Wow, stalker much?" she said as she walked away.

"For the last time, I'm not a stalker; I was concerned for your safety," I sighed.

I saw her lightly smile. Damn that smile. I have no idea what the hell is going on with me. I want to touch her, and I want to feel her bare skin against mine. Shit, this is not good. Maybe I made a mistake by bringing her here. Am I leading her on? We're just friends, and I hope she understands that. I wanted to beat my head against a wall and knock some sense into it. I took in a deep breath. Ellery sat down and sipped her wine. I needed to speak with a friend of mine, so I told her I'd be right back. I walked a few feet away and talked to Paul about the company I was trying to acquire. My eyes kept wandering to her as she sat there and looked so beautiful. I watched her lips wrap around the edge of the wine glass with each sip she took as they left an imprint of her lipstick. Paul noticed me staring at Ellery.

"Connor, you seem distracted," he said as he turned around and looked Ellery's way.

"Sorry, Paul, I'm listening, please continue."

"I would be pleasantly distracted if I had that beautiful woman in my sights," he smiled.

"You know what, Paul? Let's just continue this tomorrow. I have a meeting at 10 o'clock, but please call Valerie and have her set something up," I said.

He patted me on the back and walked away. I saw Ashlyn from across the room, eyeing Ellery. It was time that I got her out of here. I walked over to the table and lightly put my hand on her shoulder.

"Are you ready to leave?" I asked.

"I am if you are," she replied.

What I didn't tell her was that I wasn't coming with her to take her home. I needed to stay back and have a talk with Ashlyn. I also had to rethink this situation with Ellery. My head has been fucked up ever since I saw her, and I need to put an end to it. She deserves better than me as I'm not the man she thinks I am. I will hurt her eventually or she'll hurt me, and that's something I'm not in the market for. We walked out to where Denny was waiting for us, and I opened the door for Ellery.

"I'm going to have Denny take you home; I have something that I need to wrap up here," I said as I took her hand and lightly kissed it. "Thank you for coming with me tonight. I hope you had a good time."

She looked at me with her ice blue eyes, and I could see the disappointment in them. "I had a wonderful time, Connor. Thank you for inviting me."

She was hurt that I didn't accompany her, and for the first time, my heart ached putting her in that limo by herself. I hated this feeling, and I'm stopping it. I have no choice. It needs to be done. I walked back into the hotel to find Ashlyn and talk to her, but she was nowhere to be found. I sat at the bar in the hotel lobby and ordered a scotch to drown my feelings. A while later, as I was ready to order my second glass, Denny called.

"Denny, what's up?"

"I thought you should know that Miss Lane forced me to drive her to the beach."

"What! I gave you orders to take her home," I yelled.

"Connor, you know how Miss Lane is, and she gave me no choice. I'm almost at the hotel to pick you up."

"Doesn't she know how dangerous it is for a young woman to be on the beach at night, by herself? Her disregard for safety is ridiculous!" I hung up the phone and walked outside as Denny pulled up to the curb.

"Drive me straight to the penthouse so I can pick up the Range Rover," I said as I got inside the limo.

"I'm sorry, Connor, but she left me no choice. She's a very stubborn girl, and she said if you have a problem with it, then she'll deal with you herself," he lightly smiled.

"Is that so? She said that?"

Denny nodded his head. "Like I said before, Connor, you've met your match with Miss Lane."

We pulled into the parking garage, and I hopped in the Range Rover and drove to the beach. It was only about a 10 minute drive. I was furious at her for doing this. How dare she defy my orders and put Denny in that position to disobey me.

Chapter 7

I put the Range Rover in park and got out. The air was quite warm for this time of year. I looked out into the ocean as I was searching for Ellery. The ocean looked beautiful at night with the moonlight shining down, illuminating each wave that pushed its way to the shore. I can see why she wanted to come here. I saw her down by the edge of the water as the light of the moon fell down upon her and illuminated her silhouette. I could hear a light laughter coming from her as her feet touched the water. She was so full of life; and a free spirit. I stood there with my hands in my pocket as I cleared my throat.

"What the hell do you think you're doing?" My voice angered.

She stood still and turned to look at me. "What are you doing here, Connor? Don't you have things to wrap up?"

"I'm here because you didn't make it home and forced my driver to disobey my orders," I said in an abrupt tone.

"Well, it was such a beautiful night, and I wanted to be here; it's my favorite place to visit."

"There's a time and place for that Ellery, and now is not the time."

"I'm sorry you feel that way, but I'm not done here yet, and I'm not leaving."

"Let's go now, Ellery," my voice commanded.

"Don't be so grouchy, and if you want me to go, then you'll have to catch me," she laughed as she started running down the beach.

"For fuck sake, Elle, you're pissing me off!" I yelled as I started to chase after her.

I was catching up to her. I could tell she was becoming out of breath as she started to slow down. I came up behind her, picked her up, and put her over my shoulder. I'm glad it was dark so she couldn't see my half smile. She was kicking and screaming as I was carrying her through the sand.

"Put me down, Connor Black!"

"Not a chance! You'll just run again, and I'm done playing games."

"I won't, I promise. I'm out of breath anyway," she said.

I knew she was out of breath, so I gently put her down. She immediately sat herself on the soft sand in that expensive designer dress. I couldn't believe what I was seeing as she held her hand out to me and asked me to sit next to her.

"I'm not sitting in the sand in this tuxedo," I said.

She looked out into the night ocean waters and softly spoke, "Live a little, Connor, life is too short."

Her words were serious. She wasn't playing anymore. Against my better judgment, I sat down next to her. She didn't look at me, but the corners of her mouth were slightly turned up. We sat in silence for a moment. I was staring out at the water, trying to see what she saw. She came here for a reason, and now something was on her mind. I was just about to ask her if she was ok when she started to speak.

"It was my 16th birthday when I was diagnosed with cancer. Hey, happy sweet 16! Guess what, you have cancer."

I was stunned by what she had just said. Why was she telling me something so personal? I gulped because I didn't know what to say. Her voice was soft, and her eyes were focused out in the distant ocean waters. I wanted to wrap my arms around her and hold her tight, but I couldn't. I was afraid of her reaction. I reached over and lightly took her hand in mine as I whispered, "You don't have to do this." I watched her take in a sharp breath as she continued.

"I couldn't bear the thought of my father having to go through that torture and pain again like he did with my mother, so I decided I was going to spare him from having to."

"Ellery," I whispered as I leaned closer to her. I still had her hand in mine, and she didn't try to pull away. The feeling inside me was overwhelming as I softly rubbed her warm skin with my thumb.

"He was going out on one of his drinking binges, and I knew he wouldn't be home until the middle of the night, if at all, so that was my opportunity to put my plan into action. I filled the bathtub with hot water, laid back, and took a razor blade to both my wrists. Can you believe it was the one night he forgot his wallet and came back to the house? Talk about fate, right? He found me and called 911. I almost didn't make it; I had lost so much blood."

I couldn't say a word. I was choked up as I just sat there holding her hand. I was feeling her pain, and it hurt me so much to know that my friend, this beautiful woman, went through something so terrible.

"I guess God had other plans for me. I went through a year of chemo and went into remission. I was given a second chance at life, and for that, I'm grateful. Like I said yesterday, I was young and stupid, and I made a terrible mistake."

The overwhelming need to hold her finally won. I let go of her hand and put my arm around her, pulling her into me. She rested her head on my shoulder.

"That's why you have this overwhelming need to help others, isn't it?" I asked her as I lightly kissed the top of her head. "You're a good person, Ellery Lane," I whispered in her ear.

Tonight was a turning point for me. Ellery let her guard down and showed me her broken side. I knew when I saw the scars on her wrists that she had a troubled past. I never dreamed she would have to fight cancer. She closed her eyes as she left her head resting on my shoulder. She was exhausted, and it was late. I needed to get her home. I picked her up from the sand and carried her across the beach. She put her arms around my neck and laid her head on my chest. I held her tight. I needed her to feel safe with me. I opened the door to the Range Rover and gently laid her in the front seat. She started to stir so I whispered to her, "Sleep, angel."

I pulled out of the parking lot and drove to her apartment. I kept looking at her as she slept peacefully. She looked like an angel. Everything I tried to bury tonight came back to the surface and drowned my fears with a bit of hope. Maybe, just maybe, something more could come of our friendship one day. I pulled up to curb of her apartment. Her purse was lying next to her so I opened it and grabbed her keys. I got out and walked around to the passenger side, and I opened the door. I carefully picked her up as she put her arms around my neck, and I carried her to the door. I inserted the key, unlocking the door and lightly kicked it open with my foot. I carried her down the hallway to her bedroom and gently laid her on the bed. I looked around the room and saw a blanket in the corner. I walked over, picked it up, and covered her with it to keep her warm. I stood over her while she slept and ran the back of my hand down her soft cheek. "Sleep well, angel, and sweet dreams." She didn't move or make a sound.

I walked out of the bedroom and stood in the middle of her apartment. I looked around at the practically bare space that is her home. It reminded me of a box. With the sale of her paintings, she would be able to move into a bigger and better apartment. I made the decision that I was going to help her find one.

***

The next morning after my shower, I sat on the edge of the bed and looked at my cell phone, debating whether or not to text Ellery. I looked at my watch, and it was still early, but I decided to send one anyway.

"Hi, I hope you slept well. I just wanted to see if you were up and how you were feeling."

As I hit the send button, I could hear voices coming from downstairs. Who the hell is here at this hour in the morning? I walked down to the kitchen where I found Ashlyn talking to Denny.

"Ashlyn, what are you doing here? Do you see what time it is?" I asked in an irritated voice.

"Good morning, Connor. You look quite handsome this morning," she smiled as she walked over and adjusted my tie.

I rolled my eyes and walked to the coffee pot. "Answer the question, Ashlyn."

"Phil asked me to get these papers to you. He said he was sorry, but he won't be in the office until later, and he said you needed them for your meeting. So I told him I would deliver them personally to you."

She stood beside me and reached across to grab a cup. I sighed as I moved out of her way. "Thank you for delivering the papers, Ashlyn, now you can leave."

"Connor, why do you have to be so heartless? I'm riding in with you. Why should I pay for a cab when we're both going to the same place?"

I took my coffee and headed into my office to look over the paperwork before my meeting at Black Enterprises. My phone chimed and there was a text message from Ellery.

"Good morning, Connor. I slept well, and I'm feeling fine; thank you for your concern. I hope you have a terrific day, and don't work too hard!"

I smiled as I read her words. I quickly replied. "I'm glad you're feeling fine, and I always work hard; it's why I'm as successful as I am."

"I believe that, and thank you for taking care of me last night. I owe you one!"

I looked at my watch, and if I didn't get going, I was going to be late for my meeting. I quickly responded back to her. "Consider it repayment for when you got me home safe. I have a meeting I need to get to. TTYL!"

"Bye, Connor."

I stepped out into the hallway where Ashlyn was waiting for me.

"Denny is waiting in the limo for us," she said.

"That's where he waits every day, Ashlyn," I sighed.

We climbed into the limo, and Ashlyn made her attempts on me. She leaned over and grabbed my tie.

"Why don't we get together tonight and have some fun? It's been way too long, Connor, and I'm going through withdrawals," she whined.

I removed her hand from my tie. "I have plans for tonight. I'm sorry."

"You always have plans lately," she whined. "This doesn't have anything to do with that girl you were with last night, does it?"

"Ellery doesn't have anything to do with it. I've explained to you a thousand times that I've been busy. You work at Black Enterprises; you know how hard I've been working trying to secure the acquisition of that company in Chicago."

She reached over and grabbed my hand. "Connor, you need to take a break. I worry about you."

I pulled my hand away. "Remember the rules, Ashlyn," I scowled. She turned away and looked out the window. I could see Denny glaring at me from the rearview mirror. We finally arrived at Black Enterprises, and Ashlyn stepped out of the limo and onto the sidewalk. I followed behind her. As I got out of the limo, I adjusted my tie that she messed with. I looked over into the crowd of people, scurrying to get to their destination and saw Ellery a few feet away, standing in the middle of the sidewalk, and staring at me as she held a Starbucks cup in her hand. She lightly smiled and waved. I was furious at that moment because she must have seen Ashlyn getting out of the limo. The look on her beautiful face was sad. God knows what she must be thinking right now. She tried to fake her smile, but she couldn't hide the fact that she was hurt. I saw the pained look on her face when she looked at me. I couldn't force a smile because I was upset that she saw us like this. I wanted to walk over to her, hug her, and tell her how much I enjoyed last night, but I could only managed a small wave as I walked into the building. Fuck, what am I going to do now? I hurt her again, just like last night when I put her in the limo by herself to send her home.

***

My meeting had ended on a positive note, and I was in a fairly good mood. I had an idea, so I sent a text message to Denny.

"I will be having dinner tonight with Miss Lane. I believe she told me last night that she gets off work at 6:00 pm. I need you to pick her up from her place of employment and bring her to The Steakhouse where I'll be waiting for her."

"Does she know she's joining you for dinner?" he asked.

"She will when you pick her up."

"Very well, Connor."

I got the impression from that last text that Denny didn't believe Ellery would have dinner with me tonight.

I wrapped up the day and looked at my watch. It was already 5:30 pm. I stepped out of the office and hailed a cab to the restaurant. I sat in a booth and waited for Ellery to join me. I wanted to talk to her about what she saw this morning. I didn't know how I was going to explain it, but I had to think of something quick. It was 6:30 pm, and Denny should've been here by now. Just as I was about to pull my phone out and call him, I noticed him walking towards me.

"Miss Lane told me to tell you she's not available this evening and that she has plans. She also said that if you want to have dinner with her, then you should pick up the phone and ask her," he started to laugh.

"I'm glad you're finding this amusing, Denny."

"I'm sorry, Connor, but she doesn't take orders from anybody. She's one-of-a-kind."

I shook my head and looked down. "She's mad about this morning. I know she is. You're right, Denny, she is one-of-a-kind, and I need to make things right. Take me to her apartment," I said as we exited the restaurant.

"She's not at her apartment," Denny said.

"How do you know?"

"I followed her after she declined your dinner invitation. She's dining alone at a pizza place called Pizzapopolous."

"Then it looks like I'm having dinner there tonight."

I stood in front of the window and watched her as she sat at a small table, fumbling for something in her purse. She looked just as beautiful as she did last night. I walked through the door of the small restaurant and sat down across from her. She looked up at me and rolled her eyes. That attitude of hers was arousing.

"So this is where you want to have dinner?" I asked.

She cocked her head to the side. "Yes, Connor, this is where I'm having dinner tonight, and I don't believe you were invited."

I put my hand over my heart. "Ouch, that stings, Ellery. I invited you to dinner, and you turned me down, so I took it upon myself to join you."

"How do you know I want company?" she asked.

I put my hands on the table and folded them. "I don't, but since I'm here, we might as well dine together," I said as I looked around the restaurant.

She shook her head and lightly smiled. I opened up the menu and glanced at it as the waitress stopped at our table to take our orders. I used to eat pizza when I was a kid. I haven't had it in years and I wasn't about to start now. Just as I placed my order for an antipasto salad, Ellery reached over and grabbed the menu from my hands.

"You can't sit in a pizza place and only get a salad." she said.

The waitress was eyeing me and wouldn't stop to look at Ellery. She cleared her throat to get her attention.

"We'll have a large deep dish with pepperoni, mushrooms, and black olives, and a large antipasto salad with an order of bread sticks," she smiled.

I brought my finger up and rested it on my lips, "Do you actually think I'm going to eat that pizza?"

"I don't think you are; I know you are," she smiled.

Damn that smile. I'm finding it very difficult to say no to this girl. It's like she has some control over me, and I just can't help it when I'm around her. The waitress brought the pizza and set it in the middle of the table. I looked at it and then at Ellery who was putting a slice on my plate. I grabbed my fork and knife and started to cut into it when out of nowhere, she startled me.

"What, are you kidding me?! Put that down right now, Connor Black!"

"What? What the hell is wrong?"

"You are not eating pizza with a fork and knife," she said as she leaned over the table and took them from my hands.

"Then how the hell am I supposed to eat it?" I frowned.

"Like this; pick it up and bite into it," she said as she chewed.

"That's disgusting, and don't talk with your mouth full."

She cocked her head, and a smirk came upon her face. "If you won't do it, then I will," she said as she grabbed the pizza from my plate and held it to my mouth.

"Bite," she demanded.

I raised my eyebrows at her, "Do you have any idea how sexy that sounds?" I winked. That was the sexiest thing coming from her, and I started to get aroused.

I couldn't deny this beautiful woman who was holding a slice of pizza in my face, so I opened my mouth and took a bite. It was worth it just to see the smile on her face.

"My turn," I smiled back at her.

"Your turn for what?" she asked.

I took the pizza and held it up to her mouth.

"Bite," I demanded.

I couldn't help but smile because she was so damn cute when she took that bite. We sat and talked about art while we ate pizza, salad, and bread sticks. I was having a great time in Pizzapopolous, sharing pizza with Ellery. A part of me was glad she turned me down for the first dinner invitation.

Her phone rang and she answered it with a strange look on her face. I pulled out my phone to check my messages, and I looked up to see a tear running down her cheek. Her face turned from happy to pain in a matter of seconds. Without even realizing what I was doing, I reached for her hand that was resting on the table. She was as white as a ghost when she hung up the phone, and I became worried. She had received the devastating news that her aunt and uncle were just killed in a car accident. She said she needed to get out of there as she quickly stood up from her chair. I threw some money on the table and followed her out of the restaurant. She looked confused as she stepped onto the sidewalk. I put my arm around her and held her as she stumbled on the sidewalk a couple of times. She was in shock, and I needed to get her into the limo so she could sit down.

I helped her into the back seat and climbed in beside her. I didn't say a word; I just wrapped my arms around her and pulled her into me to let her know that I cared. She clenched my shirt in her hands and started sobbing into my chest. I kissed her on her head and held her tight, letting her cry for as long as needed to.

Chapter 8

When we arrived at her apartment, I followed her inside and lightly closed the door. She headed to the kitchen area and asked me if I wanted some wine. I politely declined because I had a meeting with Paul in about an hour. I asked her if she was ok because she was standing at the kitchen window just staring out into the world. She opened the bottle of wine, poured some in a glass, and turned around, placing one hand on my chest.

"Thank you, Connor. I want you to know that I truly appreciate you being here for me."

I raised my hand and brought it to her tear soaked cheek and gently wiped away a couple of tears that were left as I said, "I know you do, and you're welcome." All I wanted to do at that moment was brush my lips against hers. I wanted to take her pain away, but I couldn't. We're friends, and I won't cross that line, at least not yet. She gently smiled at me, patted me on the chest, and told me to go to my meeting.

"If you need anything, anything at all, please don't hesitate to call me," I told her as I pressed my lips against her smooth forehead.

I walked out of her apartment and started heading towards the limo. This poor girl has experienced more death than she should have in her life. I couldn't let her be alone tonight. My head was telling me one thing, but my heart was telling me to bring her home with me. I walked back up to her apartment and knocked on the door.

"Hey, what are you still doing here?" she asked.

"Pack a bag because you're staying with me tonight," I said as

I walked through the door.

She looked at me with a stunned look. "No, I'm not; I'm staying right here."

Why can't she just listen to me for once? "Elle, for once, just once, please do as I say," I sighed.

Her face became angered. "I'm not a child, Connor, and frankly, you can't order me around. I thought we had this discussion already?" she said.

I didn't want to argue with her, but she wasn't staying in this apartment alone tonight. I noticed her easel in the corner of the room, so I walked over to it and stared at the canvas that sat upon it, trying to get up the nerve to say what I needed to say.

"I don't think you should be alone tonight after the news you received, and my place has a guest room. I would feel better knowing you weren't alone."

Her attitude instantly changed, and she told me to wait while she packs a bag. Sitting on the easel was an unfinished painting of the bride and groom from Central Park. Even though it sat unfinished, the scene before me was breathtaking. I could look at the couple in the painting and see their happiness. The thing I've noticed about Ellery's paintings is that she knows how to capture the present emotion of her subjects. I wondered what a portrait of me would look like if she painted one. As Ellery returned, I smiled at her, grabbed her bag, and we headed out the door.

She sat in the limo next me and stared out the window. I made a phone call to Paul and rescheduled our meeting. She turned and looked at me.

"You shouldn't have cancelled your meeting for me, Connor,"

she softly spoke.

I put my arm around her, "My meeting can wait." She laid her on my chest, and it felt good to have her there.

***

We arrived at the penthouse, and I took her bag up to the guest room. When I came back downstairs, I noticed her staring at the black and white photographs that were hanging on the wall. When I told her I took them, she seemed very surprised. She proceeded to ask me if I decorated the penthouse. I could tell the more we talked, the better she felt. I told her about my sister, Cassidy, and she was shocked again. I guess it's because I've never talked about anything or anyone in my personal life. I headed over to the bar.

"Drink?" I asked her.

"Shot of Jack, please," she said. My eyes widened as I looked at her.

"Are you sure?" I asked in disbelief.

"Does that surprise you?" she laughed.

I reached for a shot glass as she made herself comfortable on the bar stool. "It doesn't, well, maybe it does; I just don't know any women who do shots of Jack Daniels straight."

"You do now," she said as she threw back the shot. I was in awe of this girl, this woman that was sitting across from me. She put the shot glass down on the bar and cocked her head.

"I thought you didn't do sleepovers, Mr. Black?"

I looked at her and grinned, "I don't, Miss Lane. I never have, but tonight I made an exception for a friend because I felt she shouldn't be alone."

I poured another shot of whiskey and held up the glass. "Another shot?" I asked.

"Are you trying to get me drunk?" she smiled seductively.

Damn that smile. I put my hand in my pocket and cocked my head to the side. "Should I be?" I grinned. She threw back the second shot and sat down on the couch. She looked worried. I sat down next to her with my glass of scotch and asked her if she was ok. She looked up at me with her angelic blue eyes and smiled.

"I was just thinking about how I can visit my mom and dad's grave when I'm back in Michigan."

"When was the last time you visited them?" I asked.

"Just a little over a year ago. I stopped by for a visit the day before Kyle and I moved to New York."

Just hearing his name made me angry. I'm not sure why. I should be thanking the bastard, because if he wouldn't have left, then I never would have met Ellery. I looked at her as she stared straight into my eyes and spoke about how she wants to be cremated when she dies. I narrowed my eyes at her and told her to stop talking like that. It was something I didn't ever want to think about. She continued to go on about how she doesn't want people to mourn over her, and she wants them to remember the good times they shared. She was really beginning to irritate me with all this talk about death. I told her to stop because she was talking as if she was going to die tomorrow. Then she said something that frightened me.

"You never know what each day will bring, and that's why I believe that nothing lasts forever."

I got up from the couch and took her hand, helping her up.

"Ok, I think Mr. Daniel's has gotten to you. Let's get some sleep; I have to work in the morning."

I led her upstairs and showed her to the guest room. I turned around and grabbed the door knob, "Good night, Elle, sleep well," I spoke as I walked out of the room and down the hall to my bedroom.

I took off my clothes and climbed into bed. I laid there, thinking about Ellery and how serious she was about her own death. How could she think of such things? The more I thought about it, the more it made sense; death has always been a part of her life. I tossed and turned. I tried to get comfortable, but I couldn't. I got out of bed and slowly walked down the hall toward her room. I stood outside the door and listened; there was silence. I'm sure the shots of Jack helped her sleep. I made the decision that I was taking her to Michigan as I didn't want her going alone.

The next morning, I showered and headed to the kitchen to make a pot of coffee. I called the bakery down the street and had a dozen bagels delivered. I wanted to make sure Ellery had something to eat when she woke up. I sat down at the table and opened my laptop. I had some emails to go over and meetings to reschedule for when I came back. Not too long after I sat down, Ellery came walking into the kitchen. I looked at her, and my heart started to beat rapidly. She was wearing black yoga pants that hugged her hips and ass perfectly and a pink tank top that was way too sexy on her. She had her hair up in a high ponytail. Damn, I was getting aroused again just looking at her. I needed to get my mind off her body and tell her I'm taking her to Michigan.

"Good morning, Ellery, I hope you slept well," I smiled.

She walked over and poured herself a cup of coffee and sat down across from me.

"There are bagels over there; please have one."

She politely declined. I sighed and told her she had to eat.

"I never eat when I first get up, but don't worry, dad, I'll have one in a little bit," she said in a cocky way.

I tried not to smile, but it was inevitable, because even first thing in the morning, she was a smart ass. She stared at me as I was typing. I looked up and over my laptop at her.

"What are you doing?" she asked.

This was my opportunity to tell her about our road trip to Michigan. I was a little nervous about how she was going to react.

"Just sending some emails and rearranging some meetings."

"Did you over-schedule or something?" she asked in cute way.

I looked up at her as she took a sip of her coffee. "You question everything, don't you?" I asked. She looked up at the ceiling and smiled, "I guess I do."

I asked her what her plans were for the day, and she told me that she was going to volunteer at the soup kitchen. She said that no matter what their problems were, they were homeless and needed help. Her kindness and charitable nature really had an effect on me. I've never met anyone like her. I finished up what I was doing and closed my laptop.

"I rearranged my meetings because I'm taking you to Michigan," I said as I sat and waited for her reaction.

"What?" she asked.

I know she likes to argue, but she wasn't winning this one. I got up from the table and set my cup on the counter. "It's not up for discussion, Elle; we're leaving tomorrow morning, and we're driving."

"Driving? That's a 10 hour drive, Connor!" she exclaimed.

I looked at her from across the kitchen as she stared at me with a shocked expression on her face. "Do you have a problem being in a car with me for 10 hours?" I casually asked her and was afraid that she was going to yes.

"No, but…"

I walked over to the table and stood over her. She looked so beautiful, sitting there drinking coffee and giving me an attitude about driving. It took everything I had not to reach out and run my finger along her jaw line or kiss her as she lifted her head and looked at me. It was getting harder to resist her. I didn't even know if she wanted me. I need to call Dr. Peters and see him before we leave tomorrow.

"No buts; we're going by car, and I'm driving," I said as I smiled at her and left for the office.

As I stepped off the elevator and into the parking garage, Denny was walking towards me. "Denny, I'm glad you're here early. I wanted to tell you that I'm giving you the next few days off."

"Ok, Connor, but may I ask why?"

"I'm driving Miss Lane to Michigan for her aunt and uncle's funeral, and we're leaving tomorrow morning."

Denny looked at me and smiled. "Was it her idea that you take her?"

"No, and I didn't give her any other choice. I told her I was taking her and that it wasn't up for discussion."

Denny continued looking at me. "She was ok with that?"

I rolled my eyes as I walked to the Range Rover. "She didn't really argue too much. I'm driving myself to the office today. Take Miss Lane home or wherever she wants to go, but I do have a meeting at 1:00 pm across town, so I'll need you to pick me up."

Instead of heading straight to the office, I called Dr. Peters and asked him if he was available to see me. I needed to talk to him about this upcoming road trip. He told me to come right in since his first appointment wasn't scheduled for another hour. I walked into his office and sat down in my usual chair.

"Good morning, Connor. Is everything alright? You said it was urgent."

I took in a deep breath as I ran my hand through my hair. "Remember that girl I told you about at our last session?"

"Yes, I believe her name is Ellery; correct?" he asked as he looked at me intently.

"Yes, that's her. Well, her aunt and uncle were recently killed in a car accident, and I'm taking her to Michigan for the funeral."

"That's good, Connor. So, why don't you explain to me where your relationship with Ellery stands?"

I shifted in my chair. "Ellery and I are friends and nothing more. I'm doing this for her because I don't want her going alone, and she should have someone there for her."

Dr. Peters got up from his chair and walked over to the coffee pot. "Would you care for some coffee, Connor?" he asked.

"No, I'm good."

"It sounds to me like you're beginning to have more feelings that extend beyond friendship for her. So, your flight leaves tomorrow?"

"We aren't flying; I'm driving her there. I told her it was a road trip."

He looked at me and sat down while he sipped his coffee. "That's a 10 hour drive. You and Ellery will be alone in a car for a substantial amount of time. Are you ready for what might happen along the way?"

I brought my foot to my opposite knee and leaned on the arm of the chair. "Why are you making a big deal out of this, Doc? It's a simple road trip with a friend who just lost her aunt and uncle. That's it, nothing more."

"Connor, you can keep convincing yourself of that all you want, because if you truly believed that, you wouldn't be sitting in my office, talking to me about it," Dr. Peters sighed.

"I got up from the chair and stood in front of the window. "I can't stop thinking about her, and it scares me. She confessed her deepest secret to me the other night. She told me about her past."

"She isn't keeping secrets from you. She wants you to know about her past, and she trusted you enough to tell you. I think you're fighting your true feelings. Have you discussed anything about you or your past?"

I walked over to the large bookcase and stared at the hundreds of books he had sitting on the shelf. "I told her about my sister and my nephew."

"That's it? Connor, you have to open up to her if you want any kind of relationship. Take it one day at a time. I think the two of you being friends is a very good start, and from the sound of it, you're very good friends already."

I walked over to the chair and grabbed my coat. "Thank you, Dr. Peters, but my time is up."

"I want to see you again when you come back from your road trip!" he yelled as I walked out the door.

Chapter 9

Shit, look at the time, and where is Denny? I paced back and forth in my office looking at my watch. Just as I was about to head out of the building, my phone rang, and it was Denny.

"Denny, where the hell are you, man?!" I yelled.

"Connor, I apologize, but I had to drive Ellery to the hospital," he said calmly.

"What, what do you mean?!" I asked in a panic.

"She said she fainted at home and hit her head. I saw her on the street, trying to hail a cab with her hand over her eye, and I stopped. Connor, the cut is pretty bad."

I can't even explain what I was feeling at that moment. I was worried sick about her. I felt this overwhelming need to rush to her side and comfort her. I flew out of my office and told Valerie to reschedule my meeting. Ellery was more important.

I climbed in the back of the limo and told Denny to hurry up and drive me to the hospital. I saw the blood soaked towel on the front seat, and I instantly felt sick.

"Please tell me she's ok, Denny." I said with a worried tone.

"She's going to be fine, Connor, just relax. She needs a few stitches, and she'll be alright."

I sat there in silence as the trip to the hospital seemed to take forever. When Denny finally pulled up, I got out and ran to the reception desk, asking where Ellery was. The receptionist directed me down the hall and to the last room on the right. I took in a deep breath, and as I opened the curtain, Ellery looked at me. Her eyes lit up when she saw me. I walked over to her and asked her what happened as I gently stroked the area above her cut. My heart ached, seeing her sitting there and bleeding. She put her hand on my arm and told me that she was fine. Maybe I was making a bigger deal out of it than it was, but it upset me to see her hurt and in pain. I met Ellery's friend, Peyton, and she told me that she had heard a lot about me. I was surprised to hear that Ellery had talked about me.

Dr. Beckett came in, and I immediately grabbed Ellery's hand and rubbed it softly with my thumb as he put four stitches above her eye. Her skin was soft, and it felt good to touch it. I wondered if the rest of her skin was as soft, and I wanted to find out. When Dr. Beckett was finished, he told Ellery that someone needed to stay with her tonight and monitor her for a concussion. Peyton tried to say she was staying with her, but I already made the decision that Ellery was staying with me. There was no way I was leaving her side tonight. Peyton didn't seem too thrilled with the idea. She mentioned something about a girl's night, and when Ellery turned her down, she looked disappointed. I was surprised by Ellery's decision, but we were leaving in the morning, and she probably figured it would be easier if she stayed with me.

As soon as Peyton left, I helped Ellery from the bed. I couldn't help but still be worried about her.

"Why would you pass out like that? Is there something wrong?" I asked.

"I just took too hot of a bath," she said as she grabbed her purse.

"You need to be more careful," I told her as I lightly took her arm, and we walked out of the room.

She lightly smiled at me and briefly put her head on my shoulder. We were walking down the hall when a doctor, who Ellery seemed to know, stopped us. A worried look took over her face, and she seemed nervous. He asked her what happened and then ask how she was feeling. She told him she tripped over something in the hallway and that she was feeling well. She seemed like she was in a hurry to end their conversation. I asked her who he was, and she said she saw him a couple of months ago for a bad cold. She seemed agitated that I was asking questions, and I felt something wasn't right.

**

I took her back to her apartment so she can pack what she needed for our trip to Michigan. I couldn't shake the feeling that there was something that she wasn't telling me. I kept thinking about how she told that doctor that she'd tripped over something in the hallway instead of just telling him the truth. I walked to her bedroom and stood in the doorway with my arm up on the door frame. She didn't see me at first as I stood there and watched her pack. I could stare at that beautiful woman all day. She looked up and smiled at me.

"Why did you lie to that doctor and told him you tripped over something in the hallway?" I asked.

"I don't know. I wasn't going to tell him I fainted. He would make a big deal about it and want me to get a bunch of tests done. That's what doctors do," she replied.

"You said you took too hot of a bath," I said, still standing in the doorway.

She stopped packing her bag and looked at me. I could see the anger in her eyes. "I did, Connor, now let it go for fuck's sake. You talk about me asking a billion questions, but it's different when it's you, right?"

I could see that I had upset her, and that's the last thing I wanted to do. I walked over to her and put my hands on her shoulders. "I'm sorry. I didn't mean to upset you," I said as I looked into her pained eyes. She took her hands and cupped my face. They were so soft against my skin and it made me weak. I wanted to take her hands and softly kiss them. I wanted to taste her and feel her.

"I'm sorry that I raised my voice; I'm just tired," she said.

She let go of my face and turned around to zip up her suitcase. I wanted more of her, and I couldn't stand it anymore. I grabbed her arm and turned her around, pulling her into me and holding her tight. She needed to know that I was sorry. This was our first real hug, and it felt so good. To completely hold her and feel her entire body against mine was something I'd wanted to do since I first saw her. I didn't say a word and neither did she. She kept her arms wrapped around me and her head on my shoulder. I took in the scent of her hair as it was arousing me. What was I doing? If I didn't stop this, something was going to happen. So, I broke our embrace and told her we better get going.

I picked up her suitcase and walked into the main living space of the apartment. Ellery excitedly told me about the sale of her paintings and how she was on her way to quit her job when she fainted. She was so excited about the sale of her paintings. Her eyes were dancing all around as she told me. I just hope she doesn't get mad when she finds out that I'm the one who purchased them. As we were about to leave, Ellery's phone rang. She asked me to grab a piece of paper out of her desk drawer so she could write down the address of the funeral home. I opened the drawer, found a blank piece of paper, and handed her a pen. I noticed a piece of paper sitting on top of some magazines that looked like a list. She had some things crossed off. I took notice that she wanted to go to Paris. I would have to take her there someday. It's a beautiful city, and I want to be the one to show her. She hung up the phone and looked at me as I held the list in my hand.

"What's this?" I casually asked her.

She walked over to me and took it from my hands. "Just a list of things I would like to do in my lifetime. I wrote it after Kyle moved out, kind of a new start on life list." She took it from me and put it back in the drawer. We walked out and to the limo where Denny was waiting for us.

***

I took her suitcase up to the guest room and she followed me, falling onto the bed. I set her suitcase in the corner and walked over to the bed. She had a big smile on her face as she laid there. I took in a sharp breath because of the images running through my head seeing her lying on her back. I had visions of her lying there naked with me on top of her. Stroking her and feeling every inch of skin. I had to quickly get it out of my head. I asked if she liked the bed, and she replied that she loved it. Damn that smile and what it does to me.

It was around dinner time, and I asked her if she was hungry. She had a long rough day, and I'm sure she didn't eat. I asked her if she wanted to order Chinese food, and she said it sounded delicious. I took her hand and helped her up from the bed. We headed down to the kitchen, and I pulled a menu out of the drawer. I sat beside her on the bar stool and leaned in closer to her as we shared the menu.

"What do you like?" I asked her.

"I like just about anything; surprise me," she smiled.

I took out my phone and placed the order for delivery. I got up from the stool, grabbed a bottle of wine with two wine glasses, and led her to the living room. We sat on the couch, Ellery facing me. She caught me off guard when she looked at me seriously and said she wanted to know more about me. She said she felt our friendship was one-sided. I think in a way she was right. I haven't told her anything about all the women in my life or about Amanda and Ashlyn. I've only told her bits and pieces about me that I know wouldn't hurt her. She's been hurt enough, and she didn't need me adding to her pain. I looked at her and ran my hand through my hair.

"You're right, and I'm sorry; I just don't like to talk about my life with anyone. It's not that it's a bad life; I'm just a very personal person, and I like it that way."

She looked down in disappointment, so I leaned over and cupped her chin in my hand. I lifted it so that she was looking into my eyes. "Give me some time; this friendship thing is new to me. You need to understand that I've never been just friends with a woman before."

She wasn't going to stop because she brought up how Ashlyn and I are friends. It made me nervous that she thought about her. I don't want Ellery thinking about Ashlyn, and if I tell her about our relationship, she's going to leave. I can't and won't let her go.

"It's different with Ashlyn, and I don't want to discuss it now," I said as I looked at her intently.

Just then, the doorbell rang, and I got up to answer it. I brought the food with a couple of plates and silverware over to the couch. I've never eaten on the couch before, but it seemed like the

110

right thing to do with Ellery. She was so casual about everything. I handed her a fork, but she asked me for chopsticks instead. I looked in the bag, pulled out a pair, and handed them to her. I opened up the Mongolian beef and started to put some on my plate. Ellery gave me a weird look.

"What are you doing?" she asked.

I looked at her strangely because what did it look like I was doing? "Um...serving dinner," I said.

She shook her finger from side to side as she took the carton from my hand and told me to grab the extra set of chopsticks. I tried to explain to her that I didn't know how to use chopsticks, but she wouldn't listen, she never does. She told me she was going to teach me how to use them. I grabbed my fork back from her, but she grabbed it out of my hands and threw it across the room. I looked at her and sighed; she won again. She took my hand and placed the chopsticks properly between my fingers. Her touch sent shivers down my spine, and I didn't want her to stop. She guided my hand into the container as I picked up a piece of pork.

"See, it's not hard with the proper training," she smiled.

I smirked at her as she held a piece of beef with the chopsticks and brought it to my mouth. I graciously took it and then held the piece of pork I had up to hers. She smiled that beautiful smile and took the piece of pork, but bit down on the chopsticks and refused to let them go. I laughed and took in this amazing moment we were sharing. It suddenly felt so right, and it scared the shit out of me. We ate, laughed, and drank wine. When we finished, I couldn't help but stare at her and gently stroke the area above her cut.

"Does it hurt?" I whispered.

"Not anymore," she said.

I could tell she had something on her mind. "What are you thinking about?" I asked.

She took my hand and held it to her face as she softly kissed it. My body tightened, and I took in a sharp breath as her warm, soft lips touched my skin. She didn't let go, and I didn't want her to.

"I was just thinking about how lucky I am to have a friend like you," she smiled.

Damn that smile. I pulled my hand away because she was arousing me, and I couldn't take it anymore. "We need to leave early in the morning; we should get some rest," I told her.

She agreed and headed up the stairs. I asked her if she wanted a pain killer before she went to bed. She said she was fine and didn't need one. I went to my room and shut the door. Miss Ellery Lane had me so sexually frustrated that I needed to take care of myself. When I finished, I put on my grey silk pajama bottoms, and as I was leaving the bedroom, a text came through from Sarah.

"Connor, I know I'm not supposed to text you, but it's been a while, and I was hoping you'd be up to some wild fun tonight."

"You're right, Sarah, you're not supposed to text me unless I text you. I'm not up for anything, and please don't text me again."

I put my phone down and headed to Ellery's room. I lightly knocked on the door, and she told me to come in. I tried not to look too much at her as I didn't need to be getting aroused again which I knew would happen looking at her in that little nightshirt she was wearing. I sat down in the chair opposite the bed and reclined it back. I was staying in her room tonight, and she wasn't going to argue with me.

"What are you doing?" she asked.

112

"Getting some rest," I replied. I could sense an argument coming on.

"Here?"

"Yes, do you have a problem with that?" I asked her.

"As a matter of fact, I do mind, Mr. Black."

I sat up and looked at her. "Why? The doctor said you need to be watched for a concussion. How am I supposed to do that if I'm in the room down the hall?"

"I'm fine, and besides you can't sleep all night in that chair. You'll be hurting in the morning, and we have a 10 hour drive to Michigan," she said.

"I'm following the doctor's orders, Miss Lane, so deal with it. You're not getting your way with this one."

"Now, you're making me feel bad. At least come sleep in the bed."

My eyes widened. Was she serious? "I don't think that's a good idea, Ellery."

"Why not? We're friends. Peyton and I sleep in the same bed when we have sleepovers, and my bed is tiny compared to this one. You have your own side way over there," she pointed. "If you don't, then I'm leaving, and you know I will."

"You're not going anywhere, and I'm not sleeping in that bed," I said.

She threw the covers back, got out of bed, and started to put on her yoga pants. I jumped up from the chair and grabbed her arm. "Stop it, Ellery, you need your rest," my voice was angry.

I took in a long sharp breath, "Fine, I'll sleep in the bed, just please get back in it and leave those pants on." She smiled at me and climbed back into bed. I walked to the other side, climbed in, and turned the other way. Don't get me wrong, I want to sleep in the same bed as her. In fact, I want to do a lot of things with her in bed, but I'll be damned if I ruin this relationship that we have right now. I closed my eyes and whispered to her, "You are the most stubborn and defiant person that I've ever known, Ellery Lane."

"So I've been told, Mr. Black, good night."

"Good night, Ellery," I smiled as I drifted off into a deep sleep.

Chapter 10

I opened my eyes, and the first thing I saw was Ellery. She was lying on her side and facing me. I laid there for a moment, staring at her and watching her as she slept. I still needed to pack a few things, and I wanted to make her breakfast before we head out. I carefully got out of bed, trying not to wake her. As I made my way to the door, I heard her stir beneath the sheets. I turned around and looked at her, still sleeping peacefully, as I walked to my room. I took a shower and finished packing the little bit that I had left. As I made my way to the kitchen, my phone started ringing. I looked at it, and Ashlyn's name appeared. She was the last person that I wanted to talk to, especially now with Ellery right upstairs. I answered and tried to make it as short as possible.

"Ashlyn, I can't talk right now; I'm in the middle of something," I said.

"I need to see you, Connor, and I need to see you now."

"That's too bad, Ashlyn; I have to go out-of-town for a few days on business."

"I'll come over right now, and I can send you off feeling really good."

"No, you can't; I don't have time. Don't you dare come over here; I'm leaving. I'll call you as soon as I get back," I yelled.

"Connor, it seems like it's been forever, and I'm really getting pissed off," she whined.

I changed my tone with her because I needed to get her off the phone before Ellery came downstairs. "I know it's been a while, but I can't help that; I've been busy."

"Does this have anything to do with that blonde bitch you've been with?"

"No, she has nothing to do with it. I've been working. I softened my tone with her, "Ashlyn, we'll get together as soon as I get back.""

"Promise me, Connor," she said.

"I promise. I'm going to send an envelope over with Denny; I'll talk to you soon."

I can guarantee that's one promise that I have no intention of keeping. I needed to tell her what she wanted to hear to get her off the phone, and I couldn't risk Ellery hearing me.

Breakfast was almost ready, so I headed up the stairs to see if she was awake yet. I heard the water running in the bathroom, so I knocked on the door. I told Ellery to make sure the water wasn't too hot. Somehow, I didn't believe her because she had a really bad habit of never listening to anyone. I leaned up against the wall and waited for her to come out. I heard the shower turn off, and a moment later, Ellery opened the door and jumped.

"Shit, Connor; you scared me," she said.

Seeing her standing there in nothing but a towel was the most beautiful sight that I've ever seen. Her skin was still damp from the shower; her hair wet and wavy, and the short towel was barely covering her perfectly shaped body. Her legs were long, lean, and perfectly sculpted. She stood there staring at me.

"I'm sorry; I just wanted to make sure you didn't take too hot of a shower. I didn't want you getting dizzy and pass out again. You do have a habit of not listening to anybody," I said with a smile.

She rolled her eyes at me and said ouch. "See, I told you not to roll your eye at me, and you didn't listen!" I yelled as I walked down the hallway. She smiled at me as she shut the door. Damn that smile.

I went back downstairs and fixed her a plate of eggs. She came down and sat at the island. I slid the plate in front of her, and she looked at me with a surprised look on her face. She asked me if I made everything myself, and I told her that I had. She seemed surprised at the fact that I can cook. I brought my plate and sat down on the stool next to her. She looked over at me as she took a bite of her eggs, and with a smirk on her face, she asked me if she had harmed me in any way last night. I wanted to tell her that I had wished she would've, but instead I decided to play with her a bit.

"No, in fact, you put your arms around me, started rubbing my chest, and calling me Peyton. I was quite turned on."

The look on her face was amusing. Her jaw dropped, and her eyes widened. She was so damn cute that I couldn't help but smile. She knew at that moment that I was joking, and she went to playfully smack me on the arm. I grabbed her hands before she could hit me and looked at the scars on her wrist. Our playful mood turned serious as I stared at them for a moment. I dropped her hands, got up with my plate, and headed towards the sink.

"My scars really bug you, don't they?" she asked in a serious tone.

"They sadden me, that's all," I replied as I put the plate in the dishwasher.

"Why, Connor? I didn't even know you when this happened. Why would my scars sadden you so much?" she asked.

I kept my back turned to her as I stared out the window. "It saddens me that someone could think so little of their life to want to do such a thing." I know that was the wrong thing to say, and I probably shouldn't have said it.

"I told you why I did it, and it wasn't because I thought so little of my life. I did it to lessen the pain for my father, and how dare you, Connor Black," she started to cry.

She got up from the stool and walked out of the kitchen. I didn't mean to upset her, but I had. I ran after her, grabbed her, and pulled her into a warm embrace.

"I'm sorry, I didn't mean it; I swear I didn't. I just get sad when I see them because it reminds me of what you went through," I whispered in her ear. I regretted every word that I had said. She looked up at me as I gently wiped away a few tears that had fallen from her eyes.

"It's ok; let's just forget about it and head out," she said.

I put my forehead on hers. "I'm an insensitive bastard."

She lightly smiled as she whispered, "You're in luck as I'm quite fond on insensitive bastards."

My first thought was to kiss her lips. I wanted to feel them against mine, but I had to hold myself back. It was getting harder and harder each day to control myself with her, especially after last night. So, I opted for her head instead. I kissed her gently on the head and smiled at her. When the moment passed, we headed to the Range Rover to start our road trip to Michigan.

I threw our bags in the back as Ellery settled in comfortably. As I started driving, I looked over and noticed that she was staring at me. She didn't care that I noticed, because every time I glanced over, she was still watching me.

118

"Why are you staring at me?" I grinned.

"I was just wondering about Connor Black, that's all."

I sighed and looked back at the road. She wasn't going to give up until she found out more about me. I know I need to open up to her, and I will; just not right now. She put her headphones on and stared out the passenger window. I could tell she was irritated with my response. I tapped her on the shoulder; she looked at me and took her earphones off.

"Are you going to ignore me the whole way there?" I asked her.

"Are you going to tell me a little bit about Connor Black?" she smiled in a cocky way.

My god this girl was starting to piss me off, but in a sexy way. I sighed and tried to think about what I should tell her or better yet, where I should start. She turned her head and put in her headphones again. I was not about to be ignored by her, especially for the next 10 hours because she's too damn stubborn to respect my privacy. I reached over and yanked out one of her headphones.

"Hey, what the hell, Connor?"

"Take those things out you stubborn girl, and I'll talk," I smiled.

She knew she won, and I bet she did it on purpose. There was no getting around not telling her something about me or else she would make me suffer. I started with the story about my twin brother, Collin and how he died when he was seven years old from a virus that attacked his heart. After I was finished explaining the story about Collin, I told her about Cassidy and her son Camden. I explained how Camden is autistic, and that he's the reason my company and I are involved with the charity for autism. She gave me a sympathetic look as she put her hand on my shoulder and started rubbing it. She cared; I could see it in her face and in her eyes. Ellery is the most caring and helpful person that I've ever known. I went on to explain to her about my father and how he started grooming me for Black Enterprises when I was thirteen years old. I told her all about Harvard, how I took over my father's company when I was twenty-eight years old, and how I've doubled the company's profits over the past two years. It wasn't hard talking about my personal life to Ellery. I didn't think I would be able to do it as I've never discussed anything about my life with anyone. She was easy to talk to, and I could tell she was happy with the information I gave her. That was until she spoke the unspeakable.

"What about past relationships?"

I pressed my lips together and took in a deep breath, I don't talk about my past relationships; there's no point, and why revisit the past? I don't have a girlfriend, nor do I want one." The comment just fell out of my mouth, without even thinking about it first. She looked away after I said that and then back at me.

"Why don't you? Even if you've been hurt before, you just have to pick yourself up and move on. Everyone's been hurt at least once in their life, some more than others, but you have to make a choice what to do with that pain," she said.

"It's not that simple, Ellery; trust me," I said as I continuously stared at the road ahead of me.

"So, you don't ever want to get married or have children and do the whole perfect family thing?"

I looked at her with a serious look, "No, I never want any of that, and to quote you, nothing lasts forever."

"You really need to stop quoting that, Connor. I think you took it the wrong way."

"Regardless of which way I took it, I already told you that I don't do relationships, and I mean that," I said.

She looked out the window, "I know."

I couldn't tell if she was hurt or put off by my comments. I don't know why she would be hurt, and it's not like she wants any of that bullshit. I'll admit, maybe it isn't all bullshit, but it scares me. We made small talk for a while, and she kept putting one headphone in my ear then asked me if I liked her music. She seemed to be ok, and she was having fun, making me listen to her songs. We had different taste in music, that's for sure. But I played along, because every time she put on a different song and asked if I liked it, she smiled. Damn that smile.

***

We had already been driving about four hours, and I needed to stop for gas. I pulled off the highway and stopped at the first gas station that I saw. Ellery had fallen asleep about 30 minutes before and woke up when I stopped the Range Rover.

"What's going on? What are we doing?" she asked sleepily.

"I'm going to fill her up and then we'll stop for something to eat," I replied.

I got out and walked over to the gas pump. Ellery opened her door and got out, stretching her back and legs. She walked over to where I was standing and kissed my cheek.

"What was that for?" I asked.

"It's just a thank you for telling me about your family," she smiled.

I smiled back as she told me she was going inside the store to pick up a couple of things. I finished pumping gas and headed inside to find Ellery. I saw her standing in the candy isle, looking over the vast amount of junk food in front of her. She was so engrossed in the chocolate that sat before her eyes; she didn't notice me walk up behind her.

"You're going to fill your body with this junk?" I asked.

She quickly turned around as she stumbled, but I caught her in my arms. "Ellery, are you alright?" I asked as I held her close to me.

"I'm fine; I just got a little light-headed," she replied as she held her head.

I continued to hold her until she felt better. "I knew we should have waited an extra day to leave. You're not ready to travel yet. You need more time to recover from your fall." I was pissed off at myself because I played around with the idea of leaving tomorrow instead. She kept her head on my chest and told me to stop being overprotective and that her light-headedness was probably caused from the pain medication she took. I found that odd because I didn't see her take any pain meds. I started to worry about her; in fact, I've been worried about her since she fainted. I told her that I was finding us a hotel, and that we were stopping for the night so she could rest. We were ahead of schedule, and we'd be in Michigan tomorrow with plenty of time. She told me she wanted to drive for a couple of more hours and get something to eat before we stopped for the night. She pointed towards the front door and asked me to get her a basket.

"You aren't seriously buying that much, are you?" I asked.

"Ok, Mr. Black, if you must know the truth, it's my PMS time."

I took a step back and put my hands up, "Whoa, enough said."

She grinned as she took the basket and filled it with chips, chocolate, and pop. I stood there and watched her with a horrified look on my face. I don't think I've ever seen anyone eat that much junk food. The women I'm used to practically starve themselves.

"Hey, you're the one who wanted to take me on this road trip. I'm just trying to keep the peace because without these foods for a woman at that time of the month," she waved her hand, "Well, you don't really want to know."

We walked over to the checkout, and she placed the basket on the counter. The cashier overheard our conversation, then she looked at me and said, "Trust her; we girls are two sheets short of psycho when it comes to our special little time."

I just stood there and looked at both of them, speechless, as she rang up the food. The cashier gave the total, and Ellery looked at me.

I looked at her in confusion, "Really? You want me to pay for this crap?"

The cashier leaned over the counter and looked me straight in the eyes, "Remember, two sheets short of psycho."

I pulled out my wallet and paid as I mumbled under my breath. I took the bag and headed out. She climbed in the Range Rover, and we headed for the interstate. I looked at her and shook my head.

"What?" she smiled.

"You're crazy; I just wanted you to know that," I said in a serious, but playful tone.

"Aw, sweetie, I know, but I promise it's only for a few days," she laughed.

I tried so hard to hold back a smile, but I couldn't. She was just too damn adorable, and my feelings for her were getting stronger by the minute.

Chapter 11

While driving along the interstate, we saw a sign for multiple restaurants. I got off the highway and asked Ellery where she wanted to eat. She asked me to surprise her as she liked just about anything. I asked her if she was sure, and she nodded her head in response. I had a craving for seafood as I saw the restaurant on the left. I turned into the parking lot, got out of the car, and opened the door for Ellery. I held my arm out for her as she hooked hers around mine, and we walked into the restaurant. The hostess informed us that there was a 30 minute wait; however, Ellery didn't seem to want to wait. I told her 30 minutes was nothing as I grabbed her hand and led her to the bar to have a drink while we waited for our table to free up.

As we took our seats at the bar, the bartender set down some napkins and leaned on the bar in front of me. I won't lie; she was an attractive woman, but not my type. I could see Ellery eyeing her from the corner of my eye. She had a 'back off' look on her face as she stared at the attractive bartender. I wanted to test her and see if she would get jealous.

"What will it be, handsome?" The bartender asked.

I leaned in closer to her. "I'll have a sex with the bartender," I flirtatiously smiled.

"One sex with a bartender coming right up, stud," she winked.

Ellery gasped, and by the look on her face, I could tell she was pissed. I waited for her to say something to me, but she didn't. She looked at the bartender and did the unthinkable.

"Um, sweetheart, when you get his drink, don't forget to bring those luscious boobies over here," she smiled.

My eyes widened as I slowly turned my head and looked at her. I couldn't believe what she just said. "Ellery, what the hell are you doing?" I whispered.

"What? Am I embarrassing you, Mr. 'I'll have sex with a bartender'?"

The bartender walked over and handed me my drink. She looked at Ellery, and asked her what she wanted in an irritated way. Ellery looked at her and pouted, "Don't you think it's only fair that you give me the same kind of service that you're giving him? Why should he be the only one to get to see your boobies?"

I was so embarrassed. I couldn't believe she did that. I threw some money on the bar and stood up, "Come on honey, I think our table is ready."

I grabbed her hand and shook my head. She looked at me and smiled. I leaned over and whispered in her ear, "Point taken, you bad girl." My plan had obviously backfired on me. This girl was not a force to be reckoned with, that's for sure.

"You love it, Mr. Black, and you know it," she said.

I did love it, and I hated myself for it. This girl is everything that I never thought I wanted. She breaks every rule I have.

The waitress showed us to our table and handed us the menus. I looked it over then watched Ellery as she looked at hers. I asked her what she was going to order, but she said she wasn't sure. The waitress brought us our drinks and asked us if we were ready to order. I closed the menu, and Ellery looked at her, biting down on her lip. It was then that it hit me, she didn't like seafood. I looked at the waitress and asked her to please give us a moment. I was in disbelief that she agreed to have dinner here.

"You don't like seafood, do you?" I asked.

She looked at me and shook her head while biting her bottom lip.

"Why didn't you say something?" I said as I ran my hands through my hair.

"Well, I wanted you to have what you wanted." She said innocently.

I sat there and stared at her. I tried to think of why she would agree to come here for seafood when she didn't like it. It's because she was a kind and generous woman who thought of other people first. I remembered the times she showed me new experiences, so I decided I was going to be the one to show her something new this time around.

"I'm going to order for us," I smiled as I waved for the waitress to come back. "We will start with an order of calamari, crab legs, and a lobster tail for each of us. Also, please throw in an order of broiled scallops."

The waitress looked at Ellery as she managed a slight smile. I crossed my hands and placed my elbows on the table, leaning forward so I was closer to her.

"Remember the times when you made me eat things; the pizza, hot dog, and let's not forget the use of the chopsticks?"

"Yes, I do, and I'm fine with everything you ordered," she said.

"We'll see about that," I smirked.

She leaned over the table, "You're a vicious man, Connor

Black."

"Not as vicious as you are, darling," I whispered.

Just as Ellery leaned back in her seat, the waitress came over and set the calamari in the center of the table. Quickly, Ellery took out her phone and placed it on her lap. She was looking down at it and typing something. Suddenly, her eyes widened, and I couldn't help but laugh.

"You Googled 'calamari' didn't you?" I asked.

She nodded her head as she took a sip of her coke, and I could see the fear in her eyes. I felt really bad for what I did. I stopped laughing and looked at her intently.

"You don't have to eat it, I'm sorry," I said.

She told me it was ok and that she was going to try it. She took a piece of calamari with her fork and looked at it. She took a bite and started to make the most adorable faces. I reached in my pocket and pulled out my phone. This is a moment that I didn't want to forget. She tried everything I ordered and was a great sport about it. She even told me that she actually enjoyed everything. We laughed and talked throughout dinner. Her laugh was as much of a turn on as her smile. She was fun to be around, and she made me feel human. That's the only way I can describe it, because I've never been happier than I am when I'm with her. We finished eating, and as we exited the restaurant, I put my arm around her and pulled her into me. She put her hand on my chest and laid her head on my shoulder. I wanted her as close to me as possible.

I was used to staying at the best hotels around the world, and I wouldn't settle for anything less. I drove out of the way to find a Ritz Carlton. I pulled up to the entrance and let the valet park the

Range Rover. We walked into the hotel and up to the reservation desk where I gave them my last name and reserved the Presidential Suite. The concierge called over the bellhop, and he took us to the elevators.

"Good evening, Mr. and Mrs. Black, and welcome to the Ritz Carleton," he said.

I started to explain that we weren't married, but Ellery quickly interrupted me and started playing some game with him.

"Thank you so much. What my husband is trying to say is that we won't be staying long."

As soon as the elevator doors opened and we stepped into the suite, Ellery turned and looked at me. "The Presidential Suite, really, just for one night?" I saw this as an opportunity to play her game.

"I will have nothing but the best room for my beautiful wife. Isn't my wife beautiful?" I asked the bellhop with a wide grin.

"Yes, sir, she's very beautiful."

"Darling, husband, make sure you tip this nice young man well," she smiled.

I pulled the cash from my pocket and started looking for a twenty-dollar bill to give the young man. Ellery came up behind me and grabbed a one hundred-dollar bill and handed it to him.

"Do you have a wife or girlfriend?" she asked.

"Yes, I do, thank you, ma'am, and thank you for your generosity," he answered.

"Go buy her something beautiful, perhaps a nice necklace."

I looked at her and clenched my jaw. I was in utter disbelief that she gave him a one hundred- dollar tip.

"Thank you, ma'am, sir, thank you," he said excitedly as he walked out shutting the door behind him.

"Really, a one hundred-dollar tip?" I asked her.

"Well, it's what you tipped the cab driver."

"Cab driver, what are you talking about?" I asked confused.

"The night I brought you home, I had to pay the driver, and I didn't have enough money, so I went in your wallet and gave him a hundred; that was before you told me that you were going to fuck me really hard."

My jaw dropped and horror swept over my face. "I said that to you?" I asked very embarrassed.

"Yeah, but you were drunk, so I forgave you," she smiled.

Damn that smile. "A one hundred-dollar tip, Ellery?" I kept saying as I started walking towards her. She had an excited look in her eyes.

"Connor, relax, it's only money, and you said yourself that you have plenty of it," she said as she ran behind a chair. I started to chase after her around the suite. She was screaming as I kept saying over and over, "A hundred dollars?"

She ran into the bedroom, and I chased after her. I caught her and threw her on the bed. We both were smiling as I straddled her and had her arms pinned above her head. We were both out of breath as I just stared into her beautiful, ice blue eyes. The feelings I had at that moment overtook me. I've never felt so strongly for someone before. All I know is that I wanted her. I needed to feel her. Her lips were begging to be kissed as mine were begging me to oblige. My heart was racing, and my body ached for her. As I held her wrists, I lowered my head, and gently brushed my lips against hers. I stopped and held her gaze; it wasn't enough, I needed more. I let go of her wrists and softly stroked her cheek with the back of my hand. She brought her hands to my head and lightly ran her fingers through my hair. I was highly aroused, and there was no hiding it. I could feel the rapid beating of her heart, and it was at that moment that I knew she felt the same way about me as I did about her. I brought my lips to hers once more and fell onto her as she parted her lips, allowing our tongues to meet for the first time. Kissing her was amazing; it was everything I knew that it would be. I took my time exploring her mouth and licking her soft lips. I wanted her to feel me and feel the love I was giving her. I gently held the sides of her face with my hands and started tracing her jaw line with my tongue. Suddenly, the images of Amanda, lying dead on the floor and covered in blood, flooded my mind as did all the other women I've used and had sex with. What the hell was I doing? How could I cross the line like that? I wanted her so bad, but I couldn't risk losing our friendship. She was too important to me. I abruptly broke our kiss, pulled back, and sat on the edge of the bed, running my hands through my hair.

"I'm sorry, Ellery, but I can't," I said.

She sat up on the bed behind me. I couldn't bring myself to look at her and see the hurt and rejection she must be feeling. I was appalled by the words that she spat at me.

"Why not, Connor? Is it because I'm not one of your whores?"

She knew about the other women and never let on that she did. I got up from the bed and walked across the room.

"You're not a whore, Ellery, and I just can't."

"Please just tell me what's wrong and why you don't want me," she pleaded.

It was breaking my heart to have to stand here and do this to her. "I do want you, Ellery, and that's the problem; I want you too fucking much."

"How's that a problem?!" she yelled.

I turned and looked at her with rage in my eyes. Maybe if I tell her about the real me, she won't want me and this will all be over. "You don't want to know the real me. I'm not a good person; I use women for sex. I can't have real relationships; I don't want to."

"We don't have to have a relationship; we can just be friends with benefits," she said.

I couldn't believe she would stoop to such a level that she would sleep with me with no strings attached. I would never do that to her, and I would never use her that way. She took a step closer to me and whispered.

"Connor, please; I need you." A single tear fell from her eye.

"Don't, Elle, don't do this to me, to us; I can't sleep with you."

She turned and walked out of the bedroom, telling me to fuck off. The tone of her voice was angry and hurt. I followed her out of the room as she was about to walk out the door. She put her hand on the doorknob and started to turn it. There was no way I was letting her walk out of this room and possibly out of my life.

"Don't you dare walk out that door, Ellery!" I yelled.

She stood there for a moment with her head down and then started to open it. I came up behind her and put my hand on the door, slamming it shut. I grabbed her arms, turned her around, and pushed her up against the door. I needed to make her see the kind of man I really am. She looked at me with fear in her eyes, and it killed me that she saw me that way. However, she needed to understand how much I love her and how I couldn't allow myself to hurt her by messing up our friendship.

"I fuck women for the pleasure, that's it. There's no emotion for me when I fuck them; there never has been!" I yelled as a single tear fell from her eye.

"I seduce them, use them, fuck them, and leave them. Is that what you want? Is that how you want me to treat you? You're different, Ellery, and you scare me. You make me feel things that I've never felt before. You're all I think about, both day and night. I feel empty inside when you're not around. Don't you understand? It isn't supposed to be this way, and if I sleep with you, this will all be ruined."

Suddenly, the fear was gone from her eyes, and it was replaced by empathy. I couldn't look at her anymore because of the tears, and it was tearing me apart doing this to her.

"What happened to you that made you this way?" She asked in a soft whisper.

I continued to look down, still pinning her body against the door. It was my fault that we were in this position, and it's time that she knows the truth. If she wants to leave after I tell her, then I'll let her go, and I'll never see her again. Dr. Peters is right; there can no longer be any secrets between Ellery and me. Our friendship has come too far.

"I had a girlfriend when I was 18. She started to become

obsessive and wanted to spend every waking minute with me. It became too much to try to keep her happy and, it led me to feel like I was suffocating, so I broke up with her." I paused and looked up at her as my eyes began to fill with tears.

"She committed suicide two days later. She left a note, explaining that if she couldn't have me, then she didn't want to live and told everyone to blame me for her suicide." I let go of her arms, taking her wrists, and turning them over.

"You see, this is why I feel sad when I see these on you. It's a reminder of what I did, and how I killed her." She gasped at my words as she broke my grip and cupped my face in her hands.

"You did nothing wrong, Connor. It wasn't your fault that she killed herself. It was her weakness and inability to cope; you cannot blame yourself."

"I swore then I would never fall in love or get emotionally involved with another woman, but with you, it's too late. I'm already emotionally attached, and I'm doing everything I can to stop myself, but I can't." I turned away from her; my breathing was rapid. This was her opportunity to leave, and I was willing to let her go so she can be happy, but she didn't leave.

Ellery walked up behind me and wrapped her arms around my waist. "I'm emotionally attached, and everything inside me said to stay away, but I see a side of you that I don't think you let other people see; a sweet, tender, and caring man who would give his world for someone that he cares about."

I let out a breath. She wasn't leaving; she was staying. She understood and didn't care because she just wanted to be with me, and I wanted to be with her. My secret was out, and she didn't run. I turned around and looked at her. I saw the sadness in her eyes, and I wanted to take it away. She shouldn't be sad; she should be happy.

I pressed my lips against hers and kissed her passionately. Our tongues danced together as I picked her up and carried her to the bedroom. My heart was racing, and my body ached for her, to touch her, and be inside her. I sat her gently on the bed as I lifted up her shirt and took it off. I took off my shirt and unbuttoned my pants, never taking my eyes off her. I never wanted to take my eyes off her again. She stood up, took off her jeans, and threw them on the floor. She laid down on the bed in just her black lace bra and matching thong. I stood there in awe of this amazing woman as I looked over her every curve. I never wanted anyone or anything so bad in my entire life.

"You are so fucking beautiful," I whispered as I ran my hand up and down her perfectly sculpted stomach. I climbed on top of her as she wrapped her arms around my neck. My lips met hers for a brief second until my tongue began to explore her neck. She moaned and tilted her head back to give me full access. She arched her back as I took down her bra straps and exposed her breasts. A groan escaped me as I lightly sucked each hardened nipple and ran my tongue in circles down her perfect body. She pressed her hips against me, letting me know she wanted more. I wanted to devour her. I felt like I was going to lose my mind because I wanted her and needed her so badly.

As I was licking and stroking every inch of her perfect body, she took her hand and pushed it down the front of my pants. I moaned out of excitement. Her hand was soft as she wrapped her long fingers around my cock and stroked it up and down. I lightly traced the edge of her panties as my fingers made their way to her swollen and aching clit. Her breathing was rapid as she softly moaned and said my name. I circled my fingers around her tender spot before gently inserting them inside. "You're so wet, Ellery;

god, I want you," I moaned as our lips joined together. She continuously moaned as I moved my fingers inside her in a delicate in and out motion. She was ready to come, and I could feel her wanting to explode. She started to scream my name as I softly circled her clit with my thumb, releasing all of her sweet passion to me. I've never been more turned on in my life, and I needed to be inside her.

I tore off my jeans and underwear and threw them across the room. "I promise I'll be gentle with you. If I get too rough, please promise me that you'll stop me," I told her. I was scared that I was going to lose all control with her and hurt her. She nodded her head as I climbed on top and gently inserted myself inside her.

I stared into her eyes with each slow and steady thrust. "What are you doing to me, Ellery?" The corners of her mouth curved up as she pulled me down to her, and we kissed passionately. Once I was fully inside her, my movements became faster. She panted with each thrust. Her hands traveled down my backside as she dug her nails into my back, exciting me more than I already was. I wanted this moment to last forever. I wanted to stay like this for eternity and never pull out of her. She felt so warm and so good. This moment was right for both of us. She needed me just as bad as I needed her. I brought my mouth to her breasts; sucking and lightly biting each nipple. I could feel her swell and preparing for her next orgasm, making my moans become louder and my thrusts more forceful. I took her leg and brought it up to my waist, making penetration more deep and intense. "Come for me, Ellery; come, baby," I whispered in her ear. Her breathing became fierce as she screamed my name, and her body shook in ecstasy.

"Christ, Ellery, you feel so good." I moaned as I yelled her name while filling her insides with my come. It was the most incredible and pleasurable feeling, and even though I've had sex a

136

million times, this was different; this was new.

I looked at her, panting and out of breath as she stroked my face with her hand and pulled me down onto her. I wrapped my hands around her head and buried myself in her neck. Our rapid heartbeats began to slow down, as did our breathing. I gently pulled out of her and fell to my side. I took my hand and softly pushed her hair away from her face so I could see all of her beauty.

"You're amazing," I smiled.

"You're amazing," she responded.

We laid there and talked about how beautiful our love making was and how I felt different. Ellery explained to me that it was because I made love to her with passion and emotion. She was right; I poured every emotion I had into her. I fell for Ellery Lane the moment I saw her standing in my kitchen, and now I fell in love with her. For the first time in my life, I fell in love with someone, and it scared me. I pulled her closer and held her tight until we started round two.

Chapter 12

I wrapped my arms around her as she slept. I held tight because I never wanted to let her go. I lay and stare at her as she sleeps; her perfect mouth slightly open as she takes in tiny breaths. She's peaceful now, and I need to make sure that she stays that way. I couldn't help but softly run my finger along her jaw line. I made my way to her mouth and gently traced the outline of her perfectly shaped lips; lips that were so soft, alluring, and begging to be kissed. I couldn't stop staring at the woman to whom I've given my whole heart. She stirred among the sheets and opened her eyes. I smiled as they looked up at me innocently.

"Good morning," she smiled.

"Good morning, baby," I grinned as I lightly kissed her forehead. "I hope I didn't wake you."

"No, you didn't wake me, but may I ask why you're staring at me?" She asked with such innocence.

"I'm staring because I never want to take my eyes off you. You're someone who deserves my full attention at all times," I replied as I softly ran my hand down her cheek.

She tightened her grip around my waist as she laid her head on my chest.

"I feel safe when I'm with you, Connor. I've never felt safer in my whole life," she whispered as she kissed my skin lightly.

I closed my eyes for a moment because she took my breath away. I've never felt so needed, and no one has ever needed me the way Ellery does. I need her like I need air to breathe. I need her like I need a heartbeat to keep me alive.

She moved up closer to me, and then covered her mouth with her hand. She was embarrassed about morning breath, but I didn't care. I rolled her over on her back and started kissing her. She stopped me and looked at the clock, saying that if we didn't get out of bed, we were going to be late. So, I had a better idea. I slid out of bed, and she bit down on her bottom lip as she stared at me, fully naked and standing in front of her. I smiled as I held out my hand to her.

"It looks like we'll have to shower together to save time," I said.

She quickly took my hand, and I led her to the bathroom. I turned on the water and kept it between hot and warm, but not too hot because I didn't want Ellery passing out again. I was going to make sure that never happened again. She stepped in first, and I followed. We stood there as the water ran down our bodies, wetting our skin. I took the soft sponge and the bottle of shower gel that was compliments of the hotel and opened it. I took in the vanilla scent and held it up to Ellery so she could smell it. She smiled as she took the shower gel from my hand and poured it on the sponge I was holding. I started to wash her slowly, starting with her breasts as I moved the sponge in soft circles around her nipples. She moaned as she took my cock and stroked it up and down, moving her hands in a steady motion. A groan came from the back of my throat as I continued washing every inch of her torso. She had me so excited and hard that I needed her right then and there.

"Connor, I need you now, please," she begged me.

I turned her around, and pinned her arms against the shower wall, and took her slowly from behind, kissing her neck as I moved in and out of her. I let go of her arms and cupped each breast in my hands, rubbing and feeling them as she sexily moaned. Nothing was sexier than seeing her against the shower wall. I could barely control myself.

"Are you ready, Elle?" I whispered as I wrapped my arms around her waist.

She moaned with each deep thrust. "Yes, come with me, Connor," she begged. Hearing her say those words were all I needed to hear. I pushed myself harder into her as I filled her up with my warmth. Her body shook as I held her tight, and we both sank to the shower floor, holding each other in pure bliss.

Once we were able to get ourselves out of the shower, I stayed in the bathroom to shave, and Ellery went into the bedroom to get dressed. I walked into the room and found Ellery sitting on the edge of the bed. It looked like something was bothering her. I stood over her and ran my hand through her wet hair.

"What's wrong, baby?" I asked her.

She looked up and smiled at me. "Nothing's wrong; I'm just sitting here, wishing that we could stay another night in this beautiful hotel room."

I smiled and held my hand out to help her from the bed. "Don't you worry; there will be plenty of beautiful hotel rooms in our future." I meant every word I said to her. I envision a future with Ellery. I never thought it would be possible to love someone so much. I've kept my heart closed off for so many years, but now I know it was because she was the one who was meant to open it. She looked at me and tears began to fill her eyes.

"Ellery, what's wrong? Why do you look like you're going to cry?" I asked as I wrapped my arms around her.

"I'm just so happy, that's all; you've made me so happy," she whispered.

"You've made me happy too, baby; I can't even tell you how much," I said as I squeezed her, not wanting to let go. I kissed her on head and broke our embrace. If we didn't get out of this hotel room, we weren't going to make it to the funeral home on time. I grabbed our suitcases, and we headed out of the hotel.

We were driving along the interstate, taking turns listening to each other's music when my phone started ringing. I had it sitting on the console that sat in between me and Ellery. We both looked over at it at the same time as Ashlyn's name appeared on the screen. I took in a sharp breath because I knew Ellery was going to ask about her, and I was in no way ready to discuss my relationship with Ashlyn. I hit ignore and braced myself for the question I knew Ellery was going to ask.

"Who is she, Connor?" She asked as she reached over and turned off the radio.

"I knew you were going to ask me," I heavily sighed.

"Ok, then you must tell me about her if we're going to move forward."

Her tone was calm but commanding. I took her hand and held it up to my lips, "I don't want to talk about her right now, Ellery. This isn't the right time or place to do that." There was no way I was ruining this trip by talking about Ashlyn. I had planned on explaining everything to her when we got back to New York.

"Fine, I'll wait, and we'll discuss her later. But whatever you tell me will be ok because things with us are different now, and we're putting all our baggage in the past, right?"

I looked over at her and smiled, "You bet we are."

"I have a question for you," she said as she took the wrapper off her Twix bar. "Denny told me that you've been different since you met me."

I rolled my eyes. Why is Denny telling her things like that? I'm going to have to talk with him. "Denny shouldn't be saying things like that, but it's true. I was intrigued by you the minute I saw you in my kitchen. When I woke up and heard someone making a lot of noise, I walked downstairs to yell at whoever it was for being so loud. Imagine my surprise when I saw this beautiful stranger, standing there making coffee."

"Yes, but you yelled at me about your rules."

I shrugged, "Well, I thought that I'd brought you home from the club; I'm sorry about that." She smiled and playfully smacked me on the arm. "When you told me what you did for me and gave me quite the attitude, it was that moment I knew I couldn't let you walk out of my life. Denny knew it as well because I kept talking about you without realizing it." She laughed and reached over to kiss my cheek, but instead she shoved the Twix bar in my mouth. I smiled as I took a bite.

We finally arrived in Michigan, and I noticed Ellery stiffen when she saw the sign. I reached over, grabbed her hand, and gave it a gentle squeeze to let her know that everything was going to be ok. I know this place isn't a very happy memory for her; she's experienced more pain here than happiness. Ellery reached in her purse to grab her ringing cell phone, and it was Peyton. Ellery put her on speaker as Peyton was telling us all about her and Henry's evening together. Ellery wasn't bothered by how graphic Peyton was being because she was used to it. Even though I haven't known Peyton very long, I liked her. She was a firecracker like Ellery, and I could see why the two of them are best friends. Peyton told me to live a little and to take Ellery to bed and show her all my sexiness. This was my opportunity to get back at Ellery for the incident at the seafood restaurant. I told Peyton that I already did and that Ellery made me do things to her that even shocked me. The look on Ellery's face was priceless after that, and so was her smile. Damn that smile.

We pulled into the parking lot of the funeral home, and Ellery put her hand on my arm. I knew this was going to be hard for her, and I could only imagine what she was feeling at this moment. We both got out of the Range Rover, and Ellery took a deep breath.

"This is the same funeral home where we held the services for my mother and father," she said as we stood in front of the double doors that led inside.

I put my arm around her. "You don't have to do this; you can call your cousin and tell her you got sick or something."

"No, that's the coward's way out. I can't escape reality. Besides, I have you with me," she said.

As we walked inside, we were greeted by Ellery's cousin, Debbie. It was unfortunate that we had to meet under these circumstances. I gave her a hug as well as my condolences. She led us to the room where her mother and father were laid out. I held Ellery tight as we walked up to the caskets. I had an image of her standing in this very room in front of the casket that held her mother. Tears almost stung my eyes just thinking about it. She was only 6 years old at the time, and having to experience that was awful. Even though she had nobody to protect her then, I'm here to protect her now and heal her from all the pain that she experiences in life going forward from this moment.

Ellery kneeled down in front of the caskets and prayed. I clutched her shoulders with my hands to comfort her. Once we

144

were done paying our respects, we walked around so Ellery could catch up with some relatives. She seemed to being fine until we began to hear the whispers of people talking about her and her father. Ellery heard someone say that she wouldn't have attempted suicide if they would have taken her away from her father. She was enraged as she stormed up to them, shoved her scarred wrists in their faces, swore at them, and then told it wouldn't have mattered. That's my girl. It upset me to hear that bullshit they were talking about, but Ellery was someone who can take care of herself, and she certainly did. She made no qualms about being heard. I grabbed her hand, telling her that it wasn't worth it, and then led her outside to cool off.

"I must say, you can put on quite a show," I smiled as I hugged her to lighten her mood.

"I'm sorry, I just couldn't take anymore; I knew this was going to happen if I came back here," she said as she buried her face in my chest.

"It's ok, you've said your goodbyes to your aunt and uncle, you told off a few people, and now we can go; unless you want to stay?" Ellery shook her head and said she wanted to leave.

We hopped into the Range Rover, and I had my GPS search for a luxury hotel nearby. Ellery laughed and told me to reserve a room at the Athenuem Suite Hotel. I smiled because that's the first hotel that came up on my GPS, so I reserved the Presidential Suite. I asked her where she wanted to go. I knew she wanted to visit her mom and dad's grave, but I wasn't sure if she needed to go somewhere else first. Our fingers were interlaced as she brought my hand up to her mouth and lightly kissed it. She was an amazing woman, and she made me feel so good.

We stopped at the flower shop, and I bought the flowers for

her parents' graves. She became angry at me when I wouldn't let her pay; that's the one thing that I loved most about her. She doesn't love me for my money; it never did matter to her. She would rather buy something herself. I don't care; I plan on spending every last dime that I have on her. She's more than worth it, and I want to give her the world.

Ellery led me to where her parents were buried, and I stepped away to give her some privacy with them. I overheard her talk about me to them and how she believes that I would do anything for her. I smiled because she was right; I would do anything and everything for her, and I believe she would do the same for me as well. I know she loves me. Even though neither of us has spoken those three words yet, I can feel her love every time she looks at me, holds me, kisses me, and makes love to me. She's completely taken over my heart and soul like I knew she would when I first laid eyes on her. I walked over to her, helped her up from the grass, and took her in my arms.

"You're far too young to have experienced so much death, Ellery; it hurts me to know what you've been through," I whispered as I kissed her head. "I can't even imagine losing my parents, especially at such a young age. You amaze me with your strength, Ellery, because I don't know if I could have made it through if I was in your place." She let go of me and bent down to pull some weeds that were surrounding the grave area.

"That's something you decide whether or not you're going to do. You can move on and try to live your life as normal as possible, or you can make the decision to let go of life and let sorrow consume you. I'm a big believer of fate, and I believe God took my dad so his pain and suffering could end, and he could be with my mother again."

This woman amazed me. Her strength and hope was incredible. I was in complete awe of her, and I planned on spending the rest of my life showing her. "You're amazing; I don't know what I did to deserve to have you in my life," I said to her as I stroked her long blonde hair. She stood up, wrapped her arms around my neck, and kissed me. I picked her up and carried her to the Range Rover.

"What are you doing?" she asked with a smile.

"I'm taking you for ice cream," I smiled back as she buried her head into my neck.

We stopped at a local ice cream parlor and got two cones. We sat across from each other at a wrought iron table inside the shop. She was turning me on the way she was licking her ice cream, and she knew it because she was smiling as she was doing it. Damn that smile. I've found myself being in a constant state of arousal when I'm with Ellery. Even when I'm not with her, I still am because I'm constantly thinking about her.

"You better hurry up and eat that because we need to get to the hotel immediately," I said.

"Why the hurry, Mr. Black? Are you anticipating something?" She grinned.

"You have no idea what I'm anticipating, Ellery, but I will say it involves some panty ripping," I whispered so no one would hear.

She quickly got up from the table, grabbed the ice cream cone from my hand, and threw both of them in the trash. She grabbed my hand and led me out of the ice cream parlor.

"You better make good on your promise, Connor," she whispered in my ear before getting into the SUV.

Chapter 13

We arrived at the hotel and took the elevator up to the Presidential Suite. The expression on Ellery's face was exquisite as I opened the door, and she walked in. I walked over to the fireplace and turned it on. Ellery walked over to me and wrapped her arms around my waist. "You feel so good," she said.

I turned around to face her and held her tight. "Not as good as you feel, baby," I whispered as I buried my nose in her neck, taking in her arousing scent.

"Dance with me," she smiled.

"I would love to dance with you, but let me put on some music first." I walked over to the stereo that sat on the table by the window and turned it on. I walked back to where she was standing and wrapped my arms around her waist. We held each other and slowly moved to the soft melody that was coming from the radio. This moment was surreal, and I didn't think that I could become happier than I already was. We didn't need words; we knew how the other felt just by the way we gazed into each other's eyes.

"There's no place I'd rather be than here with you," she softly spoke.

I leaned in closer and brushed her lips with mine. I lightly nipped at her bottom lip as she smiled. Our kiss turned passionate as we continued moving to the music. I slowly unbuttoned her blouse and pushed it back off her shoulders until it fell to the floor. I moved my hands along the curves of her beautiful body until I needed to feel more. I took my hand and ran it along the inside of her upper thigh as I pushed up her short black skirt. A moan escaped her as I touched the lace around her thong. She unbuttoned my pants and moved her hand down them, taking my entire length in her hand. God, she felt so warm. I undid her black lace bra and threw it on the floor, and then she took my shirt over my head. I held her tight, feeling her soft, naked breasts pushing against my bare chest. I gently laid her on the floor in front of the fireplace. I pulled her skirt from her waist while kissing her stomach and making my way down her body. I softly kissed and licked the inside of each thigh, stopping at her sensitive spot. I looked up at her with a smile as I grabbed the sides of her panties and forcefully tore them off her.

"I promised you panty ripping," I said.

"You certainly keep your promises," she seductively smiled.

I brought my mouth back to her inner thigh, running my tongue in circles as she ran her fingers through my hair. She was already wet and wanting me. I softly kissed my way to her clit as she moaned and arched her back the minute my tongue touched her. She had me so aroused that I was about to come right then and there. I felt around her, taking in her wetness and desire for me. I inserted my fingers and leisurely moved them in and out of her as my mouth engulfed her swollen parts until she came. Her body tensed as her hands tightened their grip around my head. I moved on top of her, kissing her and letting her taste what I do. I couldn't wait anymore; I needed to be inside her as bad as she wanted me to be. I took my throbbing cock and pushed inside her. She smiled and yelled out at the pleasure she felt. The warmth of the fire was heating every inch of our bodies as we made passionate love for over an hour.

After our passionate love making, I wrapped us in a blanket as we stared into each other's eyes. I ran my finger up her jaw line and behind her ear. I wanted to tell her that I loved her, but I was too nervous and scared. I've never said those words to anyone except my family, but they didn't count. So instead, I asked her if she was hungry as I kissed her bare shoulder.

"Yes, I'm hungry for you," she smirked.

I took in a sharp breath as I began to get aroused again. I stroked her cheek with my fingers, "I'm always hungry for you, but we'll eventually have to eat real food. I hate to break it to you, baby, but we can't survive on sex alone."

She pouted, and I started to tickle her. She giggled and grabbed my hands to try and get me to stop. I loved watching her laugh like that. I finally stopped when she said ouch because her cut started to hurt. I softly kissed her stitches and got up to order room service. I went to the bedroom and put on a pair of black pajama bottoms while Ellery put on a robe. It wasn't too long before our room service was delivered, and we were enjoying a nice dinner. I was a little concerned as I looked at her, and she seemed a little pale.

"Are you feeling alright, Elle? You look a little pale." I asked with concern.

She told me she was fine. She said she was a little tired, and she winked at me as she said I was to blame for that. She did have a long and emotional day, so I can understand her being exhausted. I was just ready to suggest we go to bed for the night and relax when she looked at me seductively.

"Would you care to join me for a hot bath, Mr. Black?"

"I would love to, just not too hot; I don't want you passing out," I smiled.

The bathtub was large enough for four people. I started the water and took off my pajama bottoms, got in, and laid back against the tub, making room for Ellery. We've showered together, but this is our first bath together and the thought of her wet, naked body lying against mine was highly arousing. I watched her as she twisted up her hair and put it in clip so it didn't get wet. I loved her hair up. It showed off her elongated sexy neck that I love to kiss so much. She removed her robe and let it drop to the floor as she walked to the tub. She was so damn sexy, and I wanted to spend every minute letting her know how sexy she is. She slid into the tub and laid her head against my chest. I put my arms around her and took in the softness of her damp skin. I couldn't help myself as I started to gently kiss her neck; it was inviting and alluring.

"I love it when you wear your hair up."

"Is that so?" She smiled as I continued to plant small, delicate kisses down her neck.

"You have no idea how bad I wanted you that night of the charity event. I did everything I could to restrain myself and not take you in the bathroom to have my way with you."

"I wish you would have," she said as she continuously moved her finger up and down my arm.

"No, you don't. I would have been too rough, and I might have scared you off."

"You can never scare me off," she said as she turned her head to face me. She placed her hand on the side of my face. "Infinity is forever, and that's what you are to me. You are my forever, Mr. Black."

I swallowed hard because she was bringing tears to my eyes. I was so moved by her words. I traced the outline of her lips before I kissed her.

"There's no limit to what I wouldn't do for you. Just ask, and it will be done, no matter the sacrifice," I said while looking into her blue eyes.

Her eyes began to swell with tears as she traced my lips with her finger. "Those are the most beautiful words that anyone has ever said to me."

"They're true, every last word," I whispered as our lips met one last time, and we made love before heading off to bed.

***

Morning had come, and I opened my eyes as the sun peeked through the sheer curtains that hung perfectly on the windows. Ellery was snuggled against me as our legs were wrapped around each other and tangled in the sheets. She stirred and moved her hand down my chest as she looked up me and smiled. I kissed the tip of her nose.

"Morning, baby," I said.

"Good morning, babe; I want to wake up like this every day. I love waking up in your arms." Hearing her say that made me very happy. I was afraid she thought things were moving too fast with us.

"I can't think of a more perfect way to start off the day than waking up with you in my arms," I smiled as I kissed her lips.

We both got up when we heard a knock on the door. I put on my pajama bottoms and opened the door. It was our complimentary breakfast. As we were enjoying breakfast and coffee, Ellery received a text message from her ex-boyfriend, Kyle. She seemed concerned because he was in Michigan, and he wanted to see her. I told her it was fine and to tell him where we were. I couldn't shake the feeling that Ellery was really upset by his text message. She didn't tell me, but I could see the anguish in her face. We headed to the bedroom, got dressed, and packed our bags to head back to Michigan. It wasn't too long before Kyle knocked on the door.

Ellery sighed and let him in. He had a surprised look on his face when he saw me. I smiled, waved, and said hello. He wanted to talk to Ellery in private, but she had refused. I said it was ok and that I'd be in the bedroom if she needed me. She nodded her head, and Kyle thanked me.

After about 10 minutes, I heard Ellery yelling at Kyle. I decided to wait it out a little bit to see if she would calm down before I went out there. When she didn't, but instead continued to get louder, I stepped out of the bedroom and overheard Kyle asking her if she had told me something. I walked over to where they stood.

"Tell me what?" I asked as I looked at Ellery. She was pleading with Kyle to be quiet for both their sakes. I didn't know what the hell was going on. All I knew was that Kyle was trying to tell me something, and Ellery was scared shitless; I could tell by the look on her face. Kyle didn't listen to Ellery and looked directly at me with cold eyes. I looked over at Ellery as tears started streaming down her face.

"She has cancer, but she refuses to go and get treatments; she's just going to let herself die. That's why I left her. I couldn't sit there and watch her die," he said.

I froze. I didn't believe it. Kyle looked at Ellery, said he was sorry, and he walked out the door. My heart started racing and it felt like it was going to jump out of my chest. I looked at Ellery as her tears flowed freely from her eyes. I was too scared to hear the answer to my next question.

"Ellery, is that true?!" I yelled.

She flinched at my raised voice and nodded her head. "Yes, it's true," she cried.

I clenched my fists and tightened my jaw. "You've known your cancer was back even before I met you, but you still hid it from me after everything we've been through? What kind of person are you?!" I screamed at her. I didn't know what I was doing. I was confused and in disbelief. My skin grew hot, and I felt like I couldn't breathe.

"Please, Connor, let me explain," she pleaded.

I was so angry that I couldn't see straight. "Explain what? What's left to explain? Were you just going to tell me one day that you were dying? And why the fuck aren't you getting any treatment?" This didn't make any sense to me. Why would she just refuse treatment and let herself die? Who does that sort of thing?

"Please, calm down, Connor," she pleaded.

"Calm down? You expect me to be calm when I just found out that the woman I love and want to spend the rest of my life with is dying? I don't want to hear anything from you. You make me sick, Ellery. I can't do this; I can't even look at you." I was blinded by rage, and my emotions were out of control. I turned towards the bedroom. Ellery followed after me and grabbed my arm.

"Please, Connor, don't do this; let me explain."

I jerked my arm away, and she fell back onto the floor. I turned and looked at her, my voice now calm, but pained. "Your dizzy spells and your tiredness, it's all part of the cancer. You're getting worse, and you knew it, but you still didn't tell me. I bared my soul to you. I told you things nobody in this world knows. I shared myself with you. How could you do that to me, Ellery?" I asked as my eyes filled with tears. I walked to the bedroom and slammed the door.

I paced back and forth across the floor. My breathing was still rapid, and my heart felt like it had been broken into a million tiny pieces. There was no way that I could drive with her back to New York, so I pulled out my phone and booked her on the next flight back to New York. I grabbed my bag and opened the bedroom door. As I was walking towards the door, Ellery jumped up.

"Connor, wait, please," she begged.

I turned around and pointed at her, "Stay away from me. I booked a flight for you back to New York; it leaves in two hours, so compose yourself and be ready. I'm driving back by myself. I can't stand to look at you right now, let alone ride in a car with you for 10 hours." I walked out of the hotel room and left the love of my life alone, scared, and crying. What kind of person was I? I questioned myself as I got inside the Range Rover and gripped the steering wheel as tight as I could. I picked up my phone and dialed Denny.

"Hello, Connor. How's your trip going?" he asked.

"Denny, Miss Lane will be arriving on a flight from Michigan in about four hours. She's on flight #282, and I need you to pick her up, then drive her back to her apartment."

"Is everything ok, Connor? You sound upset," he asked.

"Miss Lane and I will not be seeing each other anymore, and I don't want to discuss it. I just left the hotel, and I'm heading back to New York. Just make sure you pick her up from the airport and take her home."

"Very well, Connor. I'll be there to pick up Miss Lane."

"Denny," I said before he hung up.

"Yes, Connor?"

"She's probably going to need you to comfort her when she steps off the plane. Please be there for her," I said.

"No problem, Connor. You know I'm very fond of Miss Lane."

I hung up the phone and pulled out of the hotel parking lot. My mind was racing and reliving the conversation with Kyle over and over. I was blinded by rage when Ellery confirmed she has cancer and that she's not seeking treatment for it. I know I said some pretty mean things, but I'm so angry, and I feel betrayed. I wondered if she was ever going to tell me that she's sick. I knew something was off with her from the start, but I never dreamed her cancer came back. I turned my phone off. I didn't want to talk to anyone or hear anything. I was trying so hard to hold it together because the last thing I needed was to fall apart. I couldn't stop thinking about her sitting on the floor and the look on her face when I yelled at her. I couldn't stop thinking about the fear in her eyes right before Kyle told me. She's alone, but there was no way I could stay there with her. What she did to me was so fucking hurtful. I don't know if I'll ever be able to forgive her. Tears started to fall down my face as I was driving down the road. I glanced over and saw a field to the right. I pulled over to the side of the road, got out of the Range Rover, and started running towards the field. I felt a few raindrops hit my face. I ran until I couldn't run anymore. I stopped in the middle of the field and screamed. The hurt and betrayal I felt was unreal; something I've never experienced before. The sky opened up, and the rain came pouring down upon me as I dropped to my knees and sobbed. My heart physically ached, and my chest felt like it had been punched. I felt like my life had just been ripped away from me.

I got up from the ground and headed back to the Range Rover. I was soaked, cold, and I needed to change into some dry clothes. I opened the back, grabbed my bag, and threw it on the front seat. I climbed in the back seat and changed out of my wet clothes. I had a towel in my bag that I used to dry off my body and hair. After I put on some dry clothes, I climbed in the driver's seat and took in a deep breath. I needed to call Peyton to tell her what happened and find out if she knew Ellery was sick. I called my associate, Scott, and had him get Peyton's number. As soon as he called me back with it, I dialed her number as I pulled onto the road.

"Hello," Peyton answered.

"Peyton, its Connor Black, and I need to talk to you."

"Connor, is everything ok? Is Elle ok?" she asked in a panicked tone.

"I have a question for you, and I want you to be honest with me, please."

"Connor, you're kind of scaring me here. What the fuck is going on?"

"Did you know that Ellery's cancer came back?" There was silence on the other end.

"No, Connor, I didn't know that. She never said a word to me about it."

I could tell Peyton was telling the truth, and I hated that I was the one to tell her, but I needed her to be there for Ellery, so I had to explain what happened.

"Kyle came to the hotel room in Michigan and told me that Ellery's cancer is back. He also said that she's refusing to get treatment, and that's why he left her, because he couldn't sit there and watch her die."

"What a fucking douchebag," she said. "And what do you mean she isn't getting treatment?"

"She won't get treatments, because she said she can't go through it again. Peyton, I said some horrible things to her, and I left her. I booked a flight back to New York for her, and I left her alone in the hotel room. I'm having my driver pick her up from the airport and drive her home. She's going to need you when she gets there. I need you to be with her and make sure she's ok and safe."

"Connor, are you ok?" she asked.

"I don't know, Peyton. I feel all fucked up inside, and I don't know if I'll ever be able to forgive her for keeping this from me."

"You're hurt and upset right now; I get that, but if you love her like I think you do, that's what will get you through this."

"I have to go, Peyton. Please just be there for Ellery."

"I will, Connor. Don't worry about her; I've got this."

I hung up and continued driving. My head was pounding and the sting of tears still clouded my eyes. My head was a clusterfuck with everything that had happened. How could I be the happiest person alive a day ago, but the most miserable person alive today? I drove straight through to New York. The only stop I made was to get gas.

When I finally made it home, I stepped off the elevator and

into the darkness of my penthouse. It felt lonely because the last time I was here, Ellery was too. I threw my keys on the table in the hallway and walked over to the bar. I grabbed the bottle of scotch, a glass, and walked upstairs to my room. I threw back my glass and downed the first shot. I needed the alcohol to stop the pain. I got up from the bed and made my way to the bathroom. I needed a shower. I stepped inside and stood under the hot stream of water that ran down my body. I was both physically and mentally exhausted. I put my hands against the shower wall and lowered my head. I felt lost and never more alone in my life. I stepped out of the shower and wrapped a towel around my waist. As I walked into the bedroom, I stopped and stared at Ellery's paintings. I bought them so I could feel closer to her, but at that moment, I didn't; I only felt further away. I sat on the edge of the bed and looked at my phone. I was surprised that she didn't try to call me. I think after what I said to her and in the tone I said it, she was probably scared. I turned my phone off, because I didn't want to be bothered by anyone. I picked up the bottle of pills that Dr. Peters gave me and decided to take one to help me sleep. I poured another glass of scotch and downed it with the pill. I got up, walked to my dresser, put on a pair of pajama bottoms, and climbed into bed. I laid there until a single tear fell down my face as I fell fast asleep.

Chapter 14

The next morning, I rolled over and opened my eyes, staring at the empty bed next to me. I reached over to grab my phone from the nightstand and turned it on. I wasn't supposed to be back from Michigan yet, but I gave strict instructions to Valerie not to bother me unless someone was dying. I knew my company would be in good hands with Phil, my vice president. A text message from Ashlyn came through. Shit, I can't deal with her, especially now.

"Connor, I know you're out of town, but I was hoping we could get together when you come back. I need you so bad, and I miss our friendship."

I need to get her out of town for a while. I didn't even want to hear her voice, let alone look at her. I called Howie from our Florida office and told him to find her something to do for a couple of weeks. He said that one of their assistants just quit, and they needed someone to temporarily fill in until they replaced her. I told him she'd be there tomorrow. I got out of bed and dialed Paul.

"Connor, how's your road trip going?" he asked.

"Paul, I need you to do something for me. Howie called. Apparently, one of their assistants just quit, and I want you to send Ashlyn there for a couple of weeks to fill in. Have the plane fueled and send her on her way."

"Ok, why the urgency?" he asked.

"The urgency is that Howie needs an assistant right away."

"I got it, Connor. I'll call her now and put her on the plane," Paul said before he hung up.

I threw my phone on the bed and walked to the bathroom. I splashed some cool water on my face and looked at myself in the mirror. My eyes were bloodshot and swollen. I also needed to shave, but I didn't feel like it. I walked back to my phone and dialed Dr. Peters. I needed to see him right away.

"Connor? I'm surprised to hear from you," he answered.

"I need to see you right away, it's urgent."

"Is everything alright?"

"No, it's not, and that's why I need to see you immediately."

"Can you come to my office around noon?"

"Dr. Peters, I don't think you understand. I'll pay you triple your fee if you'll see me within an hour."

"Fine, Connor. I'll see you in an hour."

I threw on a pair of jeans and a t-shirt, then headed downstairs. My phone rang, and as I looked at it, Ashlyn's name appeared. Damn her.

"Yeah, what is it, Ashlyn?" I answered.

"Why the hell are you sending me to Florida?!" she spat.

"Calm down, Ashlyn. It's only for a couple of weeks. One of the assistants quit, and they need someone to fill in right away. You're the first person I thought of because you've worked with them on other projects. Howie's excited to have you."

"Are you trying to get rid of me? Because if you are, Connor, so help me…"

I needed to remain calm because she was pissing me off, and I wasn't in the mood for this.

"Ashlyn, listen to me, pack your suitcase, get on the company plane, go to Florida, and when you get back, we'll go out. It will be your choice, and we'll do whatever you want to do."

There was a moment of silence on the other end. "Fine, Connor, but you better be ready for me when I get back because we have a lot of making up to do," she spoke.

"Yep; have a safe trip, Ashlyn," I said as I hung up.

I quickly dialed Howie. "Howie, change of plans; I want you to keep Ashlyn on board for a month, and I don't want her back in New York until I say."

I need her out of the way and out of my life while I figured out what direction my life was heading. The pain in my heart was still there, and Ellery was still on my mind. I missed her already, and I wondered if she was ok. I heard footsteps enter the kitchen, and I turned around to see Denny standing there. I ran my hand through my hair as I looked at him.

"She told me everything, Connor," he said.

I sighed. "I can't talk about this right now, Denny. I have an appointment that I have to get to. Let's have dinner tonight."

"Dinner sounds good. Do you need me to drive you to your appointment?" he asked.

"No, I'm driving myself. Let's meet at The Pier around 6:30 pm," I said as I grabbed my keys and headed towards the elevator. As the doors opened, I stopped and turned to Denny.

"How was she?" I asked, not knowing if I really wanted to

know the answer.

Denny looked at me sympathetically before he responded. "She was a total mess, Connor. How did you think she was going to be?" I shook my head and stepped on the elevator. I rubbed my forehead as the doors shut, and Denny stood there looking at me.

***

"I thought you were on a road trip to Michigan?" Dr. Peters asked as I walked into his office.

"Let's just say that the trip got cut short," I replied as I stood in front of his large office window.

"Judging by the way you look and the way you're talking, something bad must've happened. Sit down, and let's talk about it."

"I don't want to sit down; I'm fine standing here." I took in a deep breath, "Ellery dropped a bomb on me."

"Continue," he said.

"She has cancer, and she's known about it before we even met. She didn't tell me, and she's refusing to get treatment, so she's just going to let herself die and to hell with everyone and anyone who loves her."

"What did you do when you found out?" he asked.

I turned around and looked at him. "I yelled and said some really nasty things to her, then stormed out. I put her on plane back here while I drove back alone. There was no way I could be alone with her in a car for 10 hours."

"I can understand that. Just a few days ago you told me you
164

were just friends taking a simple road trip. Did you sleep with her?"

I walked over to the chair across from him and sat down. "Yes, we slept together, and I wish we wouldn't have because it wouldn't be this hard."

"It wouldn't have mattered if you slept with her or not. You're in love with this woman, and don't you dare try to deny it," he said as he pointed his finger at me.

"You're right; I'm in love with her. I gave myself to her after I promised I would never give myself emotionally to any woman, and she took what I gave her, then ripped it to pieces. How do I ever get over the fact that she lied and hid a huge secret from me?"

I got up from the chair because the more I thought and talked about it, the angrier I became. "I told her about Amanda and everything that happened. I told her about how I use women for sex and then throw them away."

He took off his glasses and looked at me. "Was that before or after you slept with her?"

"Before I slept with her; why the hell does it matter when I told her?"

"You told Ellery what kind of man you are, and you warned her. You told her about your past, which you've never shared with anyone besides me, and she still wanted you. She obviously loved you enough and saw something inside you to continue the relationship."

"Damn it, Dr. Peters. This is different; I'm not dying!" I snapped.

"I'm not defending what she did was right, Connor. She

should have told you from the beginning about her illness, but she had her reasons; just like you had your reasons for keeping quiet about your past. Please tell me you told her about Ashlyn."

I started to pace back and forth across the room. "No, I didn't tell her about Ashlyn. She kept asking me, but I kept putting it off. I wasn't ready to tell her yet."

"Interesting," Dr. Peters said as he rubbed his chin. "You weren't ready to tell her about Ashlyn, and she wasn't ready to tell you about her illness. You two have some serious issues to work out."

"We have nothing to work out. We're not together anymore. I just want the pain to stop so I can move on with my life."

"Pain is a part of loving someone, and it's something that just doesn't go away. I don't believe you've given up on her. I know her secret hurt you, and I know you're in a lot of pain, but I think the two of you can work through this. My professional opinion is that you and Ellery need each other in more ways than one. This is the first girl since Amanda that you've let into your life. Have you stopped to ask yourself why that is? Why Ellery Lane? Of all the women you've seen and been with over the past 12 years, you chose her. You saw something rare and special in her, and you couldn't stay away. Her keeping this secret from you is a big deal, and I'm not condoning it, but I wouldn't let it completely ruin you. Take some time to think about it. Your emotions will go through different stages. Right now, you're hurting pretty bad, next, you'll be angry, but that's ok. Be angry, Connor, because you'll never begin to heal if you're not. Just don't let it cloud your judgment or consume you."

He walked over to me and put his hand on my shoulder.

166

"You'll be ok. Time heals all wounds, and you need to give it time."

I nodded my head and walked out of his office. He was right; I needed time to think, but my head was so clouded that I didn't want to think about anything besides going to a bar and drinking my troubles away. I looked at my watch, and it was only 2:00 pm.

I headed back to the penthouse and grabbed my gym bag. As I was heading towards the door, Claire walked in.

"Connor? I didn't expect you back for a few more days," she said.

"There was a change of plans, Claire," I said as I stepped in the elevator.

"Do you want me to cook for you tonight?!" she yelled from across the hall.

"No, I'm dining out tonight," I said as the elevator doors shut.

***

The gym was crowded more than usual today. I changed into my workout clothes, put my iPod on, and jumped on the treadmill. The treadmill I was on was facing the window that looked out onto the streets of New York City. Guns N' Roses was playing on my iPod as I ran fast. I was doing ok until their song 'November Rain' began to play. I should have played the next song, but I couldn't bring myself to turn it off. The lyrics reminded me of Ellery and our situation. I needed to keep it together for fuck sake; I'm in a public place. As I was running and staring at the crowds of people walking down the street, I saw her. She stopped in front of the window and pulled out her phone from her purse. She looked like I did, broken and pained. She was still beautiful, and it hurt to see her. She started walking down the street again, and I wanted to run after her, but I couldn't. I needed space and time, and so did she.

I wanted to do some laps around the pool by myself, so I paid the manager a great deal of money to close the pool for a couple of hours. I did a few laps and sat in the water while I tried to catch my breath. I loved to swim. The water was a place of escape for me. I felt like I could put myself in a different place when I was in the water. The last time I played with Collin was in the water at the beach. That was one week before he died. I think about him almost every day. I sit and wonder what it would be like if we ran Black Enterprises together. I know my life would be different with him around. When I was down or got in trouble for something, he'd always say, "Chin up, Connor. Tomorrow's another day." I didn't think about it that night I was with Ellery at the beach, but being near the water made me feel closer to Collin because it was the one thing he loved so much. I decided to do just one last lap around the pool as it was almost time to meet Denny for dinner.

Chapter 15

Denny was already sitting at the table, waiting for me when I arrived at the restaurant. I sat down as the waitress came over and smiled at me.

"May I get you something to drink?" she smiled as she tilted her head.

"I'll have a double scotch." I said without as much as a grin.

Denny was glancing over the menu when he said, "A double scotch, huh?"

I picked up the menu from the table and opened it. "It's not like it's too early or anything."

"I didn't mean anything by it, Connor," he said.

"I know you didn't, Denny," I said still looking down at the menu.

"Do you want to talk about what happened?" Denny asked as he closed his menu.

The waitress came over and set down my double scotch in front of me. Denny and I ordered our meals, then she took our menus and walked away. "Not really," I answered as I took a sip.

"She loves you, Connor, and I've known you long enough to know that you're in love with her as well."

I picked up my glass and lightly swirled the liquid around. "If she truly loved me, she would have told me that she was sick."

"And if you truly loved her, you would have told her about Ashlyn, because I damn well know that you haven't."

I sighed as I took another drink. "You sound like my therapist. I saw Ellery today," I said as I looked up at him. "I was on the treadmill at the gym, and she stopped in front of the window."

"Did she see you?"

"No, she stopped to pull out her phone to look at it. She looked frail and sad."

"Of course she did, Connor. She loves you, but you walked out on her. You left her all alone in a hotel room in Michigan," he spat.

I leaned across the table. "I know what I did, and I regret it. I was in shock and very angry by what I had just found out. The only thing I saw was my future dying, and I couldn't deal with it, so I left. Do you think it was easy for me just to leave her there? Do you know how many times I almost turned around to get her?"

"I understand how hurt you are, but it's time to be a man, Connor, because she needs you. Regardless of what she did or didn't do, she's sick, and she's alone," Denny spoke.

"I know that, but I need time as well. I'm not that much of a heartless bastard."

"That has yet to be decided," Denny smiled.

I glared at him as we ate dinner and continued to talk about Ellery. I looked at him seriously as I needed him to do something for me.

"I need you to keep an eye on Ellery for me. I want you to follow her and report back everything you find out."

"Connor, that's just not right," he said.

"If you don't do it, then I'll hire someone else. I trust you, Denny. I know she means something to you, and I know you're just as worried about her."

"I want to know where she goes, who she's with, and what she's doing. Most importantly, how she's doing."

"Fine, Connor. If that's what you really want, then I'll do it. But I don't think that it's right. I think you need to talk to her yourself."

"I will in due time. I appreciate you doing this for me. You know you're like a father to me, Denny," I said.

He smiled as he looked at me. "I know, and you're like the son I never had."

I smiled at him as we got up from our seats and left the restaurant.

As I was driving back to the penthouse, my sister Cassidy called.

"Hey, Cass. What's up?"

"I just wanted to talk to my big brother. We haven't heard from you in a while, and mom was starting to get worried."

"I'm fine, Cassidy. Please tell mom that I've been busy with the Chicago purchase, and that I haven't had a chance to call her."

"You know how she gets when you don't keep in touch," she said.

"Tell her I'll be over Sunday for dinner, and kiss Camden for me."

"I will. He misses you, Connor," she spoke softly.

"I miss him as well, and tell him that I'll see him on Sunday. I'll come early, and we can take him for a walk along the trail."

"He'll love that. I'll see you Sunday, Connor."

"Bye, Cass. Take care."

I miss my family. I don't see them as much as I should, and it's my fault. They would love Ellery. It's too bad they won't get to meet her anytime soon. The emptiness in my heart and the silence of my soul is too much to bear. I decided to stop by Ellery's apartment before going home just to----hell, I don't know why, but before I knew it, I was parked across the street from her place. Her curtains were closed, but I could see a small stream of light coming from the sides. I could see a shadow of someone sitting in the corner. I know that's where she keeps her easel. I bet she's painting. I slowly pulled away and headed home.

I arrived at the penthouse and headed straight to the bar. I poured myself a scotch and sat down with my laptop on the couch. I opened up my email, and the first one I saw, sitting on top, was one from Ellery. I took in a deep breath and prepared myself for the hate words she probably said. I wouldn't blame her after what I did to her.

Dear Connor,

I hope you're reading this and didn't delete it before you opened it when you saw my name. If you are, then you'll see this is my heartfelt apology to you. Words cannot explain how sorry I am for not telling you about my illness from the start. I never meant for us to get as close as we did for that very reason. The night I took you home, I had every intention of leaving and never looking back; if I had, we wouldn't have met, and you wouldn't be hurting right now. I will never forgive myself for not telling you the truth.

I believe in fate, and it was fate that brought us together. I told you I was saved for a reason, and I think it was to save you. You have a beautiful heart and soul, and you don't deserve to never love someone. You will never know what you've done for me, and how you've changed my life. I never would have experienced love the way I have with you, because what you showed me, and how you made me feel, was a first for me in my lifetime. I never loved Kyle. I was with him because he was there, and I was afraid of being alone. Loneliness is what my whole life was made of. My decision to not receive treatment at the time was out of pure selfishness on my part, and I've come to understand that now. I want to thank you for your love and kindness. If I had one last breath left, I would use it to tell you how much I love you, because I do, and I always will.

Love forever,

Ellery

I closed my eyes, and my heart just shattered even more than it already was. My eyes started to sting with tears as I got up and threw my glass at the wall. I paced back and forth across the room, running my hands through my hair. I'm so angry and that email made it worse, because after everything I did and said to her, she still loves me. All she had to do was tell me from the start. Why the fuck didn't she tell me?! I screamed. She said not getting treatment was selfish on her part. I wonder if she's going to start treatments. I looked at my watch, and it was too late to call Peyton, so I sent her a text message.

"Peyton, has Ellery decided to start treatments?"

"I don't want to get in the middle of this between the two of you, but yes, she has an appointment with the doctor tomorrow morning."

"Thank you, Peyton."

"No problem, Connor."

I poured myself another scotch and headed upstairs to bed. I laid there and scrolled through the pictures of Ellery that I took at the seafood restaurant. We were so happy that day. As I was scrolling through the pictures, I came across one that Ellery took of the two us in the Range Rover. The only thing I could see in that picture was her dancing blue eyes and that smile. Damn that smile. It gets me every time. I reached over to the nightstand and grabbed the bottle of sleeping pills. I took one and laid back. The only thing in my head at the moment was the email she sent me. I couldn't stop thinking about her words, and how much pain was in them. She was hurting just as bad as I was, and I want so badly to talk to her and forgive her, but it's too soon. I need time to process everything and figure out what to do. If I don't take time and just rush back to her, things aren't going to work out. I closed my eyes and tried to shut down my brain. Eventually, I fell asleep.

***

I spent the next week doing nothing but working. I'd go into the office at 6:00 am and not leave until 11:00 pm. The acquisition of the Chicago building was getting close, and there was still a lot of work and negotiating to be done. As promised, I spent the day with my family. Cassidy and I took Camden for a walk down the nature trail. The leaves were starting to change and fall from the trees. It was beautiful at this time of the year, and it felt good to spend some time at the place I grew up. However, even being surrounded by family couldn't ease the pain in my heart. Cassidy could tell something was wrong, and she wouldn't stop asking. I told her it was work related and not to worry. She told me I needed to find myself a great girl who will take me away from all the

174

stresses of Black Enterprises. I smiled because I wanted to tell her about the time I spent with Ellery, but then I would have to explain the horrific details of what happened, and I wasn't about to go there. After a good family dinner, a good football game, and some great conversation, it was time for me to head home.

The next morning, I decided to leave the office and go to lunch at a deli that was down a couple of blocks. I pulled out my phone to check the time of my afternoon meeting as I collided with someone. We both looked at each other at the same time, and I gasped when I saw it was Ellery. My heart started racing as I lightly grabbed her arm because she almost fell over.

"Connor, I'm sorry; I didn't mean…" she softly spoke as she wouldn't even look at me.

"No, it's my fault. I should have been paying more attention," I said.

We stood in front of each other awkwardly and then she pulled away and said she had to go. I stood there and watched her turn the corner as fast as she could. My heart felt like it was in my throat, and the pain I felt intensified even more. I missed her so much, and running into her and touching her arm only made it worse. I spent the rest of the day reliving our little collision and the look on her face when she saw it was me.

I was sitting in my office, scrolling through pictures, when Denny called.

"What's up, Denny?"

"I thought you'd want to know that Ellery will be starting chemotherapy in a couple of days."

"What time?" I asked.

"9:00 am," Denny replied.

"Thank you, Denny. I'll need you to drive me. I'll see you later."

I wasn't about to let Ellery go through chemo alone. I was still angry at her for not telling me about the cancer coming back, but I love her, and I can't forget about her. She needs someone to help her and to be there for her, so I made a promise to myself that I would be the one, no matter the consequences. I was in deep thought when Ashlyn messaged me.

"Connor, Howie wants me to stay for another two weeks. Please tell him no. I want to come back to New York."

"Sorry, Ashlyn, but if that's what Howie wants, then you have to do it. It's part of the job, and if you refuse, then I'm afraid you won't be able to work for Black Enterprises anymore."

"I hate you, Connor Black."

I didn't even respond to that because I was hoping she meant it. But I know she didn't because it isn't the first time she said it. I put my phone down on the desk and moved some stuff around so I could be with Ellery during her treatment. It's going to be hard on both of us.

I called the hospital and got the name and number of a good homecare nurse. After speaking with her for 30 minutes, I decided she was good enough for Ellery. She came highly recommended, and I offered her a great deal of money to become Ellery's private nurse. I arranged for her to pay daily visits to her and take care of her. I also made arrangements to be available on the days of her chemo treatments so I can take her to and from the hospital. I looked at my watch, and it was already after 10:00 pm. I shut down my computer, locked up my office, and headed home.

Chapter 16

Today is Ellery's first chemotherapy treatment. I got up, showered, got dressed, and headed to the kitchen for coffee. Denny was already sitting at the table, eating the breakfast Claire had made.

"Good morning, Connor. Can I make you some breakfast?" Claire asked.

"Good morning, Claire. I'm just going to have some coffee," I replied.

I sat down at the table across from Denny as Claire brought me a cup of coffee and a plate with banana bread on it. I looked up at her and smiled.

"I made it at home last night, and I know how much you love it," she smiled.

I got up and gave her a kiss on the cheek. "Thank you, Claire. As always, I appreciate you taking care of me."

Denny looked at me intently. "Are you ready to see her?" he asked.

"I don't know," I answered as I took a sip of coffee. "I don't know how she's going to react when she sees me."

"Well it's going to be a bit awkward since the two of you haven't spoken since the day you left her."

I looked at him as I took a bite of banana bread. "Do you really need to keep bringing that up?"

"I'm just saying that maybe you should have called her before today. You're just going to show up unexpected, and she's probably going to kick you in the balls," Denny said.

"Nice, Denny. Thanks for the vote of confidence, and I don't think she'd do that."

"Have you met Ellery Lane?" Denny laughed.

I rolled my eyes and got up from the table. I put my cup and plate in the dishwasher, then looked at my watch. It was 8:30 am, and Ellery's chemo begins in 30 minutes.

I climbed into the limo, and Denny drove me to the hospital.

"Good luck, Connor," Denny said.

"Thanks, Denny; I'm going to need it," I said as I climbed out of the backseat.

I walked into the hospital and followed the signs to the cancer treatment center. I stepped through the doors of a large waiting room. The receptionist asked if she could help me, and I told her I was here for Ellery. A nurse was standing there looking over a chart and overheard me.

"You're here for Ellery Lane?" She asked.

"Yes, I'm Connor Black."

She looked at me and tilted her head. "She said that nobody was going to be here with her."

I pursed my lips together, "She isn't expecting me."

"Are you the husband, friend, or boyfriend?" she asked.

"It's complicated, but I'm her friend," I replied.

She smiled and waved her hand for me to follow her down the long hallway. We approached a large room that was filled with oversized chairs, IV poles, and curtains. She took me to the fourth chair and opened the curtain.

"Someone is here to see you," Nurse Bailey smiled.

Ellery looked up from her phone and a wave of shock hit her face. "What are you doing here, Connor?!" She asked quite rudely.

To see her sitting there in her yoga pants and a baggy sweatshirt was a sight for sore eyes. Her hair pulled up in a high ponytail was killing me because I love it when she wears her hair up.

"Hello, Ellery," I said calmly.

She looked back at her phone. "I asked you a question," she snapped.

I could tell she was pissed, but I didn't care. "Nobody should have to go through this alone," I said as I sat down in the chair next to her.

She pointed out that she wasn't alone, and that she had Nurse Bailey as she continued looking at her phone. She wouldn't even look at me, and it was seriously pissing me off. I grabbed her phone out of her hand and put it in my pocket. Needless to say, she wasn't happy.

"What the hell, Connor?!" she yelled.

She was just about to spit fire at me when Nurse Bailey came over and inserted a needle into her port. I took a deep breath because I couldn't imagine what she was thinking or going through when that needle went in. "Cheers," she smiled at Nurse Bailey.

She turned and looked at me; her blue eyes that once sparkled and danced were now dull and pained.

"I'm here as your friend, Ellery," I said as I so desperately wanted to take her hand in mine.

"Can I have my phone back, please," she asked holding out her hand.

I reached in my pocket and handed her the phone. Our hands touched as she took it from me. Her skin was as soft and warm as I remembered. I wanted to make it very clear to her why I was here.

"This is how this is going to work," I spoke. "I'm going to bring you here every week and then take you home. I've hired a private nurse to come to your apartment daily to tend to you and make you comfortable."

She asked me why I was doing this, and I simply explained to her that I owed her for the night she took me home from the club. She was giving me that darling attitude of hers and told me she was fine and that I could leave. God, I've missed her attitude. I told her that I was staying and that she was in no position to say otherwise. She gave me a dirty look and asked me how I knew about her treatment today. I explained to her once again that I can find out anything. I didn't dare tell her that I was having Denny follow her. She called me a stalker and then proceeded to read a book on her kindle. I opened up my iPad and started checking my emails. After 15 minutes of silence, Ellery looked up at me.

"You don't need to be here; I'm sure you have better things to do than sit in a room, watching people get chemo for five hours," she randomly said.

"Whether I have better things to do or not, this is how it's going to be, so let's be quiet, and don't worry about it," I replied still looking down at my iPad.

Nurse Bailey came by and asked Ellery how she was doing. I was shocked by her response. "I'm doing fucking fantastic, Nurse Bailey, because I know that probably by tonight, I'll have my head down the toilet for a good hour or two."

I looked at Ellery and then at Nurse Bailey, "Ellery, that's enough."

The nurse looked at me sympathetically. "It's alright; she's angry right now and needs to let it out. I'm used to it. I just try to make my patients as comfortable as possible."

I leaned in closer to her and whispered, "Could you please stop being a smart ass? She's only trying to help you."

She gave me a look and raised her hands to redo her ponytail. My eyes instantly went to her wrists as the sleeves of her sweatshirt fell back. I nearly gasped when I saw the tattoos; my name on her left wrist and the infinity sign on her right. Why the hell would she do that? I didn't want to say anything to her about it; I wanted to wait and see if she would tell me.

I got up and told Ellery that I'd be right back. I walked down the hall to the restroom to catch my breath. I was speechless as to what I just saw, and I couldn't understand why she would do that. As I was heading back to Ellery, Nurse Bailey stopped me in the hallway.

"Listen, Mr. Black; Ellery is going through a bunch of raw emotions right now. She's feeling sad, anxious, depressed, and most of all, angry. She's angry that this is happening to her all over again. She's angry at life right now. When she's angry, everyone around her will feel it too. It's a normal part of the emotional process of having cancer and going through the chemotherapy treatments," she said as she put her hand on my shoulder.

"Thank you, I'll remember that, and I plan on making her as comfortable as possible," I smiled.

It was a long five hours. Not because of Ellery's chemo treatment, but because of her attitude and anger towards me. I don't blame her for being mad at me. I was mean, rude, and out of line at the hotel in Michigan, and I'll find a way to make that up to her. I took her blanket to hold it for her, and she ripped it out of my hands while telling me she's got it. I sighed as she walked several feet in front of me. We approached the limo, and I graciously opened the door for her. She slid in the back seat without even looking at me. The only person who got a hello and a smile was Denny. He was thrilled to see her. I could tell he missed her as well.

She sat there, staring out the window and still refusing to look at me. I asked her how she was feeling, and she said she was fine. She obviously didn't want to talk, so I left her alone, and there was silence the whole way to her apartment. After hearing what she told Nurse Bailey about how she anticipates getting sick, I decided she shouldn't be left alone. I knew Peyton was out of town with Henry, so she wouldn't be able to stay with her.

We pulled up to her apartment, and I followed her inside.

"I want you to start packing," I said.

"For what?" she asked as she turned and looked at me.

I took in a sharp breath, "You will be staying in the guest room at my penthouse."

"I'm not going anywhere; this is my home. This is where I'm

184

staying!" she snapped at me.

"Listen to me," I said in a raised voice. "I don't want you staying here alone."

She walked over to me with a strange look on her face and put her finger to my chest. "I'm not your fucking charity case, Connor Black, and I don't need your help. Besides, you hate me anyway, why would you want to help me after what I did?" She said as she slowly turned around and walked to the sink, resting her hands on the counter.

It hurt me to know that she thinks I hate her. Maybe that's the reason for her behavior towards me today. I slowly walked up behind her. I wanted to wrap my arms around her, but I couldn't.

"Ellery, I don't hate you; please don't ever say that again. Yes, I will admit that I'm still angry, and that I probably will be for a while, but I need to put all that aside because you are my friend, and you need help. Please put your stubbornness aside, and let me help you."

"You said you hired a nurse to come here," she softly spoke with her back still turned to me.

"Well, I'm making other arrangements," I said.

She turned around and looked at me with sadness in her eyes as she agreed and went to pack her bag. I let out a sigh because I was relieved. That was easier than I thought it was going to be. She's one stubborn girl and can put up a fight until she wins.

***

I took her bag upstairs to the guest room and set it in the corner as Ellery laid herself on the bed. I could tell she loved that bed. I could see the corners of her mouth slightly curve up as she ran her hands across the comforter. I'm glad I made the decision to bring her here. I just hope I don't end up regretting it. Seeing her sitting in that chair at the hospital while getting treatment was melancholy. I never dreamed in a million years that I would be bringing home a girl with cancer and taking care of her. It wasn't me, but then again, I'm not the same person when I'm with Ellery.

I have a business dinner with Paul this evening. I told her I was going out tonight and that she's welcome to help herself to anything she needs or wants. She gave me a half smile as I turned and walked out the door. I didn't want to leave her, but Denny had agreed to stay until I got home in case something happened. I grabbed my keys and headed out the door to meet Paul.

I arrived back home around 11:00 pm and went upstairs to check on Ellery. Denny said she had been sleeping since I left. The door was opened a crack, and I peeked inside to make sure she was ok. She was sleeping peacefully. I walked to my room and changed into a pair of sweatpants and a t-shirt. I sat on the bed and opened my laptop to do some work. I had fallen asleep for a while and woke up to the sound of Ellery vomiting in the bathroom. I got out of bed quickly and headed down the hall to the bathroom. I slightly opened the door and saw her on the floor, over the toilet, violently vomiting.

"Ellery," I whispered as I took her hair and held it back in my hands. She told me to go away because she didn't want me seeing her like this. I knelt down beside her while holding her hair and told her I wasn't going anywhere until she was back in bed. About an hour later, she was finally done vomiting. She rested her elbows on the toilet and cupped her face in her hands. I walked over to the sink and wet a washcloth with tepid water. I folded it and patted it gently across her head. She grabbed the washcloth from me as I helped her stand up; she was weak. I held her arm and helped her back to bed. I pulled the covers over her, and as I turned to walk away, she lightly grabbed my hand. I turned around and looked at her as she softly spoke.

"This is nothing. You have no idea what you've gotten yourself into, Mr. Black."

I stared at her pale and pained face. I didn't know how to respond to that, so I just turned around and walked out the door, leaving it slightly open.

***

The next morning I woke up early because I needed to go to the office. I showered and put on my jeans and a button down shirt. I walked to Ellery's room, stood outside the door, and listened. I could hear her stirring in bed. I quietly opened the door and asked her if she was awake. She looked at me in a way that made me ache for her. I asked her how she was feeling, and she told me that she was ok and going to take a shower. I told her that when she was done to come downstairs, and Claire would make her breakfast. She asked me who Claire was. Apparently, I forgot to tell her that I had a housekeeper. Before she went into the bathroom, I told her I had to go to the office for a while, and I'd be home later. She said, "Ok, see ya," in a tone that was cold and flat.

I went to the kitchen and explained to Claire that Ellery was sick last night, and she may or may not want to eat. She told me not to worry, and that she would take care of her. I grabbed a cup of coffee and took it to my office to do some computer work before heading to Black Enterprises. I sat back in my chair and ran my hands through my hair. What the hell was I doing? Having her here was nice, but it was emotionally painful at the same time. I walked back to the kitchen where Claire and Ellery were talking.

"Ah, I see you two have met," I said.

"I thought you left," she said with a snotty attitude.

"I had to finish up some computer work here first, but don't worry, I'll be leaving soon."

Claire looked at her and then eyed me as I grabbed a bowl of fruit and sat the table. Claire set a plate of eggs in front of her and told her to eat up. I glanced at her from the corner of my eye as she took a small bite. I finished my fruit and coffee and walked over to her.

"I'm leaving now, so if you need anything, Claire will be here all day."

She didn't look at me. All she did was wave her hand at me. "This is going to be more difficult than I thought," I mumbled as I left.

Chapter 17

I was sitting at my desk, signing some contracts when I received a call from Denny.

"Denny, what's up?"

"I think you should know that Ellery left the penthouse," he said.

"What the hell do you mean she left the penthouse?!" I yelled.

"Claire went to check on her, and she was gone. Not gone as in moved out, but gone like she went somewhere."

"Shit, she shouldn't be going out as she still isn't feeling well. Thanks, Denny. I'll find her."

I hung up and dialed Ellery's number. After a few rings it, went to voicemail. I hung up and dialed again; it went to voicemail. I sighed as I got up from my chair and headed out of the office to find her. Damn her. Why does she have to be so difficult? I don't get what goes on in that stubborn head of hers.

I checked her apartment, but she wasn't there. I decided to check the soup kitchen, maybe she stopped there for a visit. She wasn't at the soup kitchen, so I got back in the Range Rover and put my forehead on the steering wheel. I was desperately trying to figure out where she could have gone. The clouds in the sky were rolling in, and it looked like it was going to rain. Then it hit me; I bet she went to Central Park. As I was on my way to Central Park, it started to rain. I parked, grabbed the black umbrella, and walked to the Conservatory Gardens. The rain started pouring down hard. From a distance, I saw a blanket spread out in the middle of a grassy area, and as I approached it, I saw Ellery lying down and looking up at the sky as the rain fell down upon her.

"Ellery, what the hell do you think you're doing? Are you crazy?!" I yelled from a distance.

"Aren't you the crazy one for coming out here after me?!" She yelled back.

My jaw tightened at her smart ass remark. "Look at you, you're soaked; get up now before you get sick."

"I'm already sick, Connor. What's the difference?" she laughed.

I stood there and stared down at her. It hit me hard when she said she was already sick. She was scared and living life the way she wanted, just in case the day came that she couldn't anymore. I took in a deep breath and laid myself down on the soaked blanket next to her, staring up at the sky, trying to see what Ellery sees. She looked over at me, and from the corner of my eye, I saw a small smile escape her lips.

"Why are you doing this?" I asked as I turned and looked at her.

"Because I can lay here and no one will know I'm crying," she said, looking up at the sky.

I felt a pain in my heart when she said that. She was out here, in the pouring rain, to mask the tears that plagued her face. She was trying to put on a brave front, but I knew she was torn apart inside. I reached over and put my hand on top of hers. She didn't look at me. We just laid there, staring up at the sky without saying a word. We didn't need words. Holding her hand was all the both of us needed. After a while, Ellery sat up on her elbows and said she was cold and ready to go. We stood up. I grabbed the rain soaked blanket and opened the umbrella as we started to head out of Central Park. All of a sudden, Ellery turned the other way and started to vomit in some nearby bushes. I stood behind her until she was finished. I handed her the corner of the blanket so she could wipe her mouth. I asked her to hold the umbrella as I picked her up in my arms and carried her to the Range Rover. We arrived back at the penthouse, but she still wasn't feeling well, so I carried her to the bedroom. She told me she was going to take a bath and then lay down for a while. I took a quick shower to warm up and changed into some dry clothes. I went downstairs to talk to Claire and Denny.

"I hope you weren't too hard on her, Connor," Denny said.

"I can't even explain how I felt when I saw her laying in the middle of Central Park in the pouring rain. I wasn't hard on her at all. She just wanted to be alone for a while," I said as I sat down at the table for dinner.

Denny left to go home for the night, and Claire was cleaning the kitchen when my cell phone rang, and a familiar number appeared.

"Hello, Connor Black here."

"Connor, Peyton here," she laughed.

"Hey, Peyton, what's up?" I asked as I rolled my eyes.

"I don't want you to worry, but I haven't been able to get a hold of Ellery for two days. Do you know anything?"

"Ellery started her chemotherapy treatment yesterday morning, and she's staying with me."

"WHAT?!" she screamed into the phone. "She didn't tell me anything about starting her chemo treatments so soon. Why the fuck didn't you tell me, and are the two of you back together or something?"

"I'm helping Ellery out as a friend. She doesn't have anyone else," I said.

"Excuse me, Connor, but I didn't know Ellery was starting her treatment yesterday. I never would have left if I'd known."

"I'm sorry she didn't tell you, but she probably didn't want to ruin your vacation with Henry."

"Well, sit tight, Connor Black, because I'm coming straight from the airport and kicking your ass. You should have called me and told me. Put her on the phone so I can speak to her."

"Peyton, she's sleeping right now, and I don't want to wake her up. She needs her rest."

"Fine, tell her to call me tomorrow. I was supposed to be coming back tonight, but my flight was cancelled, so I'll be there tomorrow afternoon."

"I'll see you tomorrow, Peyton. Have a safe flight," I said.

I hung up the phone and heard noises coming from upstairs. I stepped out of my office and stood next to the staircase as I thought I was hearing things. It sounded like whimpering. At that moment, I realized it was Ellery. I ran up the stairs, skipping one step in between, and as I reached the top, I saw Ellery lying on the floor, curled up in a ball, and shaking.

"Ellery, my god, what's wrong?" I said as I knelt down beside her.

"Don't touch me; it hurts," she cried as she put her hand up to me.

I didn't know what to do. Seeing her lying there like that, crying and in so much pain, was killing me. I felt helpless. I yelled for Claire and told her to call the nurse to get her over here immediately. Ellery then told me to pick her up and get it over with. I asked her if she was sure, and she nodded her head. I was so afraid to touch her; I didn't want to hurt her. I stood up and bent over, picking her up slowly from the floor. I flinched as she screamed when I picked her up. I carried her back to the bedroom and gently laid her down.

"The nurse will be here soon; she'll help you," I said as I gently brushed the hair away from her face.

She looked at me and cried. "I'm so sorry, Connor. I never wanted you to see me like this."

At that moment, when she said those words, it finally hit me why she didn't tell me about her illness, and why she's been so angry towards me. She knew what was going to happen, and she didn't want me seeing her like this. She was trying to protect me and spare me the pain of having to go through it with her. I knelt down beside the bed and lightly touched her hand.

"You have nothing to be sorry for; I'm the one who's sorry. It kills me to see you in such pain," I said as a single tear fell down my cheek. She reached up and wiped my tear with her thumb. I lightly took a hold of her wrist and looked at my name that was inked on it. I was just about to ask her about it when the nurse came in. She gave her a shot of morphine and asked me if she could talk to me in the hallway. After a brief conversation, I walked back into the bedroom and over to the other side of the bed. I sat up with my back against the headboard and looked at Ellery as she turned on her side to face me.

"Has the shot helped?" I asked her as I stroked her beautiful, blonde hair.

See gave me a half smile and said it was helping. "It isn't always going to be like this," she said. "The first three days after chemo is the worst, and then I'm usually fortunate enough to have a few days where I feel good; well, as good as can be expected on chemo." I didn't say a word. I just sat there playing with the strands of her hair, thinking about how stupid I was leaving her in that hotel room in Michigan.

"Don't get to use to doing that," she said. "It's going to be gone soon."

"I don't care. You'll still be just a beautiful," I smiled.

I know that made her feel good because she smiled at me, and I kissed her on the forehead. Even being in so much pain, her smile could still light up the room and arouse me. Damn that smile. I took a hold of her wrists and held them in front of me, rubbing the tattoos with my thumbs.

"I noticed these at the hospital when you were receiving chemo. I've been waiting for you to show me; why, Ellery?" I asked.

She looked down and slowly got out of bed. She walked over and stood in front of the window. "Because at some point, you have to realize that some people can stay in your heart, but not in your life, and this is my way of keeping you in my heart."

The tone of her voice was sad when she said that. I closed my eyes for a moment, taking in those words she just spoke. Even after everything I did to her, she still loved me and wanted to keep me close to her, and the only way she knew how was with those tattoos. I felt like the biggest bastard on earth. I got up and walked over to her, wrapping my arms around her waist and pulling her into me from behind.

"Get back in bed, and I'll bring you some tea," I whispered in her ear.

She turned herself around in my arms and kissed me on the cheek. I took in a sharp breath as it was heaven to feel her warm lips on my bare skin again. I wanted her so much, but I knew it wasn't possible. I smiled at her and left the room to get her some tea.

I set the peppermint tea on the nightstand and climbed back in bed beside her. I had to tell her about the phone call I received from Peyton.

"Peyton called me and read me the riot act," I laughed.

"Why would she do that?" Ellery looked at me with fear.

"She said she's been trying to get a hold of you for a couple of days, and when she didn't have any luck, she called me. When I told her about your chemo and that you were staying here, she started yelling and said to sit tight because she was coming straight over from the airport to kick my ass."

"Oh god, not tonight," she said as she rolled her eyes.

"No, we're in luck. She'll only be here tomorrow since her flight was cancelled," I lightly laughed.

"Good, because tonight I couldn't deal with her," she smiled.

Ellery closed her eyes and fell fast asleep in a matter of seconds. I sat there for a while and stroked her hair while she slept. I've already forgiven her for not telling me she was sick. I just hope she can forgive me for leaving her in Michigan. I ran my finger across her forehead and down her cheek, taking in the softness of her skin. I no longer cared about my life because I have a new life to take care of and worry about, and she's lying right beside me, looking like an angel. I slowly climbed out of bed so I didn't disturb her. It was late, and I needed some sleep. I put on some pajama pants and looked around for my phone. The last time I remembered seeing it was in the kitchen. I walked downstairs and retrieved it from the table. As I reached the top of the stairs, I heard Ellery crying. I carefully opened the door as she had her face buried into her pillow, sobbing. I felt a large pit in my stomach. I hated to see her cry, and I hated that she tries to hide it. I walked over to the other side of the bed, climbed under the covers, and wrapped my arms around her, holding her tight. "It's alright, baby. I'm here," I whispered as I kissed the back of her head. I'm never letting her go again.

I slept with her in my arms the rest of the night. It felt so good to hold her and sleep next to her again. The next morning, I got up, showered, dressed, and went downstairs. I said good morning to Claire, grabbed a cup of coffee, and went to my office to do some work. As I was sitting at my desk, my phone rang. It was Ashlyn. I had already avoided two of her phone calls.

"Hello, Ashlyn."

"I'm sick of this shit, Connor!" she yelled.

"What are you sick of?" I sighed.

"I'm sick of you ignoring me and not returning my calls. You promised me we could get together when I got back, and I've been back for two days and nothing. No seeing you, no sex, nothing. I'm fucking sick of it! I know damn well it has something to do with that blonde whore you're seeing."

Now, I was seriously pissed. "I'm sorry about the other night, but something came up!" I yelled. Why the hell was I apologizing to her?

"Your apologies aren't going to work this time, Connor, and next time I see that blonde bitch, I'm telling her everything about us, then we'll see how sorry you are!" she yelled before she hung up.

"Fuck!" I yelled as I threw my phone across the desk. I started to pace back and forth. What am I going to do about her? I need to get Ashlyn out of my life for good, I thought to myself. I couldn't risk her ruining things between Ellery and me, not when it's going to take time to rebuild what we lost. I was so angry that I was starting to see red.

I walked to the kitchen and saw Ellery standing next to the counter. She had a weird look on her face.

"How are you feeling? You look better today," I said.

"I'm fine," she said in a low voice as she looked down at the floor.

I hate it when she tells me that she's fine. I never know if she means it or if she's just telling me what I want to hear, and after the bullshit conversation I just had with Ashlyn, I didn't need this right now. I wanted her to tell me the truth, but unfortunately, I lost it. I looked at her from across the kitchen.

"You always say you're fine, Elle, even when you're not. Are you ever really fine? Can you ever just tell me the damn truth for once in your fucking life, so we can stop playing these goddamn guessing games? Can you say something other than 'I'm fine, Connor'? Because you know what, Ellery, it makes me sick."

I put my hands on the edge of the counter and pushed myself away from it. I took in a deep breath to calm down. Did I mean what I just said to her? I don't know if I did or not, but I do know she won't stand there and take it. I heard her walk over to me, and as I turned my head and looked at her, she slapped me across the face. I didn't move or say a word; I just stood there and stared into her anguished eyes. She turned and walked out of the kitchen. I hurt her again, and she didn't deserve it. I stormed out of the kitchen and knocked over a vase that was sitting on the counter. I left the penthouse via the front door and slammed it behind me.

I walked down the streets of New York City. I didn't know where I was going or what I was doing. Ashlyn had pissed me off by threatening to tell Ellery everything, and I can't seem to believe whether Ellery is telling me the truth about how she's feeling. It isn't her fault that Ashlyn's a bitch, and I can't get her out of my life. I blew up at her for no reason, and like the ass that I am, I hurt her enough for her to feel the need to slap me. I walked around for an hour and a half to cool off. I needed to apologize to Ellery and tell her about Ashlyn. She's been more than patient with me, and I owe it to her. I pulled out my phone and sent her a text.

"I want to apologize for my behavior. I'm on my way back to the penthouse, and we need to talk. If you're feeling up to it, we can go out for lunch."

She didn't respond back. I walked back to the penthouse and went straight up to the guest room. I stood there and looked around. I glanced over to the corner of the room, and her bag was gone. In fact, the things she had sitting on the dresser were gone as well. Claire came in behind me.

"She's gone, Mr. Black. Right after you left, she came up here, grabbed her bag, and left. I tried to stop her, but she said there was something she had to do, and she apologized."

"Shit, what the hell have I done?!" I yelled as I ran down the stairs to the living room. I pulled out my phone, but there was still no reply so I messaged her again.

"Where are you, Ellery?"

A few minutes later, she replied. "Connor, I had to leave. My being at your place was hurting you as bad as it was hurting me. The only thing I can tell you is I'm ok, and please don't worry about me. I have a few things that I need to do, and I don't know when I'll be back."

She doesn't know when she'll be back? What the hell is she doing, and where did she go? I was pissed, and I could feel my blood pressure rise.

"What do you mean you don't know when you'll be back? Where the fuck are you going? You have treatments to finish; you better get the hell back here, right NOW!"

When she didn't respond, I sent her another text. "I will find you, Ellery Lane, even if I have to travel to the ends of the earth; make no mistake that I will find you."

"I know you will my stalker," she responded quickly.

Enough with the text bullshit, I was going to talk to her. I dialed her number, but it went straight to voicemail. I bet she turned her phone off. I decided to text her one more time to see if she would respond.

"Ellery, you better answer your phone!"

There was no response, so I called her phone one more time, but once again, it went straight to voicemail. Just as I threw my phone on the table, I heard the elevator doors open and a woman's voice.

"Where is she, Connor Black?!" Peyton said as she stormed in.

I looked at her with anger in my eyes, and she stopped dead in her tracks.

"Uh oh, what happened?" she asked.

"Your best friend decided to take off and take a little trip somewhere," I said.

"Where did she go?" Peyton asked calmly.

"How the hell do I know? She just said that she had some things she needed to do, and she didn't know when she'd be back. What the hell, Peyton? You're her best friend; what the hell is she doing?"

She shook her head and walked towards me. "I don't know, Connor, but you need to calm down. We'll figure out where she is, and we'll bring her home."

"I can't calm down," I said as I turned and headed towards the bar. "She's sick, and she needs someone to take care of her."

"Why did she leave? What did you say to her?" She asked as she frowned at me.

"I yelled at her, but I didn't mean it. I was angry about something else, and I took it out on her. Damn it!" I screamed as I downed some scotch. I looked at Peyton and could see the worry across her face. "Would you like a drink?" I asked her.

"No thanks, I'm good for now," she replied. "I should get

going; I have to unpack."

I walked her to the elevator. "If you hear from her, will you please call me?" I asked calmly.

Peyton put her hand on my shoulder and smiled. "You bet I will. I know how worried you are."

Worried isn't the only thing I am. I'm pissed at her for doing this. Damn it. It's my fault that once again we're apart. I haven't even told her I loved her yet, and it's killing me because I need her to know how much I do. I had my back turned when I heard Denny.

"I already told you that you've met your match. She's just like you, stubborn."

"I know that, Denny. So, why the hell do you keep saying it?" I snapped.

"Because you need to realize that you just can't go off on people the way you do. You need to remove the number one stress in your life because she's causing you and Ellery too much pain."

I poured another drink. "I know, and I'm trying."

"Obviously not hard enough," he said as he walked out of the room.

I sighed and closed my eyes. My phone rang, and I jumped. I grabbed it. Peyton was calling.

"Hello?" I answered.

"I'm only telling you this because I know you love her, and that she loves you. If you ever tell Ellery that I called you, I will string you up by your balls and let you hang for days. Do you understand me, Connor?"

I gulped, this girl meant business. "Yes, Peyton, I promise."

"She went to Michigan to take care of a few things and hopped on a flight somewhere else. Don't ask me where because I'm not telling you. You need to figure that out for yourself."

I started to interrupt her. "Peyton..."

"Don't interrupt me, Connor. Just let me finish. She wants you to find her, but there's something she has to do first. That part I can't help you with because she wouldn't tell me what is was. She said if you find her, then the two of you were meant to be and that whatever it is she's doing will be worth it. She told me to be your friend. So, I'm being your friend and betraying my best friend. Start looking for her, and get your ass on a plane when you find her."

"Thank you, Peyton, I appreciate you calling me."

"You're welcome. I believe you're the best thing in her life, and she needs you. That's the only reason why I'm doing this. Don't let me down," she said as she hung up.

I stood at the bar looking at my glass of scotch. What game is Ellery playing? I asked myself.

Chapter 18

A few days passed, and I had my tech guy at Black Enterprises hack into Ellery's computer via the email she sent me. She had been doing some research on a 'Dr. Danielle Murphy' from Cedars Sinai Grace Hospital in California. She's a cancer specialist and Hematologist. Denny took a quick trip with me to Michigan to check out the airport Ellery was at. Peyton had told me that Ellery threw her phone in the garbage there to throw me off her trail. She knew I'd have it traced and find her in no time. I walked around and showed the different workers at the ticket counter Ellery's picture. They said they hadn't seen her until I came across a woman who said she was the one who had helped her. I found it strange because my tech guy couldn't find any flights booked for Ellery. The woman told me she couldn't give out any information regarding Ellery. I reached in my pocket and slid two one hundred-dollar bills at her and gave her a smile. She looked at me as I could tell she was thinking about something. She looked around and then leaned in closer to me as she put her hand over the bills.

"She booked a flight to California; Los Angeles to be exact."

"I couldn't find any record of that," I said.

She looked around once more. "She paid me off to put her ticket under a different name and let it go through."

I smiled at her, "Thank you."

I walked away, and Denny looked at me, smiling. "She's a smart girl, and she's playing one hell of a game. Have I told you, Connor, how much I love Ellery?"

"Knock it off, Denny," I said as I shot him a dirty look.

We boarded my plane and flew back to New York.

***

A week had passed, and I was missing her. It was killing me not to know what she was doing or what she was up to. I was in my office at the penthouse when I heard a light knock on the door. "Come in," I said. Peyton walked through the door.

"Peyton, is everything alright?" I asked in a panic.

"Everything's fine. I just stopped by to tell you that Ellery is ok physically, but mentally, she's a wreck. She misses you, and I want to know when you're going out to California to see her."

I sighed, "Her birthday's next week. I'll fly there before her birthday. There's no way I will let her spend it alone."

"Why don't you just go now? What the hell are you waiting for?" she asked.

"I'm giving Ellery time. She went out there for a reason, and I'm giving her space. Remember, she's the one who walked out on me."

Peyton rolled her eyes, "I'm going to be honest when I tell you that the both of you make me sick. Get over yourselves, and just love each other."

"I do and always will love her. Don't worry, Peyton, I'll make things right," I smiled at her as she turned and walked out the door.

Since I told Peyton that I would be in California for Ellery's birthday, I got to thinking about what I should get her. I'm going to make sure that she has the best birthday she's ever had. I remembered that time I was at her apartment, and I saw her list of things she wanted to do. It suddenly hit me; that was her bucket list. How the hell didn't I see it before? On her list, it said she had always wanted to go to Paris, so I had Valerie make up two tickets. We would be taking the company plane, so we could go whenever she wanted to and stay for as long as she wanted. I also wanted to get her a piece of jewelry; something that represented the two of us. I grabbed my coat and headed to Tiffany's.

I was looking at the necklaces in the display case when something to the side caught my attention. I asked the saleswoman if I could see it. She pulled out a beautiful bracelet. It was made up of numerous infinity symbols that were encased in diamonds. I couldn't stop thinking about the infinity symbol that was tattooed on her wrist. This bracelet was perfect for her as she was perfect for me. I walked out of Tiffany's and headed to the Apple store. Her last gift was a new iPhone to replace the one she threw in the trash.

I spent the next few days working a lot and trying to keep Ashlyn calm. It's hard work trying to make up things to keep her busy and out of my hair. In a few short hours, I'll be on my plane, heading to California to be with Ellery. I packed my bag and made sure I had her birthday presents tucked away safely. It's almost a six hour flight, and I wanted to be in L.A. first thing in the morning because I didn't know where she was staying. She went to some serious lengths to make sure she didn't leave a paper trail. I had Denny drive me to the airport at 2:00 am.

"Thanks, Denny, I appreciate you driving me at this hour," I said as I got out of the limo.

"No problem, Connor. Just bring Ellery home," he smiled.

"I will, I promise."

I boarded the plane and looked out the window as it took off down the runway and headed for California.

It was around 8:00 am when I arrived in Los Angeles. I already made arrangements to have a rental car waiting for me at the airport. I drove to the area surrounding Cedars Sinai Grace Hospital. If I'm right, Ellery is staying somewhere close by because she loves to walk. I pulled up to a set of apartment buildings and walked inside the rental office. I showed the manager Ellery's picture and asked if she was renting an apartment. The woman looked at her picture and said she had never seen her before. I thanked her and headed off to the next set of apartments. I searched four different apartment complexes in the surrounding area, and Ellery was not staying at any of them. I had one more down the block to try. I pulled up to the curb and walked around the side to the rental office. As I walked through the door, the manager gave me a strange look.

"How can I help you, sir?" he asked.

"I would like to know if this woman is renting one of your apartments," I said as I showed him Ellery's picture.

The manager told me to hold on a minute and immediately called someone to come to the office. Within seconds, another man came through the door and stared at me. I was beginning to feel a bit uncomfortable. The manager, Mason, introduced himself to me and then introduced his partner, Landon, as well. I thought to myself that they must know Ellery. I asked them again if they knew Ellery, and Mason started jumping up and clapping his hands while saying yes. I breathed a sigh of relief. I'd finally found her. I asked them which apartment she was staying in, and they told me how she had gone to the store, but she'd be back soon. They both went on and on about how much they love Ellery. I smiled at them because it was impossible not to love her. I thanked them and walked outside to wait for her. I leaned up against the black Porsche I rented and waited for her to come back.

Just as I checked my watch for the time, I saw her coming up the street. She was looking down, and it looked like she was taking the wrap off a candy bar. I smiled, because not only was she beautiful walking up the street, but also because she loved her chocolate. She looked up and came to a complete standstill when she saw me.

"You're a hard woman to find, Miss Lane," I smiled at her.

She dropped her bags on the sidewalk and ran to me as fast she could. She jumped up and wrapped her arms and legs around me as tight as she could. I closed my eyes as I held her, taking in the familiar scent that I've missed so much. I could tell she was crying as she buried her face into my neck.

"I've missed you so much," I whispered in her ear.

"I've missed you too, and I'm so sorry," she cried.

Ellery lifted her head up, cupped my face in her hands, and kissed me passionately. Our tongues met with excitement and exhilaration as our long-lost kiss left us both breathless. Tears were running down her face as I put her down and softly wiped her cheeks with my thumb.

"Let me look at you," I said while I spun her around. I grabbed her and held her tight. "You look just as beautiful as when you left."

Mason and Landon emerged from their apartment, clapping. I explained to Ellery how the three of us already met and what great friends they were. Ellery took me to her apartment. I closed the door as she turned around and stared at me. I ran my finger softly down her jaw line and over her lips.

"You have a lot of explaining to do, but first, I'm going to make love to you," I spoke softly. I brushed my lips against hers and heard her gasp as my tongue trailed down her neck. It felt like forever since I tasted her. I wanted her more than anything else. I craved her and now it was time to satisfy my need. "You taste so good. It's been too long, Ellery; I need you. I need to be inside you."

I picked her up and carried her to the bedroom, my lips never leaving hers. I set her down in front of the bed, lifted her shirt over her head, and tossed it to the side. My hands ran up and down her sides and over her hips as I unhooked her bra and let it fall to the floor. I cupped her warm breasts and fingered her nipples as my tongue explored her navel. I unbuttoned her shorts and made my way up to her breasts with my mouth, lightly nipping her hardened nipples. My body was on fire as was hers. She brought my face to her and kissed me, letting me know how much she needed and wanted me. I groaned as her hands took off my shirt, and her nails lightly dug into my back. I broke our embrace, kicked off my shoes, and tossed my jeans on the floor. I gently laid her down on the bed and hovered over her fiery body as I stared into her eyes. "You make me feel alive like no one ever has." I moved my hands from her breasts downwards until I reached the edge of her thong. I pushed it to the side and felt the warmth of her skin. She let out a moan as I slowly inserted one finger and felt her excitement. Her moan grew louder as I inserted another finger. "Ellery, you're so wet," I whispered in her ear.

"This is what you do to me, Connor. Feel every bit of it," she said. I slid in my fingers in and out of her slowly as she arched her back, forcing them to go as deep as they could. I circled her clit with my thumb and felt it swell with pleasure. My mouth found their way to her lips as our tongues joined each other and danced.

"I want you to come now, while my fingers are inside you and pleasuring you," I whispered as I softly kissed her neck. Her body started to shake as she let out a scream of pleasure. I smiled as I softly kissed her lips, "That's my girl." She reached down and firmly grabbed my hard cock in her hand, moving her fist up and down the shaft in a slow and steady motion. The feeling was amazing as every nerve in my body was tingling. "Oh god," I moaned as she moved her thumb over the tip in circular motions. She started to sit up, and before I knew it, I was lying flat on my back. She smiled as she straddled me and my cock slid in her with ease. I titled my head back as I felt her form around me. She was taut and warm as she slowly moved up and down, taking in every inch of me. I fondled her breasts and grasped her hard nipples between my fingers, tugging and rubbing them. We stared at each other as she swiftly moved her hips. I grabbed her hips as she rocked herself in slow circles. She was amazing and she felt so good. I could feel her swell around me, and that she was getting ready to come. She started moving up and down at a faster pace. She had me so close that I could barely stand it. Our breathing became rapid as she moaned when I placed my thumb on her clit and rubbed it as she fucked me. "Ellery, come with me, baby," I panted. "I want us to come together, and I want to hear what I do to you." She screamed my name as she released her orgasm all over my cock, and I filled her body with my come; never taking our eyes off each other. She collapsed on my chest, and I held her tight, letting our heart rates slow down. I kissed the side of her head, and she turned and smiled at me. She rolled off me and laid herself on her side, running her finger across my chin as I tucked her hair behind her ear. I asked her what she was thinking, and she told me how happy she was that I found her. I slowly leaned in and softly kissed her lips.

"Come on, baby. Let's get something to eat; I'm starving," I smiled.

I climbed out of bed and put on my jeans. I followed Ellery out of the bedroom. I walked in the kitchen to grab a bottle of water and stopped when I saw several brown containers lined up against the back of the counter. I quickly counted them; there was fifteen total. I got nervous and a fear crept up inside me.

"Care to explain what these are?" I asked.

"I'm in a clinical trial study, that's why I came out here." I started to interrupt her, but she put her finger over my mouth, "Let me finish." I smiled as I took her finger in my mouth and sucked on it. She giggled and continued, "I have to take these pills every day. Once a month, I go to the hospital and get a set of three injections. It's called some type of 'Immunotherapy'. I have to do this for a period of three months. Once I complete the three months, the doctor will test my blood to see if the cancer is gone; if not, then I will continue for another three months. I don't even know if it's going to work," she said as she looked down. I saw the anguish on her face and heard the sorrow in her voice. I lifted her chin so she was looking at me, "It will work; It has to work."

"It's only a trial, Connor; it's the first time it's been done on humans, so right now, I don't know what to think," she said distressed.

"You're strong, Elle. You're the strongest and most stubborn person I've ever met in my life, and if anybody can pull through this, it's you, but you have to stop running away from me," I told her as I stroked her cheek. She told me she was scared. I took her hands, turned them over, and lightly kissed both her tattoos.

"Don't be scared. I'm here, and I'm going to help you through this. Even if this trial doesn't work, it doesn't matter because I will fly you around the world and find you the treatment that will work

210

because…" I took in a deep breath, "I love you, Ellery Lane, and I will protect you." The feeling that crept inside me as I spoke those three words was amazing. Tears streamed down her face as she hugged me tight and whispered, "I love you too." I closed my eyes and nuzzled my face in her hair. I kissed her head and held her face in my hands. I brought my lips to hers and kissed her passionately. I curled my fingers under her shirt and slowly brought it up over her head, taking it off and tossing it on the floor. We smiled at each other as she led me to the couch where we made love.

Chapter 19

It was a beautiful, sunny day in Los Angeles. The first half of the day was spent in bed, and the second half was spent at the beach. After a picnic lunch, great sex in the lighthouse, and long talks, we headed for home. As we entered the apartment, I walked over to the easel that held a beautiful painting. I stood there and stared at the Cape Cod style house with an archway, a boat, and a lighthouse. The painting was stunning, and it made me smile to see such talent, especially from the woman I love.

"I have to say, Ellery, you are a very talented artist; this painting is stunning."

She walked over to me, slipped her hands in my back pockets, and put her chin on my shoulder.

"Thank you. This is a glimpse of my future; it looks so peaceful there."

"It's very beautiful. I suggest you keep this, and don't sell it," I said.

She kissed me on the cheek. "Maybe I will."

"I was going to tell you, you know," she said.

I reached for her hands and brought her arms around my waist. "Tell me what?"

She took in a sharp breath, "About coming here and seeing Dr. Murphy. I wanted to talk to you about it that day, but you were so angry; I heard you on the phone, in your office, with Ashlyn."

I looked down, "I'm sorry, Ellery. I never should have said those things to you; I was…"

"You need to tell me about her, Connor. We can never move forward if you don't, and I think I have a right to know," she pleaded.

I turned around and pressed my forehead against hers, "I know, and I will; just not tonight." I just found her, and we shared a perfect day. There was no way I going to ruin it by discussing Ashlyn. I could see the disappointment in her eyes when I told her not tonight. I hated doing this to her, and I know it's wrong not to come clean about Ashlyn, but I don't know if there will ever be a right time to tell her. I picked her up and smiled as I kissed her soft beautiful lips.

"I think we need to go to bed," I said.

"But I'm not tired," she devilishly smiled.

"Sleeping isn't what I had in mind. We won't be doing that for at least another three hours," I smiled as I carried her to the bedroom.

***

I woke up early to get things ready for Ellery's birthday. I was going to make sure this birthday is the best one she's ever had. I carefully moved her arm from me and slid out of bed. I was pretty sure she wouldn't wake up, because after last night, I knew she was exhausted. I threw on a pair of jeans and a navy blue t-shirt. I walked into the living room and over at the easel, looking at Ellery's painting once more. She mentioned last night how she'd envisioned this painting as her future, and I am going to make sure she gets it. I just need to make sure she doesn't sell this painting before my plans are complete.

I carefully opened the door and quietly shut it behind me. As I was walking down the stairs, I saw Mason coming out of his apartment.

"Morning, Mason," I smiled.

"You're up awful early. Where are you sneaking off to?" he asked.

"I was just heading down the street to that café to pick up some breakfast for Elle. Today's her birthday."

"I know, and it's so exciting! Did she mention going to the club tonight?" he asked.

"Yeah, she told me last night; it sounds like fun," I said as we both walked out the side door.

"Have a good day with Miss Elle. Please tell her happy birthday from us and to get her dancing shoes on, because tonight, we're going to bring down the house!" he excitedly said.

I laughed when we parted ways on the sidewalk. I reached the café and placed a takeout order. It didn't take too long, but I was nervous Ellery was going to be up before I got back and wonder where I was. When I arrived back at the apartment, I quietly opened the door and set the bag on the counter. I walked into the bedroom, and she was sleeping peacefully. I took off my jeans and shirt and put on my grey pajama bottoms. I walked back to the kitchen and searched her cupboards for a tray. She didn't have one, so I ran downstairs to Mason's apartment and borrowed one. I came back and arranged Ellery's breakfast on the tray. On the way back from the café, I bought her a single red rose from a vendor selling flowers on the street. I searched the cabinets for a vase and found a small one that would hold one flower. I filled the vase with water and set the rose inside. Everything was perfect.

I climbed into bed and pushed her hair back as I lightly kissed her neck. She rolled over and smiled. "Happy Birthday, baby," I whispered as I kissed her lips. She took my hand and interlaced our fingers as she nestled her head into my chest. "Thank you," she replied. I held her for a few minutes before I told her not to move, and that I'd be right back. She looked at me and smiled while biting her bottom lip. Damn that smile. I went to the kitchen, grabbed the tray and walked back to the bedroom. She looked at me with a hunger in her eyes, and I knew she wasn't thinking about food. I smiled as I walked over and set the tray on her lap. I could tell she was excited from the grin she was displaying from ear to ear. She asked me how, when, and where. I laughed as I told her it came from the café down the street. I opened my hand and handed her the pills.

"You need to take these first," I said.

She rolled her eyes at me. "I know," she sighed as she took them with her orange juice.

I picked up the fork and fed her some eggs. She smiled as she ate them. I couldn't help but stare into her beautiful eyes, because when I did, I saw my entire future in them. She took the fork out of my hand and fed me.

"It's time to open your presents," I smiled as I reached under the bed and pulled out three boxes. Her smile widened. "I love presents!" she squealed. I removed the tray from her lap and set it on the floor. I was grinning from ear to ear as I handed her the first box that contained her new iPhone. She gracefully opened it, and I watched as her mouth dropped in shock.

"Your phone number is the same as your old phone; you know the one you threw away?" I smirked. "Who just throws away their phone?" I shook my head.

"I'm crazy, remember?" she smiled.

"Yes, you are crazy, but you're my crazy, and don't ever forget that," I said as I kissed her on the tip of her nose. I handed her the next box that contained the bracelet. She gasped when she opened the box and, covered her mouth with her hand.

"Connor, I...I love it! This is the most beautiful gift that anyone has ever given me."

I took the box from her hand and took out the bracelet. I unclasped it and put it on her delicate wrist. "I love you, Ellery. Not only for whom you are, but for the person I've become because of you. This is my forever to you."

It wasn't too long before tears started to fall down her face. "Oh no, you don't! There will be no tears on your birthday, whether they're good tears or not; I forbid it. Do you understand, Miss Lane?" I asked as she started to laugh.

She wrapped her arms around me as tight as she could and met her mouth with mine. I responded, but quickly broke the kiss. I was excited for her to open the last present.

"You still have one more present to open," I said as I handed her the last box.

"You spoil me," she said.

I took her hand, brought it up to my lips, and softly kissed it. "You deserve to be spoiled."

She opened the box and looked at the tickets. She didn't say a word; she only looked at me with tears in her eyes.

"Don't do it; no tears," I commanded. But it was too late; they had already started to fall. I took my thumb and gently wiped her tears from her eyes. "I know your dream is to go to Paris; I saw it on the list that you hid in your desk, and as soon as the doctor says that it's ok to go, we'll be on the first flight there for however long you want to stay."

She climbed on my lap and straddled me as she cupped my face in her hands and stared into my eyes. "Thank you for all that you've done for me. You've made me the happiest person in the world, and I'm never letting you go." I smiled as I ran my finger along her face. I took her wrist and brought it up to my lips as I softly kissed the infinity symbol on her bracelet. "It will always be forever you," I whispered. She leaned in and brushed her lips against mine. We stayed in bed until the afternoon, and Ellery showed me how grateful she was.

***

Later that night, I arranged for a limo to pick us up and drive us to the swank bar that Mason and Landon had planned for Ellery's birthday. It was an eventful night of talking, laughing, and drinking. Our waitress was trying to flirt with me and didn't care that Ellery was right there next to me. When we were about to leave, Ellery excused herself and went to the restroom. While she was gone, the redheaded waitress came over and whispered in my ear. "I would love to have your cock in my mouth," she winked.

I looked over her shoulder and saw Ellery coming towards her. The angered look on her face told me she had enough of this girl. She walked up behind her and tapped her on the shoulder. I started to get nervous because I know Ellery, and she doesn't put up with any shit.

"Excuse me, lady; what the fuck do you think you're doing?"

"Listen, bitch; if you're doing all three of them, then there's no harm in letting me have a taste of this juicy one," she smiled at me. My look turned to panic as I saw rage in Ellery's eyes. I was going to stop this or she might end up in jail.

"Who are you calling a bitch?!" Ellery yelled.

I stepped out of the booth as Mason and Landon sat there with smiles on their faces. I grabbed Ellery's arm. "Come on let's go," I said as I quickly escorted her out of the bar with Mason and Landon following behind us, laughing. I kissed her on the side of her head, "I can't take you anywhere." She turned her head and gave me a stern look. "It's not me; it's you and these damn women you attract." I laughed as I picked her up and carried her to the car.

We arrived back at Ellery's apartment. Celebrating her birthday with her was the best day of my life, except for the day I found her standing in my kitchen. I walked into the room with a 12 inch round cake, beautifully lit up with 24 burning candles. I set it in front of her and watched her smile as she closed her eyes, made a wish, and blew them out. Her sweetness and innocence swept me off my feet and left me with a feeling that I never knew I was capable of. Her smile, her laughter, and the way she played with her hair when she was nervous were some of the things I loved most about her.

I handed her the knife to cut the first piece of cake, and she took it from my hand with her delicate fingers. I stood there and stared at her as she cut each piece with finesse. She looked at me with her ice blue eye; eyes that were mesmerizing and full of life.

"What are you thinking about?" she asked.

A smile fell upon my face as I answered, "I was just thinking about how much I love you." The words I was never able to say before, now flowed freely from my lips as easy as loving her did. She leaned over, put a dab of icing on the tip of my nose, and laughed. She wiped it off and held her finger to my mouth as I took it inside and licked it slowly. I saw the fire in her eyes like I do every time she looks at me.

I can't extinguish the fear that resides in my heart with her illness. I don't want to believe that she won't get better, but there's a tiny part of me that is scared shitless that she won't. I put on a brave front for her because she needs me. She needs me to be her rock, and I won't let her down. Mason and Landon left, and we walked to the bedroom.

I laid there in bed, checking my emails while waiting for her to come out of the bathroom. She opened the door and walked into the bedroom while brushing her teeth, frantically looking for something. "What's wrong, baby?" I asked. She mumbled something; I couldn't understand her between the toothbrush and the foam. She held up her free hand against her ear.

"Are you looking for your phone?" I asked her.

She nodded her head. I smiled as I pulled it from between the sheets. She smiled at me and gave me thumbs up as she went back into the bathroom and spat in the sink.

"Thanks, baby!" she yelled. She walked towards the bed and looked at her phone, checking her messages before she pulled back the covers and climbed in. She snuggled into my chest as I put my arm around her. This was right, too right, as she softly kissed my chest and slowly drifted to sleep.

Chapter 20

The next morning, I woke up and looked over to find Ellery staring at me. I could sense something was bothering her. She kissed my cheek and laid her head on my chest.

"What's wrong?" I asked as I held her.

"I'm scared to go today," she whispered.

I kissed her on the top of her head. "Don't be scared; I'm here with you, and I told you that I will protect you. You have nothing to fear when you're with me; I promise you that, my love."

She looked up at me and smiled. "I think we have time for a long shower before heading over to the hospital."

"You must have read my mind, Miss Lane, because I was just thinking the same thing," I smiled back.

We ate breakfast and headed out the door. I walked over to the Porsche as Ellery turned the opposite way. "Hey, where are you going?" I asked.

"I'm walking," she replied.

"No, you're not! Get in the car, Ellery, I'm driving you there."

I sighed as she kept walking down the street. I ran up behind her and picked her up.

"Connor, come on, please?" she laughed.

"Sorry, babe, but it's better to drive there because we don't know how you'll feel afterwards. You may not be able to walk home."

"You're right; I'm sorry," she said as she kissed me on the cheek.

We arrived at the hospital, and I could tell Ellery was nervous as she was biting her bottom lip. We sat in the waiting room of Dr. Murphy's office until a leggy blonde receptionist called Ellery's name and led us to a room. I put my arm around Ellery as we walked down the hall, letting her know she's safe. The blonde kept eyeing me up and down and Ellery noticed it. I was getting nervous because of what happened last night, and Ellery won't hold back. She gave Ellery a cloth gown to change into and quickly left the room after Ellery gave her an evil look. I took the gown from her hands and helped her into it.

Dr. Murphy walked in with a silver tray and three large needles. She explained to Ellery what each injection was going to feel like. She looked at me and told me that Ellery is going to need me to hold her hand. Just hearing Dr. Murphy explain to Ellery what her body is going to feel like had scared the shit out of me. I looked at her face, and she was as pale as a ghost. She was frightened, and it was my job to protect her. I turned on the bed so I was facing her, and I grabbed her hand.

"Just look at me, baby, and focus on nothing but me, ok?" I said.

She nodded her head as Dr. Murphy inserted the first needle. She squeezed my hand hard as she shrieked. When the second needle was injected, her shriek turned into a cry as she let go of my hand, clutched my shirt with her fists and screamed into my chest. My heart was breaking for her. I held her in my arms as the third needed pierced her skin, and she continued to scream.

"Please, Dr. Murphy; isn't there anything we can do for her?"

I pleaded.

"I'm sorry, Mr. Black. We have to let it run its course, but it's only temporary. I'll be back in an hour to see how she's doing; if you need anything, or she's having a reaction, you are to push this button immediately," she said as she walked out of the room.

"It's ok, baby. Just hold onto me," I whispered to her as she laid there and shook in my arms. My eyes started to swell with tears. I had to hold them back. I need to be strong for her, but seeing her like this and having to go through this pain was horrifying. I just kept telling her I loved her over and over.

***

A couple of days had passed, and we mostly stayed in bed, watched movies, and cooked together. Cooking with Ellery was fun because neither one of us were very good at it. When I sat at the table, doing work and holding meetings, Ellery would sit at her easel and paint. When she wasn't looking, I would stare at her and watch how flawlessly she moved her brush on the canvas. This is how I pictured the rest of my life with her; she's my future.

The next morning, I was up early for a brief phone meeting with Paul regarding the Chicago acquisition. Just as I hung up with him, my mom called. She wanted to make sure I was coming for Thanksgiving. I told her that I had met someone very special and that I would be bringing her to Thanksgiving to meet the family. I could tell she was excited by the way she screamed, "Connor's bringing someone home for Thanksgiving!" I guess she had the right to be excited since I've never brought anyone home for her to meet before. I hung up the phone, walked to the bedroom, and stared at my sleeping beauty. She opened her eyes and smiled at me. I smiled back as I walked over and sat on the edge of the bed.

"How are you feeling?" I asked as my finger ran down her jaw line.

"I'm feeling ok. I heard you on the phone."

"I was talking to my mother. I'm taking you home for Thanksgiving."

"Did you tell your mom about me?" she asked.

"Of course I did, and she's looking forward to meeting you. She's going to love you."

"I meant, did you tell her that I have cancer?" she asked as she licked her lips.

I sat there and looked at her because I didn't tell my mom about Ellery's cancer. I shook my head.

"Why didn't you tell her, Connor?"

My eyes traveled to the window, "I haven't had the chance, and it's not something I want to do over the phone, Elle. I think that needs to be done in person."

"So, what you're saying is that you want me to spring it on her on Thanksgiving? Hi Black family! I'm Ellery Lane, your son's girlfriend who has cancer for the second time in her 24 years of life and is nothing but a walking cancer disaster."

I got up from the bed. I couldn't believe she just said that. "Wow, Elle, you really know how to ruin a moment. I will tell her before Thanksgiving; end of discussion," I said in an authoritative tone.

"No, Connor. It's not the end of the discussion, and don't you dare take that tone with me!"

I turned away from the window and looked at her, "Are you looking to start an argument?"

"All you have to do is tell me why you didn't tell her yet," she pleaded.

I didn't know why I didn't mention it. I've been so busy with trying to take care of Ellery and conducting business at the same time. I didn't think about telling my mom about her cancer because I just want to forget about it. I looked at her and yelled, "You want to know why?! I haven't been able to do anything because I'm stuck here taking care of you!" Shit, that came out wrong, but it was too late because I could see the rage in her eyes. I turned towards the window and ran my hand through my hair.

"Stuck? You're not stuck here, Connor. I didn't fucking ask you to come here, and I sure as hell didn't ask you to take care of me."

She was so hurt by what I said, but I didn't mean it. I turned and looked into her sad blue eyes, "Baby, I didn't mean it like that."

"Get out of here!" she screamed as she picked up a glass that was sitting on the night stand and threw it at me. I ducked and shook my head.

"Fine, if that's what you want!" I yelled as I stormed out of her apartment. I took a walk to the beach. The sun was shining, and it was warm out. I needed to let her cool off before I went back and apologized. She was right; I should have told my mom about her having cancer. Ellery has every right to be pissed as hell at me. I was gone about an hour, and on my way back to her apartment, I stopped at the store to buy her a bag of chocolate.

I walked into the apartment and into the bedroom where I saw

Ellery bent down, picking up the pieces of broken glass. I knelt down beside her and lightly took her hand.

"Stop, you're going to cut yourself," I whispered as I removed the pieces of glass from her hand.

She took in a deep breath and started to say she was sorry. She didn't need to apologize. She had every right to act the way she did. I took her face in my hands, "I know, baby, and it's ok."

"No, it's not, Connor. I know this is hard for you, and I'm so sorry."

She was begging for forgiveness, but she didn't need to. I brought my lips to hers as I said, "It's ok, baby. I didn't mean what I said; it came out wrong."

"I know you didn't, and I overreacted."

I kissed her again and held her tight, letting her know that she was forgiven.

"Where did you go?" she asked.

I got up from the floor and told her to go sit on the bed. I walked over to the dresser, grabbed the brown bag, and handed it to her. "I figured this would make you feel better," I said with caution. She opened up the bag, and her eyes widened as she looked inside and dumped the chocolate on the bed.

"You are amazing and absolutely perfect! I love you," she said as she wrapped her arms around me and pulled me on top of her. "I know something else that will make me feel better," she smiled as I hovered over her.

"Are you sure you're up for it?" I asked. She lifted her head and kissed me passionately. That was the only sign I needed.

The next morning I got out of bed and made a pot of coffee. Ellery was still asleep, and I had some business I needed to take care of. I sat on the couch with my phone and opened an email from Phil, stating that there's one more meeting scheduled to finalize the deal for the Chicago Company. He said the meeting is first thing tomorrow morning and that I really need to be there. I got to thinking that it would be great to bring Ellery back to New York, so we could spend more time together, and she'd be able to see Peyton.

She stumbled out of the bedroom, rubbing her eyes and yawning as she headed towards the coffee pot. "Hey, babe, I hope I didn't wake you," I smiled. She poured some coffee and sat down next to me. I leaned over and ran my finger over her lips before kissing them good morning. I told her how I needed to fly back to New York today for the meeting tomorrow morning, and that I wanted her to come home with me. She was unsure if she could because of her treatment. I explained to her that it didn't matter, and that we'd be back here for her second treatment next month. She threw her arms around me in excitement, especially when I told her that she would be living with me at the Penthouse. I laughed when she pouted and asked me if she had to stay in the guest room. I took the coffee cup from her hands and set it down on the table. I grabbed her and pulled her onto my lap as I lifted up her nightshirt, threw it on the floor, and made love to her.

***

I was in the bathroom shaving while Ellery was still in the shower. I could smell the lilac scented body wash that she was using. It's the same scent that I've smelled since I first met her. She stepped out of the shower, wrapped a towel around her wet body, and walked up behind me, wrapping her arms around my waist and laying her head on my back. I stopped shaving and looked at her through the mirror. She had a smile on her face. Damn that smile. I turned around so her head was on my chest as I wrapped my arms around her.

"What's wrong?" I asked.

"Nothing's wrong. Can't a woman hug the man she loves without there being something wrong?" she asked.

"Of course she can," I said as I kissed the top of her head. She took her hands, placed them on my chest, and gave me a kiss. "I love you, Connor Black," she smiled. "I love you too, Ellery Lane," I smiled back and kissed her nose. "Now, let me get back to shaving," I said.

Her bathroom was small, and there was really only room at the sink for one person. Ellery decided she was going to be funny and pushed me out of the way so she could brush her teeth. She reached over to the medicine cabinet and opened it as I was in the middle of shaving. I could see the smirk on her face. She grabbed her toothbrush and toothpaste and shut the cabinet. She reached over me and ran her toothbrush under the running water. "Would you like me to move out of your way?" I asked. She looked at me as she put her toothbrush in her mouth. "No, you're fine," she mumbled. I took the can of shaving cream and put some on my hands. I started to bring my hands up to my face when she bumped into me so she could spit in the sink. I lightly pushed her back, and she missed the sink and spat on my leg. She looked up at me and tried to hold back the laughter that was dying to come out. I looked at her, then at my leg.

"Oh please! We share spit all the time," she started to laugh.

I was going to play this one cool and get her back. "It's ok,

Ellery. It was an accident," I said as I opened my hand with the shaving cream on it and planted it firmly on her cheek. Her jaw dropped as she looked in the mirror. She looked at me with that look she gets when she's going to take revenge. She grabbed the tube of toothpaste and squirted it at my chest.

"Here's a little toothpaste to go with that shaving cream," she said.

I took my finger and tried to wipe the toothpaste off as she stood there, smiling; our eyes never leaving one another. I grabbed the can of shaving cream and squirted her legs and chest with it. She jumped back and screamed.

"Need a shave darling?" I asked.

"How dare you!" she exclaimed.

I laughed as I pointed the shaving cream at her, and she ran out of the bathroom, holding her towel so it didn't fall off. I chased after her and tackled her to the ground. I rolled her over and pinned her arms above her head. I stared at her, mesmerized by her beauty. I took my hand and gently wiped away the shaving cream from her face while my other hand had her wrists locked tight. She didn't struggle. I could tell by the way she stared into my eyes that she didn't want me to stop. I was hard and wanting her again.

"I want to feel you inside me," she whispered.

I wanted to make sure that she was ready because I didn't want to hurt her. I reached down with my free hand and felt how wet she was. I pushed myself into her. She titled her head back and lightly moaned as her hands were running through my hair. I moved in and out of her slowly before I began to grind my hips and move circles inside her. The feeling was amazing, and hearing the sounds she made from pleasuring her was heightening my arousal. I hovered over her, pushing in and out with shallow thrusts as she moaned and became breathless. She started to come, and I followed shortly after, releasing myself inside her. I looked at her as her eyes locked on mine, taking in the pleasure and the beauty of what just happened.

"I think we need to hit the shower again," I smiled as I was covered in shaving cream and toothpaste.

"At this rate, we'll never get on that plane back to New York," she laughed.

I got off her and helped her up. I wrapped my arms around her from behind as we walked into the bathroom and took a shower for the second time that morning.

Chapter 21

We finally arrived back in New York, and Denny was waiting for us at the airport. I grabbed our bags as Ellery ran to Denny and gave him a hug. It made me really happy to see the two of them get along so well. I told Ellery that I had arranged for Peyton to come over around 7:00 pm under false pretenses. I didn't tell Peyton that Ellery was coming back with me; I wanted her to be surprised. I took our bags up to my room while Ellery went to the kitchen to grab a bottle of water. I set our bags on the floor and heard Ellery gasp as she stood in the doorway. I had forgotten that she had only been in my bedroom once, and that was when she brought my drunken ass home from the club. At first, I couldn't figure out why she stood there with a shocked look on her face, but then I saw her look around the room and at the paintings that hung on my wall.

"You were the one who bought my paintings?" she asked.

"Please tell me that you aren't mad," I said as I held my hands up.

"I'm not mad; I just want to know why," she asked softly.

"Look at them, Elle. They're beautiful. It was my way of being close to you when you weren't around." I was afraid she was going to be angry with me, but she wasn't. She walked over to me and hugged me tight, thanking me and telling me how much it meant to her.

She walked over to my bed and slightly giggled.

"What's so funny?" I asked.

"I was just remembering the night you were passed out on this bed, and I was straddled over you, taking off your clothes."

I smiled as I laid myself on the bed and spread out.

"What are you doing?" she laughed.

"I don't remember you doing that, and I want to, so I thought you could reenact it for me."

Ellery bit her bottom lip as she pulled her shirt over her head and threw it on the floor.

"Um, I don't think you did that," I smiled.

"No, I didn't, but I'm going to make it a little more interesting this time." I watched her as she unbuttoned her pants and took them off, throwing them on top of her shirt. She straddled me and slowly started unbuttoning my shirt. This was definitely not the way she helped me that night because I would have remembered it. "Fuck it; I need you now," I said as I rolled her off me and quickly got on top.

***

Later that night, Ellery was snuggled against me with her arm around my waist. She must have had a late night with Peyton because I didn't hear her come to bed. I reached over and lightly kissed her on the head before carefully sliding out of bed. I had an early meeting to attend in order to finalize the acquisition of the Chicago building. After I showered and got dressed, I emerged from the bathroom and saw Ellery laying there, staring at me. I smiled as I walked over to her.

"You need to go back to sleep, my love. It's way too early for you to be up," I said as I stroked her hair.

"I rolled over, and your side of the bed was empty; I didn't like it," she pouted.

"I'm sorry, baby, but I have a meeting first thing this morning."

"I know, and I'll miss you while you're gone. I hate being apart from you."

"Let's meet for lunch and do some shopping. I'll have Denny pick you up around noon," I said as I brushed my lips against hers.

"That sounds good; I can't wait," she said as a smile spread across her face.

I couldn't resist her smile, and I hated leaving her. I looked at the clock, and I had 15 minutes before I had to leave. I unbuttoned my pants and took them off.

"What are you doing?" Ellery smiled.

"Getting ready to have sex with you, but I only have about 15 minutes, so we have to be quick," I said as I took off my shirt.

"Hurry up and get that fine ass of yours in here," she said as she patted my side of the bed. Needless to say, I was late for my meeting.

***

The purchase of the Chicago building was finalized, and I was a happy man. Everything in my life at the moment was perfect. I missed Ellery, so I decided to have Denny pick me up before her. He pulled up to the building, and Ellery was waiting outside. She looked amazing standing there in black leggings, a long black sweater, and black high boots. She's perfection, and she's mine. Denny got out and opened the door for her. She slid in the seat and smiled when she saw me. I reached over and kissed her on the lips.

"Hey, baby, you look gorgeous," I smiled.

"I thought we were meeting at your office," she said.

"I missed you, and I couldn't wait."

She wrapped her arms around my neck as she kissed me. "I'm happy you're here now because I couldn't last another minute without you."

As we were on our way to lunch, my phone rang. I pulled it out from my pocket, and it was Ashlyn. I ignored the call and put my phone back in my pocket. Why the hell is she calling me?

"Aren't you going to answer that?" Ellery asked.

"No, it's just Paul. We're almost at the restaurant, so I'll call him later."

We had a great lunch and enjoyed some shopping afterwards. I bought Ellery some new clothes, and being the stubborn woman that she is, she tried to put up a fight when I paid for them, but I won that battle. We left the store and headed down the crowded street to a nearby Starbucks. We were walking hand in hand when I ran into Sarah.

"Hello, Connor. How are you?" she asked as she cocked her head.

"Sarah, I'm good. How have you been?" I nervously asked.

She eyed Ellery up and down, and her eyes instantly looked at our interlaced fingers. Sarah extended her hand to Ellery.

"Hi, I'm Sarah, a family friend of Connor's," she smiled.

"Hello, I'm Ellery, Connor's girlfriend."

Sarah looked at me for a moment and then again at Ellery.

"Well it was nice seeing you again, Connor, and it was wonderful to meet you, Ellery," she said. Sarah leaned into me and whispered in my ear, "She's perfect for you." She kissed me on the cheek, winked, and walked away. I let out a sigh of relief and squeezed Ellery's hand. We started to walk, but Ellery abruptly stopped behind me. I turned around and looked at her.

"I don't ever want to know what you did with her or who she was to you," she said.

"Ellery, she's…" I started to say.

"Connor, she's a family friend," she smiled as she led me through the doors of Starbucks.

***

Thanksgiving had arrived, and we spent the day with my family. It was good to bring Ellery to the home I grew up in, and to meet my family. My mom and dad took to her immediately, as did my sister. I didn't know how to bring up Ellery's illness. I was going to wait until after Thanksgiving when it was just my mom, dad, and Cassidy, but I didn't have to wait thanks to Aunt Sadie. My mom always said that Aunt Sadie was born with a gift. I never believed it, and I just chalked it up to her being crazy. I walked in the entrance of the kitchen, and I overheard Aunt Sadie grilling Ellery about her cancer. Ellery was trying to explain to them about her first time when she was 16. She was very nervous. I felt bad for her, and it was my fault. If I would have told my family about it in the first place, Ellery wouldn't be in this position.

I cleared my throat and walked over to Ellery. I wrapped my arms around her waist and kissed her on the head. "Her cancer came back recently, but she's in a clinical trial in California, so everything is good at the moment. She's doing fine, and she's going to be fine, so there's nothing more to discuss," I said in an authoritative tone. Ellery pulled me out of the kitchen and into the hallway.

"How could you not tell me about your Aunt Sadie?" she asked furiously as she hit me in the chest.

"Ouch, Elle, that hurt."

"That's not the only thing that's going to hurt, Connor Black."

"Promise, baby?" I smirked.

"Ugh, you make me so mad!" she whispered as she turned the opposite way.

I wrapped my arms around her and whispered, "I'm sorry; I never took much stock in what Aunt Sadie had to say. I always thought she was kind of crazy."

"Your family must think I'm a walking disaster of a human being, and they are probably wondering what the hell you're doing with me."

I squeezed her tight. "They love you; I can tell, and it doesn't matter what they think about our relationship. I love you for all that you are, nothing less, and for the record, I think you're a beautiful disaster."

She laid her head back on my chest and looked up as I leaned down to kiss her. She bit my lip. "That's for the 'beautiful disaster' remark," she said.

"Ouch, you really need to save this shit for the bedroom, Ellery; you have no idea how much you're turning me on with all your hitting and biting." She laughed, turned around, and licked my lip to soothe the sting.

Dinner was exceptional, and our family conversation was good. Ellery spent a great deal of time talking to my mother and Cassidy. Camden came up to me, took my hand, and led me to the floor to build blocks with him. All of a sudden, I heard my mom ask Ellery how we met. Panic washed over me as I feared Ellery would tell her about getting me home that night. I looked at her, and she gave me a smile that assured me that she wouldn't tell. She told my mom that we met at a club. Ellery sat down on the floor next to me and Camden, and asked if she could help stack the blocks. Camden picked one up and handed it to her. Watching her interact with him told me she would make a wonderful mother. How and when was I going to tell her that I can't have kids?

When it was time to leave, we said our goodbyes to my family and started on the road back home. "I love your family," Ellery said as she grabbed my hand.

"They loved you too," I smiled as I brought her hand to my lips.

"Do you really think so?" she asked nervously.

"Baby, I don't think; I know." She smiled as she laid her head on my shoulder.

***

Ellery was in the bathroom, washing her face as I was getting undressed. "I loved watching you with Camden today; it was so special and sweet."

"Yeah, well he's a pretty special kid," I smiled.

"Watching you with him made me think of some things," she said as she walked out of the bathroom and opened the dresser drawer for a nightshirt.

"What things?" I asked hesitantly.

"I don't know; just how good you are with him and…"

I knew this was going to happen, and I tried to prepare myself ahead of time. I guess this was the time to tell her. I instantly cut her off. "I can't have children, Elle; I took care of that many years ago."

Her back was turned to me as she opened the drawer. The minute I spoke those words, she stopped what she was doing, and I saw her take a deep breath.

"Aren't you going to respond to that?" I asked.

"Ok, why didn't you tell me that before?" she asked as she turned around and looked at me.

"I don't know, Elle. It just didn't seem to ever be appropriate."

"Was it because you thought I was going to die, and it didn't matter if I never knew?" she spoke with pain in her voice.

I instantly felt sick at her words. "How could you say that?"

"I'm sorry, I didn't mean it, and anyway, I don't want kids. With my fucked up family genes the kid wouldn't stand a chance," she said as she turned and faced the window.

I closed my eyes for a second as she said that. It broke my heart for her to think that way. I walked over and put my arms around her, pulling her into me. "Don't say things like that."

"It's the truth. My mother died of cancer, father was an alcoholic, and now me having cancer for the second time; think about it, Connor, the child would be doomed from the minute it was conceived."

238

"You're wrong, and I don't want you talking like that ever again," I said with anger.

She loosened herself from my grip. "Well, it doesn't matter anyway because neither of us wants kids, so end of discussion." I watched her as she walked over to the dresser across the room and grabbed the bottle of lotion.

"Does it bother you that I can't have children?" I asked.

"No, and like I said, it's for the best anyway, but I would like to know why you did it, Connor."

I took in a sharp breath, "Do you really want to hear the answer to that, Elle?"

"Yes, I do, since we're being honest and not keeping secrets."

I swallowed hard because I was about to relive what I had already told her back in Michigan. Then all of a sudden, before I could get the words out of my mouth, Ellery spoke.

"Since you can't say anything, let me say it for you. You were never going to fall in love, and that meant never having kids. So, why torture yourself with only experiencing half the pleasure every time you fucked a woman when you could experience the whole natural pleasure and not have a worry in the world, except being ignorant about STD's."

My face fell, and anger grew inside of me. "I'm not even going to respond to something as fucked up as that!" I yelled. "You're pissed that I can't have kids? Aren't you the one who said she doesn't believe in happily ever after and fairytale romances?!" I yelled at her across the room. She walked over to where her pants were and started to put them on.

"What the hell do you think you're doing?!" I yelled.

"I'm not staying here tonight; you're a dick, and I don't want to be near you right now."

"I'm a dick?" I laughed. I can't believe she thought I was being a dick when she started this argument.

"You're the one being a bitch and overreacting about me not being able to have kids."

"I'm a bitch because you didn't tell me about this sooner?!" she yelled back.

Anger and darkness consumed me. "You really want to go there, Ellery, about not telling each other things?"

"I regretted that from day one, and you know it!" she yelled. "How dare you throw that in my face?!"

"Then, I guess we're even!" I yelled. I was so angry at her for what she said. I needed some space to cool off. "Maybe it's best you stay in the guest room tonight, till we both cool off."

"I'm not staying in the guest room; I'm going home to my apartment that you so graciously call a box," she said as she pointed her finger at me.

"Really, Ellery, you're going to run?" I said as I waved my hand. "Why not; it's what you do best anyway."

She stormed out of the bedroom, and I just stood there. I didn't go after her. She needed some time to cool off, and so did I. How could such a perfect day turn into such a nightmare? I let her go back to her apartment to sleep it off. I'll head over there in the morning to get her and make things right.

***

The next morning, I showered, got dressed, and headed over to Ellery's apartment. I didn't sleep all night because she wasn't next to me, and I missed her. I knocked on her door, but there was no answer. I continued to knock, and still no answer. Either she wasn't home or she was ignoring me. I went back to the penthouse, thinking maybe she would show up there to apologize. As I stepped out of the elevator, I noticed her keys sitting on the table in the hall. She left her keys here which meant she didn't go back to her apartment. Worry began to settle inside me. I grabbed my phone, sent her a text and ran up the stairs to my bedroom. Now I was really pissed that she knew she didn't have her keys, and yet she didn't come back here.

"Where the hell are you?! I went to your apartment, and you weren't there."

"It's none of your business where I am; remember I'm just doing what I do best," she responded quickly.

"You are behaving like a child, and I don't like it; now get your ass back to my penthouse."

"I think we need time apart to think about what each of us said last night."

I read her text, and it hurt me to know that she wanted time away from me. She was acting like a selfish brat. Maybe she's right. She needs to know that how she behaved last night was unacceptable. So I sent her the following reply:

"I agree, and when you stop behaving like a selfish child, call me so we can talk like adults."

She didn't respond after that. I closed my eyes to try and stop the tears from falling. I slammed my fists down on the dresser and walked downstairs to the kitchen.

"Good morning, Connor. Will you and Ellery be having breakfast together this morning?" Claire asked.

"Ellery isn't here, so the answer is no," I snapped.

"Whoa, Connor, calm down," Denny said as he walked towards me.

I ran my hand through my hair. "Claire, I'm so sorry. Please forgive me," I begged.

"It's ok, Connor. Don't worry about it," she smiled.

"What the hell happened between the two of you now?" Denny asked as he handed me a cup of coffee.

"I told her last night that I can't have kids, and she didn't take it very well. We both said some pretty bad things to each other. Fuck, Denny, I love her so damn much. Why is this so hard?"

"Nobody said love is easy," he smiled.

I shook my head and walked out of the kitchen. I hated not knowing where she was. She said she thought it was best to spend some time apart. If that's what she wants, then I'll respect her wishes. When she's ready to come back, she'll let me know.

Chapter 22

The next few days were difficult. I missed her so damn much, and all I wanted to do was see her. Ashlyn kept calling me and making it a point to see me at the office. The days went by slow, and the nights slower. I buried myself in work most nights and went to dinner with Paul and Denny. Ellery's second treatment was scheduled for next week, and if she didn't come to her senses by then, I would have to go find her. I won't let her go through that alone.

I was in the kitchen the next morning, having coffee with Denny and Claire, when a text from Ashlyn came through, saying she was on her way up. I'd invited her over to talk. Today is the day that I'm getting rid of her and out of my life once and for all. I walked over to the elevator just as they opened, and she stepped out with a big smile on her face.

"I was so excited to get your call," she said as she ran her finger down my chest.

I removed her finger from my chest and led her to my office. This wasn't going to be easy, but it needed to be done, especially if I was going to have a future with Ellery. I asked her to sit down, but she refused.

"What's going on, Connor? I'm sensing some tension here?" she said.

I took in a sharp breath before I spoke. "There's something that we need to discuss, and it's going to upset you." She looked at me with daggers in her eyes.

"If this is about that blonde whore I've been hearing about, then I don't want to discuss it. I want things between us to go back to where they used to be," she said as she moved closer to me.

"First of all, Ashlyn, Ellery is not a whore, and you are never to refer to her as that again. Do you understand me?" I said in an angered voice. "Second of all, Ellery is my girlfriend, and I love her very much. And finally, things with us are over; they were over the night I met Ellery."

She stood in front of me as she cocked her eyebrow. "Is that so? Well I think I can make you change your mind." Suddenly, Ashlyn lunged at me, and before I knew it, her lips were on mine. I pushed her away as I looked up and saw Ellery standing in the doorway. My heart sank as I saw the pain and betrayal in her eyes.

"Ellery, this isn't what it looks like," I said in a panic. She put her hand up as if she was telling me she didn't want to hear it, turned around, and started to walk away. Ashlyn smiled as she watched her leave.

"See, Connor, I told you she doesn't love you like I can," she said.

Ellery stopped dead in her tracks and turned around. She had the same look in her eyes that she did that night at the bar. "Oh shit," I said as I watched her slowly walk towards Ashlyn. Ashlyn stood there with her arms crossed, and with a smirk on her face. This wasn't going to be good, and it was making me nervous. Ellery approached Ashlyn and extended her hand to her.

"I don't think we've officially met. I'm Ellery, Connor's girlfriend."

"Funny, Connor said he didn't have a girlfriend anymore when he had his hands all over me," she said as she refused to shake Ellery's hand.

Ellery looked at me as I stood there speechless. I couldn't believe Ashlyn just said that, but I have to make Ellery believe she's lying. The only thing I could do was shake my head so she knew it wasn't true. She glared at me as she began to speak to Ashlyn.

"He said that?"

"Yeah, he did, just after he kissed me and told me that it was me he loved all along, and you were just a charity case that he felt sorry for."

Shit, I can't believe she just said that. I have to stop this now or I'll lose Ellery forever. No matter what, I'm making sure Ashlyn is out of my life for good. I saw the look on Ellery's face, and the anger brewing in her eyes. It's a look that I've never seen before, and to be honest, it scared the hell out of me. I took a step back as I saw Ellery raise her fist and slam it across Ashlyn's jaw. She fell back on her ass as Ellery bent down until their faces were inches from each other.

"My advice to you is to crawl back into the whore hole you crawled out from and to never look at me or him again. If I even catch you looking in either of our directions, I will pound my fist into you so hard that even a plastic surgeon wouldn't be able to fix you," she said as she turned on her heels and started walking away.

Ashlyn held her jaw and screamed, "You're a crazy bitch; do you know that?!"

Inside I was laughing because Ashlyn deserved it, and I couldn't believe Ellery did it. She was leaving, and I wasn't about to let her go. I ran after her and grabbed her arm before she could reach the elevator. "Don't you dare take another step," I commanded. She whipped her head around and looked at me with evil in her eyes.

"Let go of me, right now, Connor, before you suffer the same fate as your whore over there."

I let go of her arm. "You're angry right now, so I'll forgive that last statement, but what I will not forgive is you taking another step and walking out that door." She told me she couldn't stay, especially after what just happened. I wasn't letting her go. The time had come to tell her about Ashlyn. As I pulled out my phone to call Denny and have him get Ashlyn out of the penthouse, Ellery pushed the button and the elevator doors opened. I grabbed her from behind and carried her up the stairs as she kicked and screamed at me to put her down. We reached my bedroom, and I threw her on the bed. I was so angry at her for trying to leave. I needed her to listen to me, and I wasn't letting her leave until she did.

"Now, sit down on that bed, and listen to me, Ellery. I'm not playing games with you anymore, and I know what you just saw hurt you more than anything else. You're going to sit there, and you're going listen to me!" I screamed at her.

"Go on then, explain to me who Ashlyn is, and why you've been keeping your relationship with her such a secret," she said with anger in her voice.

I paced back and forth across the room while running my hands through my hair. "Ashlyn is Amanda's twin sister."

"Who the hell is Amanda?" she asked.

I took in a sharp breath. "Amanda's the girl who committed suicide after I broke up with her."

246

"Keep talking, Connor; I'm listening."

"Ashlyn sought me out and came to my office about a year ago. She told me she had been kicked out of her house, and she didn't have any money or any place to go. She said that I owed her because it was my fault her sister killed herself." I stood there and watched Ellery close her eyes for a moment. This was so hard for her to hear, and it was making me sick to tell her.

"I took her to dinner. We talked, drank a lot, and we had sex. You have no idea how much I regret that day," I said as I stood there, shaking my head in shame.

"Why didn't you stop it after that night, Connor?" she asked as she got up from the bed and walked over to me.

"She kept bringing up Amanda, and making me feel guilty for what had happened. I gave her a job at my company, and we had an arrangement that we would meet three times a week after work for sex, with no strings attached."

"Wait, let me guess; she started falling for you, and she wanted more," she said.

I nodded my head. "Yes, she wanted me to stop seeing other woman and to have an exclusive relationship with her. I told her time and time again that I wasn't interested, and that our arrangement was staying the way it was." I turned my back to her and took in a deep breath.

"She threatened to do what her sister did if I didn't succumb to her wants and needs. It was that night at the club; the night you brought me home, that I told her there was never going to be anything more than sex between us."

"Damn it, Connor. Why the hell didn't you just stop seeing her?!" she yelled.

"The next morning, she called and apologized. She said she would be happy to keep our arrangement the way it was as long as I doubled her pay," I said as I turned around and faced her.

She shook her head and looked down. She walked back over to the bed and sat on it. "Are you ok?" I asked as I started to walk towards her. All I wanted to do was hold her. She was hurting, and I wanted to ease her pain.

"Don't take another step, and I mean it," she said and put her hand up as she got up from the bed and headed towards the door. "I can't listen to any more of this, Connor, I'm sorry."

"Ellery, please, we need to talk about everything," I pleaded.

"Why bother? So we can hurt each other again with our words?" she yelled.

I put my hand on her face, but she backed away and spoke. "My illness is tearing us apart. You can't handle your emotions, and neither can I. We just end up hurting each other more often than not."

She looked at me with anguish in her eyes. "I have a question for you, and I want you to be totally honest with me. Are you trying to save me to erase the guilt you've harbored over the years about your ex-girlfriend?"

The pain that shot through my body when she said that was unbearable. I stood there and closed my eyes while taking a deep breath. Did she really think that? How could she even say something like that after everything I've done and said to her? After everything we've been through, she doubts my love for her, and that hurts me the most. I closed my eyes and struggled with my next words.

"I think it's best if you go back to California, and that I remain here," I said as I turned around. I couldn't look at her anymore; it was too painful. She walked out of the bedroom and out of my life. I dialed my pilot and told him to have the plane ready to fly to California. I sent a text to Ellery.

"My private plane is waiting to take you back to California. Text Denny your location, and he will pick you up."

I walked downstairs and into the kitchen to find Denny sitting at the table.

"I took Ashlyn home. She talked about pressing charges, Connor, but I convinced her otherwise. Ellery has a great right hook," Denny smiled.

"Yeah she does, and believe me when I tell you that Ashlyn deserved it," I smiled back. "I need you need to take Ellery to my plane; she's leaving for California."

Denny walked over to me and put his hand on my shoulder. "You and Ellery are the two most stubborn people on the face of this earth, and you couldn't be more perfect for each other. Don't let your fears sabotage your relationship with her."

"I appreciate that, Denny, but she doubts my love for her, and it hurts. I don't know if I can be with someone who won't truly believe that I love her."

Denny's phone beeped. "It's Ellery, and she's ready to go," he said as squeezed my shoulder. "Are you sure this is what you want, Connor?" he asked as he started to walk away.

I rubbed my eyes and nodded my head. "At least for now, Denny," I said.

I walked over to the bar and poured myself a double scotch.

Once again, we're apart, and the pain and anguish in my heart and soul flared up. Have I given up on us? After she questioned me about being with her only out of guilt, that made me angry and almost hurt as bad as when I found out she had cancer. I sat on the barstool and stared at myself through the mirrored wall. What the hell am I going to do? I thought as I stared at the man who had changed his life for Ellery Lane.

The elevator doors opened, and for a second I thought it was Ellery. I turned around as Peyton peeked around the corner.

"Hey, Connor, where's Elle?"

"She's not here," I grumbled.

"What the hell happened this time?" she asked.

I got up from the barstool and turned to her. "I'll tell you what happened. Your best friend doesn't believe I love her, and she thinks I'm only with her out of guilt. Do you fucking believe that? After everything I've done for her and everything I've said to her, she has the nerve to doubt my love!" I yelled.

"Whoa; calm down, and don't yell at me, Connor," she said as she put both hands up.

"I'm sorry, Peyton. I didn't mean to yell. It's not your fault, and I'm sorry that I'm taking it out on you."

She walked over, gave me a hug, and then looked at me. "You're the best thing that has ever happened to Ellery, and she knows it. She has had such a hard life that was filled with more sorrow than joy. Whenever she gets a glimpse of happiness, something bad happens, so she tries to sabotage whatever it is that's making her happy before it makes her sad. She knows you love her more than anything in the world, and she's watched you change your life for her. It scares her to death because she thinks you're going to go away like everything else has in her life."

Peyton had a point, and I understood it. "Ellery punched Ashlyn in the face, and knocked her on her ass. She told her that if she ever looked at me or her again, she was going to make it so a plastic surgeon couldn't fix her," I smiled at Peyton.

She started laughing. "That's my girl! The one thing about Ellery is you don't mess with the people she loves, or she's going to kick your ass."

"I can see that," I laughed with her. "Thanks, Peyton. I'm going to give me and Ellery some time to calm down. I have some serious thinking to do."

"Well, don't think too long. She needs you, Connor, and you need her. I'll call her later and see how she's doing. Good luck," she said as she patted me on the chest and then walked out.

Chapter 23

The next few days had passed by slowly as I worked from home. Cassidy called to tell me that she and Camden were in the city for a doctor's appointment and then they were going shopping. I told her to come by when she was done, and I'd take them to dinner. I set my phone down on my desk and headed to the kitchen for a bottle of water. As I was coming back to my office, I heard my phone ringing. By the time I got back to my desk, it stopped. I picked it up and looked at it. My heart stopped when it said that I had a missed call from Ellery. She left a voicemail. I pressed the listen button and closed my eyes when I heard the voice that I had been missing.

"Hi, Connor, it's Elle. I just called to see how you're doing and how things are going. I guess you're busy, so I'll talk to you soon; bye." She was reaching out to me. I dialed her number and waited impatiently for her to answer.

"Hello?" she answered.

"Hey, Elle, I just got your message," I said in a low voice.

"Hi, Connor, I was just wondering how you were doing."

"I'm ok, and how are you?"

"I'm ok; I was just finishing up a new painting."

"I'm sure it's beautiful," I said as I smiled into the phone.

"I could take a picture and send it to you if you want."

"That would be great, thanks. I'd like to see it."

"So, what have you been up to?" she asked.

"Not much, really; I've been working a lot. What have you been up to?" I asked her, trying to sound normal.

"Nothing really, I've been doing a lot of painting."

"How are you feeling?" I asked.

"I'm ok, I guess," she said.

I looked at my watch. This conversation was hurting, and I hated talking to her over the phone knowing that things aren't right between us.

"I'm sorry, Elle, but I have to get going; Cassidy and Camden are in the city, and I'm taking them to dinner. They should be here any minute."

"Oh ok. Please tell Cassidy that I said hi, and give Camden a big hug for me."

"I sure will, Elle. Thanks for calling," I said.

"Sure, no problem; I'll talk to you soon. Bye, Connor."

I hung up just as Denny walked into my office and sat down across from me. "I heard that conversation," he smirked.

"Were you eaves dropping the whole time?" I asked.

"As a matter of fact, I was. So, tell me why you cut her off the way you did."

"I don't want to talk about it, Denny," I growled at him.

"You never want to talk about it, Connor, but you need to face reality. You either love her enough to fight for her or you don't, and if you don't, then tell her and walk away. Go back to your old life, and be the miserable prick you were."

"Damn it, Denny! Why can't you just leave me alone?! I yelled as I slammed my fists on the desk.

"Because you're family, and family always interferes in personal matters," he said as he stood up and pointed his finger at me. "You, my friend, will not destroy the best thing that has ever happened to you. I'm telling you exactly what I told Ellery the other day. Why do you think she called you? I set her straight as well, and now I'm setting you straight. Get your head out of your ass, stop feeling sorry for yourself, and get your plane over to California. I will not sit back and let you both ruin each other and what you have because the other is too stubborn to make the first move!"

I looked at him in shock. I couldn't believe Denny, of all people, spoke to me like that. I stood up, walked over to him, and gave him a hug. "Thank you," I whispered.

He patted me on the shoulder, "You're welcome."

***

I had a nice dinner with Cassidy and Camden. She asked where Ellery was, and I told her what had happened. She gave me some sisterly advice and she promised me that she wouldn't tell mom. I stared at Camden, thinking about that night that practically started all this. Ellery wants children someday, but I can't give them to her. I confided in Cassidy about it, and she told me to have my vasectomy reversed. She went on to say that her boss had it done, and now he has two beautiful, little girls. After dinner, I took Cassidy and Camden to the ice cream parlor. They were both thrilled for the treat. We took our ice cream and sat down at the small table. Being here made me miss Ellery even more.

"I'm going to ask Ellery to marry me," I said to Cassidy.

"Connor, that's wonderful! I'm so happy for you," she said excitedly.

"Don't get too excited; she hasn't said yes yet, and who knows if she even will."

"Don't be a fool, Connor. Of course she's going to say yes. Women can't resist the charm of Connor Black," she smiled.

"Very funny," I said. "I'm going tomorrow to pick out a ring and then I'm going to California."

Camden started getting fussy, and it was getting late. "I'm going to head on home," Cassidy said as she hugged me tight. "Thank you for dinner, and good luck. I love you, brother."

"I love you too, sister," I smiled as we walked out the door and onto the streets of New York. We drove back to the penthouse, and she got in her car and headed home.

***

The next day, I went into the office for a few hours to handle some meetings and then headed to Tiffany's to buy a ring for Ellery. I walked through the doors, and the saleswoman escorted me to a private room that displayed rows of diamond rings on the table. I picked up every one and examined them closely, but I wasn't seeing anything that was worthy enough for Ellery. The saleswoman told me that she'd be right back as she left the room. A few moments later, she came in, holding a black cloth in her hand. She held it out and opened the cloth which displayed a beautiful four-carat, princess cut, and perfectly flawless diamond ring, with the infinity symbol covered in diamonds on each side of the band. It was the perfect ring for her. I smiled at the saleswoman and told her I'd take it. I also told her that I wanted to engrave the band. She asked me what I wanted to say as she held a pen in her hand.

"To my love, my future, & my forever."

The saleswoman looked up at me with tears in her eyes. I smiled and handed her my credit card. She said the ring will be ready by tomorrow morning. I walked out of the store, and Denny was waiting for me at the curb. I slid in the back seat as he turned around, looking at me, smiling. He knew what I did, and he was happy. I smiled back at him and pulled up Ellery's picture on my phone. I couldn't wait to see her again. Her treatment is in two days which works out perfectly. I'll pick up the ring tomorrow morning and fly to California to talk to her and make things right before her treatment.

I decided to go to the gym and workout for a while. I was lifting some weights when I looked up, and Ashlyn was standing over me. I sat up and looked at her.

"Is your crazy girlfriend here with you?" she asked as she looked around.

"No, she isn't," I responded as I couldn't help but stare at the bruise on her face.

"I just want to apologize for saying and doing what I did. I have issues, Connor, and I feel like I'm heading down a bad road. But I am seeing a therapist, and I'm going to get my life straightened out."

I actually felt sorry for her at that moment. "You do realize that you can no longer work for Black Enterprises, right?" I said.

"I know, and I just handed in my letter of resignation today. I asked Phil not to tell you because I wanted to do that myself."

"I'm also stopping your monthly payments, but I will pay for your therapy. It's the least I can do since you're seeking help."

"Thank you, Connor," she smiled. She started to walk away and then turned around. "Tell Ellery I'm sorry and that she's a lucky woman to have someone like you to love her." I smiled and nodded my head, and then she was gone. I felt like a weight had been lifted off my shoulders. I finished my workout and then went home to prepare for my departure to California.

When I got off the elevator, Peyton was sitting in the kitchen, talking to Claire. I walked in, sat down on the stool next to her, and kissed her hello on the cheek. "Is everything alright?" I asked her.

"Everything's fine. I just stopped by to see how my friend is doing," she smiled.

"I'm good, in fact, I'm fantastic," I laughed.

Peyton narrowed her eyes at me. "The only way you'd be fantastic is if you saw or talked to Ellery. So spill it, Black; I want details."

"I bought Ellery an engagement ring today, and I'm going to propose to her."

Peyton threw her arms around me. "I'm so excited for you!"

"Don't get excited yet; she hasn't said yes, there's a possibility of her saying no."

"Ellery will say yes, Connor, trust me. She loves you too much to say no. Plus, she knows I'll kick her ass if she turns you down."

"Please don't tell her about this," I commanded.

"No worries, Connor; your secret is safe with me. I love my best friend, and I wouldn't ruin this for her," she smiled.

"Call Henry, and let's have dinner together," I said.

"Great idea, I'll call him now."

The three of us had a nice dinner out and great conversation. I really liked Peyton and Henry, and I could see the four of us hanging out together and being great friends for as long as we live.

After I got home, I packed my bag and made sure everything was ready for the morning. I climbed into bed and laid there, planning the perfect proposal. Ellery deserved the best, and I wanted to make sure it was something that she'll never forget.

Chapter 24

Tiffany's called me the next morning to inform me that Ellery's ring was ready. I threw my bag in the limo, and Denny drove me to pick it up. As I put the box in my pocket and headed back to the limo, my phone rang.

"Valerie, what's up?" I answered.

"Mr. Black, you need to come to the office. There's a problem with the Chicago building, and Phil needs you here right away for a meeting."

I sighed heavily into the phone. "Tell Phil I'll be there as soon as I can." I hung up and told Denny that we needed to stop by Black Enterprises first. I called my pilot and told him that I'd be delaying the flight for a couple of hours.

I walked through the doors of Black Enterprises and headed straight to my office. "Tell Phil I'm here, and let's get things moving," I said to Valerie.

I looked at Phil as he walked through my office door. "What the hell is going on?"

"The Chicago building caught on fire and burnt to the ground last night. I just got the call. Connor, everything's destroyed."

"Shit, are you kidding me, Phil? Do they know what started it?"

"The firefighters are saying that it was arson," he said.

I shook my head and ran my hand through my hair as I dialed my pilot. "Change of plans, we're flying to Chicago first and then California," I told him. "Let's go and see how many millions of dollars I just lost."

We flew to Chicago and met with the local police and the firefighters. They said it was definitely arson, and they'd be working hard to try and find the person who did it. They asked me and Phil a number of questions about employees, friends, and various people we know. I couldn't think of a single person who would purposely do this to me. I looked at my watch, and I needed to get on that plane to California. I told Phil to stay in Chicago for the night, and I'd send the plane back for him first thing in the morning. He needed to stay behind and fill out a bunch of paper work anyway.

The flight to California seemed unusually long. I got out of my seat to use the bathroom, and when I came back, I noticed I had a missed call from Ellery. I was arriving in California in less than an hour, so I decided that I'd call her when I landed. Upon arrival, I got into a cab and headed to her apartment. I tried to call her, but she didn't answer. I arrived at her place, and I knocked on the door. I was feeling nervous to see her again. I didn't know what to expect from her. When she didn't answer, I went downstairs to Mason and Landon's apartment. Landon came to the door, and he didn't look very well.

"Hey, Connor; it's good to see you, buddy," he sniffled.

"Hi, Landon; are you sick or something?"

"Yeah, I caught some kind of virus. What brings you here?"

"I'm looking for Ellery, but she's not answering her door."

"Her and Mason went to Club 99 for an evening out. You can find them there."

"Thanks, man, and feel better," I said as I left.

I hailed a cab, and he dropped me off in front of the club. The line to get in was long, so I pulled a hundred-dollar bill out of my pocket and handed it to the bouncer. He smiled at me and lifted up the rope. I walked inside as the music was blaring, and the floor was thumping. There was no way I was going to find her in this crowd. I decided to hit the bar for a drink before I started looking for her. As I was almost there, I saw Ellery and Mason standing there doing shots of Tequila. I stopped and stared at her from behind. The little black skirt she was wearing barely covered her ass, and she had on high black boots that came to her knees. I felt like I didn't know that girl standing there. She looked like a slut to be exact.

I decided to stay back and watch her. She downed six shots of tequila, grabbed Mason's hand, and went to the dance floor. I didn't know how much she had to drink before I got there. I followed her to the dance floor while keeping some distance. I saw a guy approach her and they started talking. My blood was boiling, and I could feel the anger rising up. They started dancing together as Ellery was grinding and moving her body up and down his. I was ready to kill. I went up and tapped the guy on the shoulder. I slipped him a fifty-dollar bill to leave and indicated that she was mine. Mason saw me across the crowd, and his eyes widened. I shook my head at him not to let Ellery know it was me standing behind her. She moved her body up and down me. She brought her hands to my arms. I tightened my grip on her hips. This girl was in big trouble with me. She turned around and shock overtook her expression as she looked at me.

"Let's go now!" I ordered.

"What the hell are you doing here, Connor?" she asked as she jerked her arm from me.

"Why don't you tell me first, Ellery?!" I yelled.

"I'm having fun," she slurred.

"You look like a total slut on this dance floor, and thank god I was here or who knows what that asshole would have done to you."

She looked away from me and headed towards the bar. I weaved in and out of the crowd, trying to catch up with her. She'd already downed one shot by time I caught up with her and picked up the next glass as I grabbed it out of her hand. "You're drunk, and we're leaving; let's go." I demanded. I threw some money on the bar and grabbed her hand, pulling her out of the bar with Mason following behind us. She tried to get out of my grip as she was screaming at me to let her go. She was so drunk, and it killed me to see her behave this way. She stopped dead in her tracks and wouldn't move, so I picked her up in the middle of the club and threw her over my shoulder. She started kicking and screaming for me to put her down.

"Ellery, knock it off or so help me."

"So help you what, Connor?!" she yelled as I put her in the cab and climbed next to her. She looked at me as I stared straight ahead. I couldn't look at her at that moment. I was too pissed off.

"You have no right!" she spat.

My angered eyes turned and looked at her. "I have no right? What the hell do you think you were doing in there? Were you trying to get yourself raped? Look at you, and the way you're dressed, you're just asking for it."

She flipped out and started hitting me in the chest. "Fuck you, Connor!" she screamed as she proceeded to beat on me.

Mason grabbed her arms as I grabbed her wrists, trying to

calm her down. The cab pulled up to the apartment building. Mason and I got out, and Ellery sat there with her arms folded.

"Get out of the cab now!" I yelled. She glared at me and then flipped me off.

"Real mature, Ellery," I said as I leaned into the cab, grabbed her arm, and pulled her out. I threw her over my shoulder and carried her straight to the bedroom, throwing her on the bed. I paced back and forth across the room while running my hands through my hair, trying to calm down.

"I can't believe you, Ellery. I came here tonight to surprise you, and I find you dry humping some guy in a club, drunk off your ass. What the hell were you thinking?"

"I was having fun instead of being cooped up in this apartment, crying over you every damn day!" she screamed.

I stopped and looked at her. I could see the affliction in her eyes, and it hurt. "Do you think this has been easy for me?" I asked calmly.

She put her hand over her mouth and ran to the bathroom. She leaned over the toilet, and I heard her vomiting. I walked in behind her and held her hair back with one hand while I softly rubbed her back with other. As she began to cry, I walked to the sink and ran a cloth under the warm water. When she was finished, I wiped her mouth with it and helped her off the floor.

"Let's get you in your pajamas and into bed. You have your treatment tomorrow," I said as I took her nightshirt out of her drawer. I walked over to her, and she grabbed it out of my hands.

"Let me help you," I calmly said.

"I don't need your help; I can do it myself!" she yelled and undressed as I watched her. She climbed into bed and pointed at the door for me to leave her room. I rolled my eyes and sighed as I grabbed a pillow and laid myself on the couch. I turned on the TV, but it was playing a DVD. The woman on the screen looked just like Ellery. I restarted it from the beginning and watched as Ellery's mother spoke to her. No wonder she went to the club and drank like that. Between watching this video and me, the girl was a wreck. I felt horrible, and I should've been here for her while she watched it. I wanted nothing more than to climb into bed next to her and hold her tight. I wanted to tell her how much I love her and that I'm here for her, but it's the last thing she wanted, so I respected her wishes and slept on the couch.

***

I woke up early the next morning and put on a pot of strong coffee. Ellery was going to need it because she was going to have one hell of a hangover. I leaned up against the counter, waiting for the coffee to brew as she emerged from the bedroom.

"Good morning; you look like shit," I smiled, trying to be funny and lighten the moment.

"Yeah, well, we all can't look as perfect as you," she frowned.

I smiled as I handed her a cup of coffee. "Do I get a hug?" I asked as I held my arms out.

"Sluts don't give hugs," she snarled as she grabbed her cup and walked away.

Obviously she's still pissed about the 'slut' remark. I was hoping she wouldn't remember that. I took my coffee, sat at the table, and waited for her to get ready. After 20 minutes, she was finally ready and she went to the cabinet to grab a bottle of Motrin.

She was having trouble opening the bottle, so I walked over to her and tried to take it from her hands to help her. She wouldn't let go and told me to go away.

***

We arrived at the hospital in silence. She walked a few feet ahead of me through the parking lot. I tried to hold her hand, but she just jerked it away. "I don't understand why you're so mad," I finally said.

"You called me a slut, Connor."

"I said you looked like a slut, Elle."

She shook her head, "Same thing, you idiot."

When we reached the office, the nurse took us promptly to the room. Ellery changed into the thin gown and sat on the bed, waiting for Dr. Murphy. She wouldn't even look at me.

"Are you even going to look at me?" I asked.

"I'm so mad at you, Connor Black, I could scream."

I walked over to her and tried to take her hand, but she pulled away. "If you think I'm going to apologize, then you're in for a surprise because I'm not. What you did last night was unacceptable and immature," I said.

"At least I didn't take the guy home and fuck him like you did with random strangers!" she spat while staring me straight in the eyes.

"Why did I even bother coming here?" I asked.

"I don't know, Connor; why the hell did you?"

Dr. Murphy walked in and looked at us. She could feel the tension in the room. "Hello, Ellery, Mr. Black," she smiled.

Ellery laid herself down on her side, and I sat on the edge of the bed, facing her. She looked at me and pointed to the chair. "You; go sit over there," she growled. I sighed and shook my head as I got up and sat across the room. She wouldn't even look at me when the first injection went in. She whimpered like before until the second injection pierced her skin, and Ellery let out a scream. She held out her hand to me, and I was by her side in a second. She clutched my shirt in her fists as I wrapped my arms around her and kissed her on the head. "You are the most stubborn person that I've ever met," I whispered. She cried as Dr. Murphy gave her the last injection. I climbed on the bed while still holding her and laid myself next to her. It felt so good to have her in my arms again. I kept kissing the top of her head as she tried to sleep for the next couple of hours.

When Ellery woke up and we got the ok from Dr. Murphy, I took her home, and she laid herself on the couch. "Are you going to be comfortable there?" I asked her, but she ignored me. I knelt down in front of her; my eyes staring into hers. "Would it be ok if I gave you a kiss? I've really missed those lips."

I laughed as she clamped her mouth shut. I ran my finger softly over her mouth and up her cheek. I leaned into her and softly brushed my lips against hers. It didn't take long before she gave in, and her lips joined mine. She parted her lips so my tongue had access to her whole mouth. The kiss was light and soft. I broke our kiss and looked at her. I didn't say anything at first. I just stared at her, taking in her beauty and thinking about how much I love her.

"I've never loved anyone like I love you, Ellery, and no matter what we've been through, or are going to go through, nothing will ever change the way I feel," I said.

Tears began to swell in her eyes as she cupped my face in her hands. "I love you too, and I'm sorry, again," she started to cry.

"I think we're going to spend our whole lives apologizing to each other," I lightly laughed.

She sat up so I could sit next to her. I pulled her onto me so her head was resting in my lap. I started to gently stroke her hair as she fell asleep. I pulled my phone out and sent a text message to Denny.

"I need you to be in California the day after tomorrow. That's when I'm proposing to Ellery. Make the arrangements for the rental of the beach, the dinner, and tent. It has to be perfect."

"Don't worry, Connor; I have Valerie and Claire helping. Everything will be perfect. I'll see you in a couple of days. Now, calm down."

I carefully lifted Ellery's head and scooted off the couch. I covered her with a blanket and went into the bedroom to call Phil. He told me that the cops were holding someone in custody that fit the description of someone lurking around the building the night of the fire. He told me not to worry and that he'll take care of things while I'm gone. Just as I hung up, Ellery came walking into the bedroom.

"I hope I didn't wake you," I said as she wrapped her arms around me.

"No, I woke up on my own," she smiled. "Who were you talking to?"

"I was talking to Phil about something that happened before I came out here."

"What happened?" she asked with concern.

I pushed her hair away from her face. "It's nothing for you to worry about. It's just business," I said as I kissed her lips. Her hands traveled down my back as she firmly grabbed my ass. I broke our kiss and smiled at her. "What do you think you're doing?" I asked.

"Just feeling that tight ass of yours, Mr. Black," she smiled. Ellery moved her hands around to the front and felt my hard cock through my jeans. "Well, we sure can't let that hard on go to waste," she said as she unbuttoned my pants and slowly pulled them down. I looked at her with a smile as she caught me off guard and went down on me. Her mouth was amazing. I closed my eyes and threw my head back as she licked every inch of my erection with her soft warm tongue. She rolled her tongue around the tip like she was eating an ice cream cone before gently wrapping her mouth around me and sliding the head against the roof of her mouth. I was already on the verge of exploding. After she had taken me in her mouth, she began slow even bobs. I started to thrust my hips back and forth and fist her hair as her sucking increased. She took her hand and gently stroked my balls. I groaned as my breathing became rapid, and I was ready to come. "Ellery, I'm going to come," I warned her in case she didn't want me to explode in her mouth. She didn't stop, and I yelled her name as I released myself. That was the best I've ever had because it came from the woman I love. Once I was done, she released her mouth and looked up at me. I knelt down and cupped her face as I kissed her passionately. We spent the rest of the night in bed having sex, discussing plans for Christmas, and drinking wine. Everything was perfect and just as it should be.

Chapter 25

I opened my eyes and noticed Ellery wasn't in bed. I thought that was odd because I'm always the first one up. Today's the day I am proposing to her, and I couldn't be more nervous. Denny had sent me a text last night and assured me everything was set and in place. I pulled the white box with the pink satin bow from under the bed and hid it behind my back as I walked towards Ellery to where she was standing in the kitchen.

She looked at me and smiled. "What are you hiding, Mr. Black?"

I smiled back and kissed her on the lips. "A present for you," I said as I handed her the box. She opened it and pulled out the white, spaghetti strap sundress that I'd picked out for her back in New York.

"I'm taking you to dinner tonight, and I want you to wear it."

"I love it," she smiled as she kissed me. "But what's so special about dinner tonight?"

"It's our last night in California until next month, and I want it to be special, especially since tomorrow is Christmas Eve."

"You're so sweet," she said as she hugged me.

I picked her up and swung her around. "I know something else I can give you that's sweet," I smiled as I carried her to the bedroom and made love to her.

***

I sent a text to Denny to make sure he was outside, waiting

with the limo. I made sure I had everything, including the ring. "Come on, babe; we're going to be late for our reservation!" I shouted across the apartment.

"Excuse me, but if you recall, I was just getting out of the shower when you decided to push me back in," she smiled as she emerged from the bedroom. I gasped when I saw her in the white sundress. She looked as beautiful as an angel that fell from the sky. "You look absolutely beautiful, baby," I said as I held out my arm to her. "Thank you, my love," she smiled. Damn that smile.

We walked outside, and she was surprised to see a limo parked at the curb. I opened the door for her, and I heard her gasp as she slid in the back seat.

"Denny, what are you doing here?"

He turned and looked at her with a smile. "It's good to see you, Ellery."

"Why is Denny driving us in California?" she asked as I sat next to her.

"I need to blindfold you," I smiled.

"Don't you think that's a little too kinky with Denny here?" she said.

"Trust me; we'll be using this in the bedroom, but for now, where I'm taking you is a surprise, and I don't want you to know until we get there," I said as I took out a black cloth and covered her eyes. "Are you ok?" I asked.

"Except for being incredibly turned on, yes," she smiled.

We arrived at the beach, and I helped Ellery out of the limo.

We walked a few feet and then I stopped, bent down, and removed her shoes from her feet.

"You're full of kinky surprises tonight, Mr. Black," she smiled.

"Trust me, Ellery, you'll love this." I picked her up and carried her to the sand. I gently put her down and asked her if she knew where we were. She guessed it, so I removed the blindfold from her eyes. She stood there and looked around to see a white canopy, sitting in the middle of the beach.

"Is it just us here tonight?" she asked.

I smiled as I kissed her softly on the cheek. "Yes, baby; I rented out the entire beach just for us."

I took her hand and led her down the beach to the white canopy. Inside the canopy, sat a round table, draped in white linen, white roses, and two chairs covered in white fabric. She stood there, taking it all in and the beauty of it all. "Connor, how and when did you do all this?"

"Do you like it?" I asked as I kissed her hand.

"I love it; you're so amazing," she smiled.

"Dinner will be here soon, so I thought we could take a walk along the water."

I took her hand as we walked along the edge of the shoreline; the water hitting our feet. I stopped and pointed to the sky. "Look over there; the sun is starting to set."

I felt an overwhelming sense of peace and comfort at that moment, and I believe Ellery felt it as well. Now was the perfect time to propose to her. I took her hands and held them as I faced her, taking in a deep breath.

"Ellery, from the first moment I saw you, I knew instantly that I needed you in my life, and I set out to make sure that happened. You kept calling me a stalker, and you were right; I did stalk you, but for good reason. You're different from anyone that I've ever met. You're strong, kind, good-hearted, forgiving, and loving. You're also incredibly stubborn, a smart ass, and very independent, and that's everything I love about you. You've certainly given me a run for my money since I've met you. You've challenged me and brought out a man that I thought I never could be. You've shown me things that I never would've seen if you weren't in my life. You've filled the void in my heart and soul that I never knew existed until you weren't by my side." Tears began to fall down her face.

"I was simply a man with no meaning until I met you, and I'm proud of whom I've become because of you. We've been through a lot together, and we will continue to go through a lot, but we'll conquer whatever life throws our way, together. I want to thank you for being my best friend, and my lover." I got down on one knee and pulled the small velvet box from my pocket. I looked up at Ellery as the tears wouldn't stop flowing down her face. "I want to be more than just your lover; I want to be your happily ever after, your best friend, your husband, and I want you for my wife. Will you marry me, Ellery Lane?" I opened the box, took out the ring, and held it up to her.

She looked at me, crying as she nodded her head. "Yes, Connor; I will marry you."

A large grin grew upon my face as I put the ring on her delicate finger and stood up, hugging her and twirling her around. We kissed passionately and then I had her look up at the sunset. "I wanted to propose here because I figured you'd want your mom to be here with us." She put her hand on my cheek as I wiped away her tears. I smiled as we watched the sunset.

When dinner was ready and being served, I took Ellery's hand and led her back to the canopy. We sat down and ate great food. We talked and laughed, and she occasionally cried, but they were tears of happiness. I held her hand across the table as she stared at her ring. "It's so beautiful, Connor."

"A beautiful ring for a beautiful woman," I said as I got up and took her hand in mine, leading her to the large white tent that was filled with fluffy pillows and blankets.

A huge grin crossed her face as she entered the tent. "Sex on the beach?" she asked.

"Yes, sex on the beach," I nodded with a smile.

I slid the spaghetti straps off her shoulders, allowing her entire dress to fall to her feet. She stood there in only white lace panties as my tongue traveled across her neck and up her jaw line before joining my mouth with hers.

"I want to make love to you all night; first here, and then at home in every room. When you walk tomorrow, you'll be reminded of our passionate night; one that I never want you to forget," I whispered. I laid her down on the soft pillows as she watched me take off my shirt, pants, and boxers. She stared at me with a hunger in her eyes. I bent down and laid myself on my side, propped up on my elbow as I softly stroked her beautiful breasts, paying special attention to each hardened nipple. She ran her hand through my hair and brought my head closer for a kiss. Our lips grew hot as our tongues were reunited with each other. My hand traveled up and down her torso and into her lace panties, feeling the wetness from her arousal.

"Christ, Ellery, you're so wet," I moaned. My lips broke from hers as I kissed each breast, making my way down to her belly button and kissing her softly between her inner thighs. I gently inserted my finger inside her, feeling the wetness before inserting another. She gasped at the pleasure and arched her back for me to go deeper. My tongue ran circles around her clit, forcing her to release her pleasure to me. I quickly placed my mouth where my fingers had been, sucking lightly and licking every sensitive area. I brought my mouth up to hers and gave her a taste of what I love so much. She reached down and took me in her hand, stroking the length of me with long soft strokes. I let out a groan as I was lightly licking behind her ear.

"Connor, I need you inside me now. Please, I need to feel you," she begged.

I moaned from hearing her say those words as I turned her on her stomach and entered her slowly from behind. "Is this how you want me?" I asked.

"Yes," she whispered.

I sat up and moved fluently in and out of her. I reached my hand around the front of her delicious body and grabbed her breasts, squeezing them and pinching at each nipple before moving my hand down and rubbing her clit. She was moaning and wanting more.

"Don't come just yet, baby, I need you to come with me."

"Harder, Connor; fuck me harder, right now!" she demanded.

I took in a sharp breath as I moved faster in and out of her at a faster pace. I was close to exploding as she screamed my name, and I felt her orgasm. "Ah," I said as I pushed myself deeper into her, releasing all my pleasure into her body. I planted small kisses up and down her back before collapsing on her. My heart was rapidly beating as I was trying to catch my breath.

"I love you," she whispered.

"I love you too, baby."

We spent a couple more hours in the tent, drinking wine, and talking. Then as promised, we made love in every room back at her apartment. It was the best night that we've ever spent together, and the happiest. As we lay together in bed, I held her hand, rubbing my thumb over her ring. It looked beautiful sitting on her finger.

"You're mine now; I hope you realize that," I said to her.

"I was yours from the moment you asked me what my name was," she smiled.

I brought her hand up to my lips as I softly kissed her ring. We were both exhausted and drifted off into a deep sleep.

***

The Christmas holiday was beautiful and well spent with family and friends. Ellery and I spent New Year's Eve hosting a party at the Waldorf Hotel with about 200 people. We rented a room for the night and rang in the New Year by making passionate love.

"What's wrong, babe?" I asked. I could tell something was bothering her.

"What makes you think something's wrong?" she asked as she looked up at me.

"I can tell when something's bothering you," I said as I lightly smiled and ran my finger across her lips. "Talk to me, Ellery; tell me what's on your mind."

"What if this clinical trial doesn't help me?" she asked.

"It will help you."

Ellery sat up and turned towards the edge of the bed, letting her feet hit the floor. "You can't be so sure of that, Connor."

I sat up and clasped her shoulders. "I can be sure because I have faith. It's a new year, and a new beginning for us, for our future, and nothing's going to take that away. You will get better, and we'll be married and have the rest of our lives in front of us. Speaking of our future, there's something I want to talk to you about." She turned and faced me. I smiled at her as I pushed her hair behind her ear and softly stroked her cheek.

"I've made an appointment with my doctor to have my vasectomy reversed."

"What? Connor, no, you can't," she said.

I looked at her and was surprised at her reaction. "Listen to me; I want this because I want a family with you, and if we can have our own child, that would be amazing. I'm not saying it'll work, but there's a 50/50 chance, and I think we should try it."

"But my genes suck, and you know it," she sighed.

I laughed and planted a kiss on her forehead. "Your genes are beautiful."

"I guess I'm just scared," she whispered.

"Don't worry, baby. Everything is going to work out; you just wait and see," I said right before we fell fast asleep.

Chapter 26

A couple of weeks later, I felt the emptiness on Ellery's side of the bed as I rolled over. I opened my eyes and noticed that it read 4 am on the clock. I looked around the dark room; the only shadow of light was coming from the clock. I got out of bed, put on my pajama bottoms, and walked downstairs to find Ellery, sitting at her easel and painting. I walked over to her as she turned her head and looked at me.

"I'm sorry, babe, I hope I didn't wake you," she said softly.

"No, you didn't wake me, but why aren't you sleeping?" I asked as I slipped my arms around her shoulders.

"I couldn't sleep. I have too much on my mind, and painting always helps me clear my head."

"You need to talk to me, Ellery. Please tell me what's on your mind," I said as I kissed the top of her head."

"It's nothing to worry about. I've just been thinking about my last treatment and where we go from there."

"We simply move forward," I said as I lifted her from the chair. "It doesn't matter what happens. We move ahead and take it one day at a time, because baby, time is all we have," I smiled as I picked her up and carried her back to bed. She smiled as she put her arms around me. I laid her on the bed and held her tight, letting her know she has nothing to worry about.

A couple of hours later, the alarm went off, and I needed to head to the office. I looked out the window, and the snow was lightly falling. I looked over at Ellery as she laid there on the bed sound asleep. I took a hot shower, got dressed, and headed to the kitchen for some much needed coffee. Denny walked in behind me.

"Good morning, Connor," he spoke. "Any word yet on the Chicago fire?"

I sighed as I took a sip from my cup. "No, not yet; they had to let the guy go because of insufficient evidence. But don't worry; I have my men working on it. They'll find out who set that fire."

"What fire?" I heard as I turned around, and Ellery was standing in the middle of the kitchen.

"What are you doing out of bed?" I asked.

"Don't worry about why I'm here; answer my question, Connor," she said as she poured herself a cup of coffee.

Denny looked at me and smiled. "Someone set the Chicago building on fire, and they burnt it to the ground," I answered her.

She sat down next me after she gave both Denny and I a kiss on the cheek. "Good morning to my two favorite men," she smiled. Damn that smile. It was too early for any of the kinky ideas that popped into my head at that moment. "Who would do that to you?" she asked with concern.

"I have no idea, Elle. That's what we're trying to find out, and I don't want you worrying about it." I wanted to quickly change the subject because I knew this would ultimately lead to an argument as I didn't tell her about it when it happened.

"I'm taking you ice skating tonight," I said. Denny looked at me and raised an eyebrow because he knew what I was doing.

"I don't know how to ice skate," Ellery said.

"Then I'll just have to teach you," I smiled. I got up from the table and kissed her on the lips. "Be a good girl today, and stay out of trouble; I'll see you later." I got out of there as quickly as I could before she could ask any more questions.

***

The snow was falling lightly as Ellery and I stepped onto the ice at the Rockefeller Center. "I'm scared, Connor. You better not let go of me," she nervously said.

"Don't worry, baby. I already told you that I'm never letting you go," I smiled as I kissed the tip of her nose. I faced her and held both her hands. Her ankles were wobbling all over the place as we moved slowly across the ice. It was a beautiful night, and a perfect scene. The trees all around the arena were lit up, casting a soft light down on the ice. People were skating and having a good time. I couldn't help but notice the couples that brought their children and were teaching them to skate. It gave me a warm feeling inside, and it got me thinking about my vasectomy reversal that I had done a couple of weeks ago. I want to have a child with Ellery someday, and I couldn't imagine not having a family with her. We've discussed that if the reversal didn't work, and if Ellery wasn't able to conceive, then we're going to adopt.

"Where'd you go, Mr. Black?" she smiled.

I led her over to the railing and wrapped by arms securely around her waist. "I was just thinking how nice it'll be when we bring our children here someday," I whispered. She kissed my cheek. "Then you'd better get moving and teach me how to skate; I don't want to look stupid in front of our kids." I laughed and let go of her. I skated a few feet away and held out my arms like a parent teaching their child to walk for the first time.

"You're crazy if you think I'm skating to you by myself," she said.

"Come on, Elle; you can do it. Just take small steps."

As I was waiting for her, and she stood there holding onto the rail, Peyton came out of nowhere and grabbed her. Ellery screamed as she lost her balance, and they both fell flat on their asses on the hard ice. Henry came up to me as we shook hands.

"Thanks for inviting us out tonight," he said.

"Thanks for joining us. I didn't tell Ellery that you two were coming; I wanted it to be a surprise."

I looked over at her and Peyton as they sat on the ice laughing. It was gratifying to see her so happy. "Have you decided what you're going to do if Ellery's treatments don't work?" Henry asked. "I've been in touch with a specialist over in Germany, and he said he'll see her if she isn't better, but he's heard great things about the clinical trial."

"I know that everything will work out, and she'll get better. Dr. Murphy is one of the best research doctors in the country," he said as he put his hand on my shoulder.

"Thanks Henry; I hope so because I don't know what I'd do if something ever happened to her."

"Don't think like that man. The universe works in mysterious ways, and look what it's done for the two of you already."

Peyton helped Ellery up and led her over to me. "Thank you for inviting Peyton and Henry to join us," Ellery said as she kissed me on my cold lips. I hugged her and turned her around so her back was against my chest. I told her to move slowly with me, one foot at a time. We skated on the ice together as I held her tight, making sure she didn't fall.

"I love you," I whispered in her ear.

"I love you too, Connor," she whispered back.

Peyton and Henry skated up to us as she gave me an evil grin. "Ellery can skate you know, and she's good at it," she laughed as she skated away.

We stopped as I turned her around, and she looked at me. "You can skate?" I asked.

She looked at me and cocked her head. "Maybe I can a little," she said. I sighed as I stared into her eyes. "So, all this time you pretended that you didn't know how to skate? Why?"

"Because I liked the idea of you holding me and protecting me," she innocently answered.

"Ellery Lane!" I exclaimed as I let go of her, and she smiled at me.

She started skating backwards holding out her hands as I stood there. "Come on, big boy; come and get me," she smiled as she took off around the rink. I skated after her as Peyton and Henry stood to the side and laughed. She was fast. I couldn't believe she tricked me, but that made her more irresistible. I caught up with her and grabbed her from behind. I pushed her up against the side of the railing and kissed her passionately. We were both out of breath as our tongues tangled, and our cold lips started to warm. "You're a very bad girl, Ellery, and I think you need to be punished," I smiled.

"You're going to punish me here, right in front of all these people?" she asked with a grin.

"No, I'll save your punishment for later when we're in bed."

She looked at me and pouted. "I'm sorry, babe, but you'll have to put my punishment on hold because you can't have sex yet."

I ran my finger across her lips, "Oh, sweetheart, what I have planned for you won't involve me having sex with you." Her eyes widened as she looked directly at me. Henry and Peyton skated over to us. "Break it up you two love birds, and let's get some dinner; I'm starving," Peyton said.

We got off the ice and headed to Pizzapopolous. It wasn't my first choice of fine dining, but Ellery and Peyton wanted pizza. It was a good night spent with friends, and even better when we got home where Ellery received her punishment.

***

I spent the next few days coming home from the office and finding Ellery sitting in front of her easel. Sometimes she wouldn't even hear me come in, and I'd stand a few feet away and watch her. When you look at her, you can tell she's in a different world while she paints. Our evenings are spent having dinner, talking about our day, laughing, and drinking. We would sit on the couch by the fire, cuddle, and watch movies. This is what my life has become, and I wouldn't have it any other way. Ellery's last treatment is in two days, and we're leaving for California tomorrow. I took her upstairs and made love to her for the first time since my vasectomy. The feeling was incredible as I moved in and out of her, knowing that every time we made love, there was the possibility of her conceiving a child. The doctor told us it could take a year or longer, if at all. I hovered over her; our hearts racing, and both of us breathless. I stared into her eyes, looking beyond

284

them into her soul.

"You complete me, Ellery. You've given me a life of happiness that I never knew existed, and I'll spend the rest of my life thanking you."

A tear fell from her eye and stopped at her cheek. I pressed my lips against it and held them there for a few seconds. She softly closed her eyes as I lowered myself on her and buried my face in her neck. She tightened her arms around me and whispered, "I love you so much, and I'll never leave you; I promise you that."

***

As we approached Dr. Murphy's office, Ellery put her hand on the doorknob and stopped. She stood there, looking down at it as if she was frozen. I put my hand on top of hers. "Baby, come on; we have to go in," I whispered.

"I know; just give me a minute, please," she said.

I removed my hand from hers and gave her the minute she needed. She took in a deep breath, turned the knob, and opened the door. We walked in and were greeted by the receptionist. She led us to the usual room and handed Ellery her gown. I sat with her on the edge of the bed and held her hand as she laid her head on my shoulder. We waited for Dr. Murphy for what seemed like hours. "Well, this is it Ellery. Are you ready?" Dr. Murphy asked as she finally walked through the door. Ellery put on a fake smile and nodded her head. I took hold of both her hands and planted them firmly against my shirt. She took in a deep breath as her hands clutched the fabric with each burning injection.

"One month from today, you'll be back here for blood work," Dr. Murphy instructed as she injected the last needle.

I nodded my head as I pulled Ellery into an embrace and

whispered in her ear, "Now we wait."

I wanted to take her back to the apartment to rest, but she insisted that I take her to the beach. I tried to reason with her, but she wouldn't listen. I'm sure she had her reasons for wanting to go at that particular time, so I took her to the beach like she asked. She walked towards the shoreline and stood in the sand, staring straight ahead at the water. I stood next to her and stared out into the water with her.

"Tell me what you're feeling, Elle," I said to her.

"I'm feeling scared, anxious, and most of all unsure. I hate this, Connor. I knew this day would eventually come. I don't know what's worse, the treatments or the waiting," she said as she continued staring straight ahead.

I put my arm around her. "You have me to take away all your fears. I know waiting is the hardest part, but the results will come back normal. You were made for me, and I will never let anything or anyone take you away. It will always be forever you."

She turned to me and buried her head in my chest. She sobbed as we slowly fell into the sand, and I held her until she wore herself out. I hated seeing her like this, and I'd do anything to take away her pain, but the only thing I could do right now was make her feel safe.

***

We spent the next month trying to live as normal as possible in New York. Ellery had her moments of doubt and broke down in my arms at the mere mention of our future together. Peyton tried to get her mind off the waiting by talking to her about planning the wedding. I wanted to set a date, but she said that she wouldn't even think about it until after the results come back. I tried to tell her that it didn't matter and that I was marrying her regardless of what the results showed. But, as usual, Ellery's stubborn, and when she has her mind set on one thing, there's no changing it. She spent a lot of her time painting and escaping into a world where, as she put it, she was healthy.

I decided to begin working on Ellery's wedding present. I want to give her the future she wants, and her painting, the Cape Cod house, is how she saw her future. The property was perfect. It was right on the beach just like in her painting. I hired rotating crews so the house and the property will be worked on 24 hours a day, 7 days a week. Ellery listened to me and decided to keep the painting rather than selling it. I told her that I would put it in storage for safekeeping until we found a place for it. I showed it to the builder and told him to replicate the painting exactly as is. The house and property have to be perfect for her as it represents our beginning and our forever.

Chapter 27

Dr. Murphy sent over a script to Dr. Taub so Ellery didn't have to wait to get her blood work done. She had lengthy conversations with Dr. Taub during Ellery's treatment period to ensure he was fully aware of everything going on. He told us that she should have the results in about three days. We flew to California the day before her results were supposed to come back. Ellery wanted to spend time with Mason and Landon. She seemed to be doing fine until I woke up at 3:00 am, and she was gone.

I rolled over and opened my eyes; her side of the bed was empty. I got up and searched the apartment for her. Where the hell is she? I thought as I ran my hand through my hair. I picked up my phone and dialed her number, but it went straight to voicemail. I sighed as I put on a pair of jeans and a shirt. I grabbed my shoes and got in the Porsche. I sat there with my hands on the steering wheel, trying to figure out where she'd go. It's 3:00 am, and she's out in Los Angeles all alone. I was pissed now, because once again, she had no regard for her safety. Then it hit me; I drove to the beach, got out of the car, and started heading towards the water. I could see a shadow of someone sitting on the sand.

"Ellery," I called out. She turned and looked at me, then back at the water. She was sitting and hugging her legs against her chest.

"I was worried when I woke up, and you were gone. Actually, Ellery, I was scared," I said as I sat down next to her.

"I'm sorry, I didn't mean to worry or scare you. I couldn't sleep, and I needed to come here."

"Why didn't you wake me up? I would've come with you. Did you walk here?" I asked in a commanding voice.

"No, I called a cab, and I didn't want to wake you. I just felt like I needed to be here, alone."

"Do you want me to leave then?" I asked her in an irritated voice.

She grabbed my hand, "No, I want you to stay with me. I don't want you to leave. I want you to watch the sunrise with me because it'll be the start of a new day, and I'm scared to death of what this day's going to bring."

I closed my eyes for a moment as I wrapped my arms around her and pulled her into me, holding her head against my chest. "You have nothing to fear, Ellery, because I'll take care of you regardless of what the results show. I'm your lifeline, and I promise to give you a healthy life and future no matter the cost or sacrifice." She lifted her head up and kissed me softly on the lips. She wasn't the only one who was scared.

We sat and held each other while we watched the sun rise over the ocean water. It's amazing to share this experience with her, and it's one that I'll never forget. She looked up at me and smiled.

"Let's go home and make love before we see Dr. Murphy," she requested.

I picked her up and carried her across the sand. "It would be my pleasure to make love to you," I smiled.

***

I grabbed Ellery's hand as we walked through the parking lot of the hospital. She was trying to put on a brave front, but I could see right through it. Denny had sent me a text, asking me to call him as soon as we receive the results. We were escorted into Dr. Murphy's office and told to have a seat. Ellery kept bouncing her leg up and down. I put my hand on her knee to try and calm her down. Dr. Murphy walked through the door and looked at us.

"How are you feeling today, Ellery?" she asked her. What the hell kind of question is that?! I wanted to say. How does she think she's feeling?

Ellery said that she was very nervous as Dr. Murphy sat down at her desk and opened Ellery's file. She looked at her and then at me.

"I am happy to report that the treatments worked, and you are in a full remission, Ellery Lane," she smiled.

My heart started racing; I couldn't believe what I just heard. Ellery's better; she's healthy and in remission. Ellery put her hand over her mouth and began to cry.

"Are you sure, Dr. Murphy?"

"Ellery, I'm positive. You have a full and long life ahead of you," she grinned.

Ellery looked at me as we both stood up and hugged each other. "Thank you, Dr. Murphy, for everything," I said.

"Yes, thank you so much," Ellery followed as she walked over and hugged the doctor.

"You two go be happy, and enjoy your lives together," she said as she walked out of her office.

We left the hospital and went back to the apartment. The first thing Ellery did was tell Landon and Mason the good news. They wanted to go out and celebrate. I took out my phone and called Denny. Tears started to fill my eyes as I spoke to him.

"She's fine, Denny. The cancer is gone, and she's in full

remission."

"Connor, I'm so happy to hear the wonderful news. I'll let Claire know. Give Ellery a hug and kiss from me, and tell her that I can't wait to see her again."

"Thanks, Denny, I will."

I walked over and hugged her. "Denny told me to give you a hug and kiss from him," I said as I kissed the top of her head. She smiled as I held her and wouldn't let her go. I couldn't let go of her even if I tried. I was so happy and thankful that she's better, and now, we can move forward with our lives together.

"Connor, you're squeezing me just a little too tight," she said.

"I'm sorry, baby, but I can't help it. I'm never letting you go, so get used to it." I loosened my grip on her and stared into her happy, sparkling eyes. I unbuttoned her pants and slid them off her hips. She smiled at me as she stepped out of them. I lifted her shirt off and threw it on the floor. I picked her up as she wrapped her legs around me, and I set her on the kitchen counter.

"I believe this is one spot where we haven't had sex yet," I smiled.

"I don't think we have, Mr. Black," she replied with a grin.

She unbuttoned my white cotton shirt and slid it off my shoulders. I kissed her on the lips before moving towards her neck. She still had her legs wrapped around me as I unhooked her bra and took it off her. My lips glided around her neck and down to her breasts. She let out a moan as I took her hardened nipple in my mouth. She reached down and unbuttoned my pants, taking my erection in her hand. She had me so hot for her. My fingers trickled down to her panties as I grabbed the string on the side and tore

292

them from her. "I promise I'll buy you a new pair," I moaned as I sucked her breasts and my fingers slid inside her. I slid my fingers in and out of her as I stimulated her clit with my thumb, rubbing it in round circles as her moans grew louder, and her breathing became more rapid. She was incredibly wet, and I needed more of her. I let my fingers slip out of her as I took off my pants and boxers. I grabbed her legs and put them up on the counter so her feet were flat against it. I grabbed her and pulled her forward so her ass was hanging from the edge. I inserted myself in her as she wrapped her arms around my neck, and I brought my lips to hers. I moved in and out of her at a rapid pace until I brought her to the brink of an orgasm. She was ready; her nails clawed down my back and into my ass as I gave one more thrust, and we both came at the same time. I let out a loud groan as I gave a final thrust into her and finished off. I put my hands on the sides of her face as I stared into her beautiful, dancing eyes.

"I love you so much, and I'm so happy everything turned out right today. I was so scared for you, Ellery," I said as my eyes swelled with tears.

She tilted her head and wiped away the tears that were falling down my face. "I know, babe, and I'm so sorry I put you through that. But we have our whole life in front of us, and we need to set a wedding date. I can't wait to marry you and become Mrs. Ellery Black," she smiled. I picked her up from the counter and held her firmly by her ass as I kissed her and carried her to the bedroom for round two.

***

We said goodbye to Mason and Landon as they drove us to the airport. All three of them cried as we said our goodbyes. I looked at Mason and Landon seriously.

"When the two of you come to New York, which I know will be frequently to see Ellery; you are to call me first to let me know because I'll send the company plane to get you. I don't want you flying commercial."

Ellery smiled at me as both Landon and Mason agreed. They were such good friends to Ellery when she first came to California, and I know she considers them family. I do as well; they're a couple of great guys, and I owe them a lot. We boarded the plane, and Ellery took her usual seat by the window. I sat down next to her as she took my hand and kissed it.

"June 15th," she smiled.

I looked at her in confusion. "June 15th? What's on June 15th?" I asked.

"That's our wedding day," she said as she kissed me.

I smiled and took her face in my hands. "June 15th is a perfect day to marry you." I leaned over and kissed her. I was happy she finally chose a date. I better get in touch with the builder and the contractors to make sure the house is done before then.

We landed in New York at 7:00 pm. There was a surprise waiting for Ellery at the penthouse when we arrive. She doesn't know it, but I've arranged to have a small party for her to celebrate the good news. I had Claire, Peyton, Cassidy, and my mom put it together. Knowing all of them, I imagine the party will be overdone. Denny picked us up from the airport, and Ellery ran straight to him. We slid in the back of the limo and headed to the penthouse. When the elevator doors opened, the penthouse was dark. Suddenly, the lights turned on and everyone yelled surprise. Ellery's eye widened, and she looked at me. I kissed her cheek and let her tend to her guests. I walked around the penthouse, and just as I thought, it was overdone, but it was nice; every time I glanced over at Ellery, she was smiling. Damn that smile. I grabbed a glass of Champagne as my mom walked over to me.

"Connor, darling, I'm so happy for you and Ellery. I could only imagine what you must be feeling right now," she said as she hugged me.

"I'm feeling extremely happy, mom. I can't even explain it to you."

"Do the two of you have any other news that you may want to share with me?" she smiled.

Ellery came walking over to us and put her arm around me. "Don't you think now would be the perfect opportunity to tell everybody that we've set the wedding date?" I whispered to her.

"Yes, it's the perfect time, so let's do it," she excitedly replied.

I took Ellery's hand and led her to the center of the room. I called for everyone's attention as they gathered around us. I put my arm around her waist and smiled at her. She told me to go ahead and announce the date. I held up my glass of champagne.

"I want to thank all of you for coming tonight and celebrating Ellery's great news. Now, we have even more news to share. I would like everyone to plan on attending our wedding and celebrating with us on June 15th!" The crowd stirred in excitement, and glasses were raised. Congratulations were said, and happiness was heard all around the room.

A couple of hours later, everyone said their goodbyes, and suddenly, the penthouse was quiet. Ellery walked over to the couch and collapsed on it. I sat down next to her and pulled her feet on my lap. I started massaging them as she smiled at me.

"Thank you for tonight," she said.

"You're welcome. You deserve a party with family and friends for everything you've been through these last few months. It's only the beginning of the many things I'm going to do for you, Ellery."

"You've already done enough, and I can't thank you enough."

"I know one way you can thank me if you're up to it," I grinned.

Ellery got up from the couch, grabbed me by my shirt, and led me to the bedroom. She thanked me for the next hour and a half before we fell fast asleep, wrapped in each other's arms.

Chapter 28

The next morning as I was sitting at my desk, I called the contractor to inquire about the house. "I fucking told you that the house better be done in three days!" I screamed into the phone. "You've had three months to get that house finished, and I paid you a lot of fucking money to see that it happened. Now you better get off your ass and get it done, because if it's not finished when I come there in three days to inspect, I will sue you and shut you down for good!" I threw my phone across the desk just as Phil walked in.

"We need to talk, Connor," he said as he sat down.

"Not now, Phil; it's not a good time."

"Well, you're going to want to hear this. It's about the fire in Chicago," he spoke seriously.

I got up from my desk and looked at him. "What? What the hell do you have to tell me?"

"They found the person responsible for the fire, and it's someone you know," he spoke.

"Someone I know? Who the hell would do that to me?" I started to get nervous.

"It was Ashlyn. She was the one who hired the guy to set the fire."

I walked to the other side of my desk and paced the floor. "Are you absolutely positive about Ashlyn?"

"Yes, Connor; the police have her under arrest. The guy finally broke down and confessed everything after the police arrested him again on some other charges."

"Alright, then it's done. I'm getting married in a week, and I don't need this. You are to handle everything. I don't want to hear another word about it until after I get back from my honeymoon."

"Aren't you going to confront her about it?" Phil asked.

"No, what's done is done. I'm sure I know the reason anyway. Now if you'll excuse me, I have a beautiful fiancée who's waiting at home for me," I said as I grabbed my briefcase and left the office.

On the way home, I thought about whether or not to tell Ellery about Ashlyn. I didn't want to upset her, but we aren't keeping secrets from each other, and if she found out that I didn't tell her, there would be hell to pay. I stepped off the elevator and into the hallway and was caught off guard by a tantalizing smell, coming from the kitchen. I set my briefcase down and walked to the kitchen to find Ellery cooking dinner.

"Are you cooking, Miss Lane?" I asked as I put my hands on her hips and kissed her.

"Yes, and you're going to eat it, whether you like it or not," she smiled.

"I'll eat anything from you," I winked. She hit me on the arm and turned to the oven. I grabbed a couple of glasses, filled them with wine, and set them on the table. Ellery took a chicken pot pie out of the oven and set it in the middle of the table.

"My mom used to make this for my dad and me. It was his favorite. I've kept the recipe with me all these years. I started making it for him when I was only nine years old," she said as she sat down across from me.

"You cooked dinner for your father at the age of nine?" I asked.

"It was either that, or he didn't eat. I always knew that would be the one dish he would eat."

I looked at her and shook my head. I couldn't believe that drunken bastard would let his child cook and use the oven at the age of nine. I needed to tell her about Ashlyn, and I guess now's as good as time as any. I decided to wait until after dinner because she started talking about the wedding. After we ate and cleaned up, I asked her to sit with me in the living room.

"I get the feeling that you have something that you need to tell me," she said.

I took in a deep breath as she laid her head down on my lap and looked up at me. "Ashlyn was the person responsible for setting the fire in Chicago."

She quickly sat up. "What? That bitch!" she exclaimed.

I took her and laid her head back down on my lap. "Listen to me, Ellery; I don't want you to worry about this. I told you because we aren't keeping keep secrets from each other. Phil is handling this for me, and I have no intentions of confronting her about this," I told her as I stroked her hair. "In fact, you are not to see her either because I know you, and you have quite a temper."

"Fine, if you don't want me to, then I'll respect your wishes, but I still think you're wrong."

I bent down and kissed her. "Thank you, baby, I love you."

"I love you too even though you're wrong," she smiled as she tapped me on the nose.

I walked through the newly built house. Ellery's painting hung perfectly above the fireplace and was the focal point of the room. "How does it look, big brother?" Cassidy asked.

"It looks great, and I think Ellery's going to like it," I replied.

"Are you kidding? She'll love it, Connor, every bit of it. It's the best wedding present anyone could ever give, and I hope to find someone like you someday."

I hugged her. "Someone's out there waiting for you; he just hasn't found you yet."

"Since when did you become so poetic?" she asked with a smile.

"I guess that's what being in love does to a man," I replied. We left the house and I headed back to the city to meet Denny for dinner. In two days, I will be presenting the house to Ellery, on our wedding night. I was nervous she wasn't going to like it, but she can make whatever changes she wants.

Denny and I left the restaurant and went to a local bar to meet some guys for a few drinks. I missed Ellery because we decided not to see each other for a couple days until our wedding day. I was having a good time, talking and laughing with the guys when my phone rang; it was Ellery.

"Hey, baby, is everything ok?" I asked.

"Everything's fine; are you having fun?"

I could barely hear her because wherever she was, the background noise was really loud.

"Babe, I can barely hear you. You're going to have to talk a lot louder."

"Is this better?" she said as she whispered in my ear.

I turned around, and with a smile, I wrapped my arms around her and hugged her tight. "What are you doing here?" I asked.

"I missed you, Connor."

"I missed you too, baby, more than you'll ever know." I looked around, and the girls Ellery went out with were gathered around the table. The guys pulled up chairs for them as I pulled Ellery on my lap. I buried my nose in her neck, taking in her scent of lilac and closed my eyes. She laughed as I nibbled on her ear.

"You smell so good; it's killing me," I moaned.

"Behave yourself, Connor; we agreed not to have sex until our wedding night."

"I know," I sighed. "It's just that I've missed you, and there's a bathroom right over there," I motioned with my head.

"No way," she said as she pushed me back. "Just think of how special it will be on our wedding night. It will be like our first time," she smiled. Damn that smile.

When it was time to leave, we all left the bar together, and I walked Ellery to the cab. I wrapped my arms around her. "Are you sure you don't want to come home with me? I miss you in our bed. You can leave in the morning and then we won't see each other again until our wedding day."

She took my face in her hands. "As much as I want to, babe, I can't. Besides, I have way too much to do tomorrow, and if I wake up with you by my side, things will happen, and I'll never get out of bed, then I'll be behind, then I'll stress out, then I'll…"

I put my finger over her lips. "Ok, I get it, Ellery, please stop." I leaned forward and kissed her on the lips. I put her in the cab, closed the door, and waved as the cab took off down the street. Denny patted me on the back. "The next time you see her, I'll be walking her down the aisle on her way to becoming Mrs. Connor Black," he smiled. "Now, let me drive you home."

When I got home, I poured myself a glass of scotch and climbed into bed. I picked up my phone and stared at the picture of me and Ellery that was proudly displayed on my screen. I already missed her, so I decided to FaceTime her. I smiled as she answered on the second ring, and her face came across my screen.

"Hello, my love," she smiled.

"Hi, baby, I just wanted to say good night."

"Do you have a glass of scotch with you?" she asked.

I held up my glass so she could see it. "I sure do. Do you have your glass of wine?"

She held up her glass of red wine and smiled. "I sure do."

"You need to go to sleep, babe, and get your beauty rest," I said gently to her.

"I was going to sleep, but some hot, sexy man called me and wanted to FaceTime; I couldn't resist."

"I just wanted to see you one last time before our wedding day. Now, put your lips up to the screen so I can kiss you good night." We puckered up and brought our lips together on the screen of our phones. "Goodnight, baby, and sweet dreams," I whispered.

"Good night, my love," she softly spoke. I ended the call, set my phone on the night stand, and slept until the alarm went off for work.

Chapter 29

The day that I've been waiting for had finally arrived. I looked in the mirror as I straightened my bow tie. I couldn't believe that in just a few short hours, I'll no longer be a bachelor. I'll be a happily married man to the most beautiful woman. If you would've asked me a year ago if I thought this day would ever come, I would've said hell no! It's amazing how much your life can change in just a little under a year when the most perfect woman in the world walks into your life.

"Connor, it's time to go," Denny said as he walked in the room. "You don't want to keep your bride waiting; do you?"

I took in a deep breath as I climbed in the back of the limo. Our wedding was taking place in the Conservatory Garden in Central Park. It's something that Ellery has always dreamed of, and she was right; it was a beautiful place to get married, just as it was in her painting.

It was a perfect day as the sun was shining brightly. When we arrived at the Conservatory Garden, people were already gathering and being seated as we walked through the Vanderbilt Gates. The rows of white chairs, decorated with bows made of tulle, were perfectly positioned. Beautiful flowers graced the aisle where a white runway was laid, leading down to an archway made of white magnolias that sat in front of a large fountain. Henry was to be my groomsman. Not only was Denny my best man, he was also walking Ellery down the aisle. I remember the day she asked him, and a tear formed in his eye as he said he'd be honored to give her away to me. I walked around and said hello to family and friends.

"Connor," my mom said as she walked over to me, "You look

so handsome. I thought I'd never see this day," she smiled.

"I didn't think that I would either, mom," I said.

My parents took their seats in the front row as Henry and I headed down the aisle to take our place in front of the archway. Denny stepped outside the gates to meet Ellery as her limo pulled up. Dr. Peters nodded and smiled as he and his wife sat down. I stood there next to Henry as a nervous wreck.

"You're not nervous; are you?" Henry asked.

"I'm nervous as hell," I replied.

He put his hand on my shoulder. "Don't be nervous. Ellery's the woman of your dreams, and you're finally making her your wife. You're one lucky man, Connor."

I nervously smiled at him. "Just wait until you're standing in my place, waiting for Peyton to walk down the aisle."

"Good point," he said as he cocked his head to the side.

The orchestra began playing as Peyton, Ellery's maid of honor, slowly walked down the aisle. I looked at Henry as a wide grin spread across his face. She looked beautiful. Following behind her was Cassidy. She looked just as beautiful as she gracefully walked towards us with a smile on her face. I took in a deep breath as the wedding march started. My heart started racing when I saw Ellery holding the arm of my best friend. She looked exquisite in her wedding gown. Her hair was up in curls that were accented by her classic long veil. Her delicate hands carried a bouquet of pink roses and small white magnolias. As she slowly walked down the aisle, she never took her eyes off mine, and her smile captivated me. She was radiant, and the most beautiful woman in the world.

She reached the archway as I stepped forward and Denny delicately placed her hand in mine. I smiled at her and saw some tears beginning to form. I lightly shook my head. She started to laugh as we stood there, holding hands, and we turned to the minister so he could begin the ceremony. He had us face each other to say our wedding vows. I took in a deep breath and stared into her beautiful blue eyes as I held her hands in mine.

"Ellery, I didn't write anything down because I didn't have to. Every word I say to you is straight from my heart and soul. I want to start off by saying that you are the most beautiful woman I've ever seen, and you look absolutely stunning. I feel like I'm the luckiest man alive to have you in my life, and not just as your best friend, but as your husband. You stole my heart from the moment you turned around and looked at me. The moment I saw your smile, I knew I was done for, and everything I thought I had believed in disappeared. You showed me love, and taught me that it was ok to love someone. We grew together as friends and then as lovers. Now, we will grow together as husband and wife. I promise to love you forever, and to never break your heart. I promise to keep you safe at all times. I promise you a world of happiness and joy, and I promise to take away your pain and sadness. You are my forever, Ellery Rose, and I love you more than words can express. You've been etched into my heart, and my heart is yours till death do us part. I will never love anyone as much as I love you."

Henry pulled the ring from his pocket and handed it to me. All I could hear were the sniffles of the guests as I slipped the delicate ring on her finger.

"Take this ring as a symbol of my eternal love for you and for the start of our new life together. I love you, Ellery." Tears fell down her face. I gently took my thumb and wiped them away as she said her vows.

"Connor, you are the most amazing man that I've ever met. You stood by me, you fought for me, and you gave me the strength to fight through one of the toughest times of my life. You never gave up on me when you should have walked away. You believed in me and our relationship and I will never forget that. You are a kind-hearted, self-less man, and I'm the luckiest woman in the world to have found you. They say everyone is born with a purpose in this world. My purpose was to find you and to love you." She let go of my hands and turned up her wrists. "The scars are gone because of you, and they've been replaced with love. You've put life back into my soul, and you've completed me. I will forever cherish this moment, and I will spend eternity thanking you and loving you."

Peyton handed her the ring. She took my finger and slowly slipped it on. "Take this ring as a symbol of my love and devotion to you as we start our new life together as one."

The minister smiled at us and he pronounced us husband and wife. I cupped her face in my hands as we shared our first kiss as husband and wife. The crowd stood up and clapped. We heard cheering as we turned and looked at the people who graciously attended our ceremony. I took her hand, and we walked down the aisle as Mr. and Mrs. Black, stopping in front of the Vanderbilt gates.

"Hi, Mrs. Black," I smiled as I softly kissed her lips.

"Hi, Mr. Black," she smiled back.

Our moment alone didn't last long as our guests soon followed. Waiters walked around with glasses of champagne for everyone. After the photographer took pictures of us in the different gardens, it was time to head to the reception. I took

Ellery's hand as we walked through the Vanderbilt gates where our horse and carriage were waiting. I helped Ellery up into the carriage and took my place beside her. We were taking a ride through Central Park for some alone time before heading to the reception.

"Do you have any idea how beautiful you are?" I asked her as I stroked her cheek with my thumb.

"I do, because you tell me every day," she smiled.

"And I will keep telling you every day because I love you, Mrs. Black. You are the most important thing in my life, and that will never change." I leaned closer and kissed her softly.

***

The reception took place in the Grand Ballroom at the Waldorf Astoria Hotel. It was elegant as 700 people joined in the celebration in honor of our wedding day. We ate the finest food and drank the most expensive alcohol. No expense was spared when it came to Ellery. We greeted our guests and walked around the ballroom, engaging in conversation as people congratulated us with hugs and kisses. The band announced that it was time for our first dance. I only asked for one thing while planning this wedding and that was to pick our song. Ellery had agreed but threatened me that it better be perfect. I told her to trust me because I already had the perfect song in mind.

I took her hand and led her to the dance floor as the song started. From the moment she heard the first line, tears formed in her eyes. "You'll ruin your mascara if you start crying now," I smiled.

"You never cease to amaze me, Connor Black, and that's why I love you so much. This song is perfect, and I couldn't have picked anything better," she said as one tear fell. I wiped away her tear and kissed her cheek.

I wanted to get Ellery out of there and to her wedding present. We said goodbye to our family and friends as we climbed in the back of the limo, and I took out a blindfold from my pocket. Ellery looked at me and tilted her head.

"Planning a little kinky time in the limo before we go back to the hotel?" She smiled.

Ellery thought we were spending the night at the Waldorf. She didn't know what I had planned for us. She didn't even know about the limo until I told her we had to leave.

"I'm taking you somewhere special, and it's a surprise, so you need to wear this blindfold," I said as I put it over her eyes.

"Aren't we spending the night at the hotel?"

"No, Ellery, I have somewhere else in mind," I said as my hand started traveling up her dress.

"You are a very mysterious man, Mr. Black," she moaned.

We finally arrived at the house, and I couldn't wait any longer for her to see it. I was reeling with excitement. "Are you ready, darling?" I asked as I took her hand.

"Yes; I was ready forever ago," she smiled.

I helped her out of the limo. I removed the blindfold, and watched her gasp at what stood before her. "Connor, what is this?" she asked. I took her hand and led her to the porch.

"This house is your wedding present. Do you like it?" I asked her as she stood there in shock.

"Like it? I love it, but I don't understand."

I smiled and gently kissed her lips. "This is our second home. We'll spend our weekends and summers here."

I picked her up and carried through the door. I put her down as I led her to the back of the house. Tears started to roll down her face as she stepped out onto the deck and took in the beauty before her. "This is what I painted," she softly spoke. I stood behind her and let her take it all in. She turned to me as I wiped away her tears.

"You don't have to say a word, Ellery, I know how much you love it; I can tell by the look on your face. This was built for you because I love you. I want to give you every dream you've ever dreamed, every happy moment you never had, every bit of love you've ever lost, and most importantly, a family. This home, our home, is my future with you, and we're going to spend the rest of our lives making beautiful memories here."

She gulped as she cupped my face in her hands and stared deeply into my eyes. "I could never understand my purpose in this world. I've had nothing but pain and loss my whole life. But now I know why God saved me the first time. It was so I could find you. Then he saved me the second time so I could love you forever. This house is perfect; you're perfect, and no one will ever take that away from us. Our love is infinite, and I'm going to spend the rest of my life showing you."

She pressed her lips against mine, and we fell into a deep, passionate kiss. I picked her up and carried her in the house. "Let's get you out of this dress, Mrs. Black," I smiled.

Our wedding night was perfect. We spent many hours breaking in our new bed. Ellery was right; the wait was worth it.

"Good morning, Mrs. Black," I smiled as she laid herself in my arms.

"Good morning, Mr. Black," she snuggled closer to me.

"We need to get up and get ready to leave for Paris," I said as I looked at the clock.

Ellery kissed me, and we got out of bed. Our shower took a little longer than expected, but it was our first morning as husband and wife, so we felt the need to celebrate. We ate the breakfast that I'd arranged and then took the limo to the airport. I hired another driver to take us because I sent Denny and his wife to Hawaii to celebrate their anniversary while Ellery and I were in Paris. We spent two weeks honeymooning in Paris. We saw all the sights, had sex in a lot of different places, and shopped until we both collapsed from exhaustion. Before we knew it, two weeks had flown by, and it was time to fly back home.

Chapter 30

ELLERY

Connor and I spent the past two months living our lives as a happily married couple. I couldn't believe how quickly the time had passed since the day I said I do. He went to the office every day while I spent my time helping with various charities and painting. My work was becoming known, and people were beginning to want more of my paintings. I was living the perfect life with the perfect man, and I didn't want anything more.

Connor stepped out of the shower and into the bedroom as I sat in bed from not feeling well. "I thought you would've joined me in the shower," he said.

"I'm not feeling well, Connor."

I saw the fear sweep across his face. "What's wrong?" He asked as he sat on the bed and stroked my face.

I quickly jumped up and flew into the bathroom to vomit. Connor followed in behind me and held my hair until I was finished.

"Looks like someone has the flu," he said. "Get back into bed, and I'll have Claire bring you up some tea."

I climbed into bed as Connor pulled the covers over me. He finished getting dressed and kissed me goodbye. I was starting to feel better as Claire came up to check on me. I told her I was fine as I got up and took a shower. I had too much to do today, and being sick wasn't an option. I received a text from Connor.

"How are you feeling, baby?"

"I'm fine. I think it was something I ate."

"Maybe it was. Get some rest just in case it wasn't. I have a meeting to go to. I love you, babe."

"I love you too, and stop worrying."

I spent that whole week not feeling well and exhausted. I was beginning to get really scared, but I didn't let Connor know. He had enough on his plate, dealing with the trial for the Chicago fire and the new building he bought in Los Angeles. I was lying on the couch when Peyton came over. She walked in and hovered over me.

"What's wrong? Why are you laying there like that in the middle of the day?" she demanded to know.

I sighed as I sat up. "I haven't been feeling well the past week."

"Elle, what do you mean? Have you seen a doctor yet?" she asked with concern.

"No, I thought it was the flu at first, but I'm so tired. I'm scared, Peyton; what if my cancer is back?"

"Don't say that, and don't think that way. What does Connor have to say about this?"

"He really doesn't know. He knew I wasn't feeling well a few days ago, but I've told him I'm fine and that I had a virus. I don't want to worry him. This is the last thing he needs on his mind right now."

"I want you to call your doctor, right now," she demanded.

"I will next week if I don't feel better," I said.

"Have you not learned from your past mistakes, Ellery

Black?" she scolded me.

She pulled out her phone and started dialing. "Who are you calling?" I asked.

"I'm calling Connor and telling him to get your sorry ass to the doctor."

I grabbed the phone out of her hand and hit end. "Peyton, stop it; I'll call Dr. Taub."

Her phone rang in my hand and Connor's name appeared. "Great, now he's calling you back," I said as I handed her the phone.

"Hey, Connor! Sorry I must have butt-dialed you. So, do you want to tell me how it felt being on my ass?" she laughed.

I shook my head and rolled my eyes. I picked up my phone, called Dr. Taub, and spoke with him directly. He told me to go to the hospital for some blood work and wait. I told Peyton we'd have to take a cab because I didn't want Denny knowing where I was going. I couldn't risk him telling Connor. We hailed a cab and headed to the hospital. Connor called as we were in the cab.

"Hello, my love," I answered.

"Hey, babe, are you having a good day?"

"I'm having a fantastic day; how about you?"

"My day is going well, but it'll be even better after I take you to lunch."

I started to get nervous as I looked at Peyton and mouthed "shit."

"Baby, as much as I want to have lunch with you, I can't."

"Why not?"

"I'm with Peyton, and we're going shopping. She came over, and she's feeling a little down, so I told her shopping will lift her spirits."

"Why is she down? Is everything ok with her and Henry?" he asked.

"Oh yeah, it's just her time of the month; you know how that goes."

"Enough said, Ellery. Have fun, and I'll see you tonight. I love you."

"I love you too, Connor, bye."

Peyton looked at me and started laughing. "You're good," she said.

We arrived at the hospital, and I headed to the lab to have my blood drawn. The nurse told me that Dr. Taub gave strict instructions to have me come upstairs to his office and wait for the results. After my blood was drawn, we stopped at the Starbucks inside the hospital and grabbed some coffee before heading up to his office. I was a nervous wreck. I felt bad for lying to Connor, but I had no choice. There was no need to worry him until I got some answers. We patiently waited in Dr. Taub's waiting room until the nurse called us into his office. Peyton grabbed my hand as we sat in the two seats across from his desk. "Everything will be fine, Elle," she said.

Dr. Taub walked in his office and sat in his chair. He looked at me and then opened his file. He looked at me again.

"I got your blood work back and everything came back

normal."

I sighed with relief. "Thank god. Then why have I been so tired lately?" I asked.

Dr. Taub looked at me and smiled. "You're pregnant, Ellery."

"Shut the fuck up!" Peyton blurted out.

My mouth dropped open as I sat there in shock. "Are you sure, Dr. Taub?"

"Yes, I'm sure. According to these numbers, you're about eight weeks along. You need to make an appointment as soon as possible with your OB/GYN and start preparing for a healthy pregnancy."

Peyton hugged me when we stepped outside the hospital. "I'm so happy for you and Connor. I know this is what you both wanted so badly."

"Connor's going to be ecstatic; I can't wait to see the look on his face when I tell him!"

I went back to the penthouse and laid down for a nap. I put my hands on my stomach and smiled. I couldn't believe there was a baby growing inside me. This was perfect timing. Connor's birthday is in a few days and telling him he's going to be a father will be the best present for him. I finally fell asleep when I felt warm lips traveling across my face. I opened my eyes as Connor was staring at me.

"Are you ok, baby? You're starting to worry me with all these naps you've been taking lately."

"I promise you that I'm perfectly fine, and there's no need to worry about me," I smiled. I pulled him on top of me and we made love before dinner. It was the best way to distract him from my naps.

***

It was Connor's birthday, and I couldn't wait to give him his gift and tell him the news. It was so hard to keep my pregnancy a secret from him. I woke him up the way any man would want to be woken up. He opened his eyes and smiled as he looked down at me.

"Happy Birthday, my love," I smiled as I took him in my mouth.

"You're a very naughty girl, but thank you," he moaned. I made sure that he was well taken care of, and that his day started off just right. I told him to stay put as I got up, walked to the dresser, and pulled a box from the drawer. I handed it to him and told him to open it. A grin graced his face as he took the watch he wanted out of the box.

"I love it, Ellery; thank you," he said as he kissed me.

"You better love it since it's the one you picked out," I said.

"Oh, is that so?" he laughed as he pinned me to the bed and started tickling me.

I laughed and squirmed as I tried to make him stop. He finally did stop but only after I told him I was going to pee in the bed. I looked at him as he laid there smiling at me.

"I have another present for you."

"Babe, the watch was enough," he said as he stroked my hair.

"I racked my brain, trying to figure out what to get the man who has everything in the world. Then suddenly, a gift, something you don't already have, fell right into my lap," I smiled.

"Oh, really? What is it?"

I brought the back of my hand to his face and stroked it up and down as I stared into his eyes. "I'm pregnant, Connor. You're going to be a daddy."

He looked at me as tears formed in his eyes. "Are you 100% sure, Elle?"

"Yes, Connor, I had the blood work done, and Dr. Taub confirmed it; Happy Birthday, daddy."

He jumped up and grabbed me. "I can't believe this. The doctor said it would take a year to conceive a child. How far along are you?"

"Dr. Taub said that I'm about eight weeks along. The way I calculated it, we got pregnant on our wedding night."

Connor hugged me tight. "That explains why you haven't been feeling well and taking so many naps. Thank you, baby; this is the best birthday that I've ever had," he whispered as he kissed me. "I can't believe I'm going to be a father." We made love for a couple of hours and then headed to the beach house for Connor's birthday party.

Chapter 31

CONNOR

It was the best birthday that I've ever had. We celebrated at the beach house with about 70 close friends and family members. I made the announcement about Ellery's pregnancy, and the whole room beamed with excitement. I still couldn't believe it myself, and every time I looked at her, she was glowing. Ellery had arranged it so the party was mainly outside between the patio and the beach. It was a beautiful summer evening. When the last of the guests left, Ellery turned and looked at me.

"I'm exhausted," she said as she fell into my arms.

"Thank you for the wonderful party," I said as I kissed her on top of her head.

"Have I told you lately that I love you?" she smiled as she looked up at me.

"You tell me every day over and over again," I smiled back as I picked her up. I held her as she wrapped her legs around me and grinned.

"I love you, and I will never let you go. We are forever, Mrs. Black, and nothing will ever change that." I kissed her as I carried her into the house and upstairs to bed.

***

Over the next couple of months, I watched Ellery's belly grow. She was just as beautiful pregnant. She was happy and had a glow about her that was felt every time she entered the room. I was lying in bed, checking my emails when she came from the bathroom and climbed in next to me. She looked at me and pouted. I cocked my head and raised my eyebrow.

"What's going on in that pretty little head of yours?" I asked, already knowing the answer.

"I'm craving some rocky road ice cream, and we don't have anymore," she pouted.

"Ellery, it's 11:00 pm. Do you really need it that badly?" I asked.

"I'm pregnant with your child, and our child wants rocky road ice cream. What do you want me to do, starve the baby to death?"

"So, what you're saying is, if I don't go and get you rocky road ice cream, our baby will starve?"

She nodded her head and pushed out her bottom lip. I nipped at it as she smiled. "I'll be right back," I said as I got out of bed and put on some clothes. I ran to the corner store and grabbed a gallon of rocky road ice cream. I arrived back at the penthouse, went to the kitchen to get a spoon, and walked to the bedroom only to find Ellery sound asleep. I stared at her and shook my head. I took the ice cream to the kitchen and put it in the freezer for tomorrow. I climbed into bed and snuggled against her back. I put my arm around her and softly stroked her belly.

***

The alarm went off, and I reached over and patted the empty side of the bed. I opened my eyes and looked around the room. I laid there for a minute and took in the aroma of something delicious baking. It smelled like banana bread. I got up, put on my pajama bottoms, and walked down to the kitchen. I stopped in the doorway as Ellery was bent over, pulling something from the oven.

"Is that banana bread I smell?" I asked with a smile.

322

"Yes, I made it just for you, babe. I got the recipe from Claire."

I walked over and cupped her face in my hands. "Thank you, sweetheart, and good morning," I whispered as I kissed her.

"Don't thank me yet until you taste it. I can't promise that it'll be any good."

I put my forehead against hers. "It'll be the best banana bread that I've ever tasted. Please don't tell Claire I said that."

I put my hands on Ellery's belly, knelt down, and kissed our baby. "Good morning to you too little one," I said. Ellery ran her fingers through my hair as I had my ear pressed against her belly. Suddenly, I felt something kick against me. "Did you feel that, Connor?!" Ellery asked with excitement.

"I sure did!" I smiled as I stood up. To be able to feel our baby moving inside Ellery was the most amazing feeling. I took her in my arms and embraced her. "I love you, Ellery Black."

"I love you more, and so does our baby," she whispered as she buried her head into my neck.

I poured a cup of coffee as she sliced the bread and placed it on the table. "Are we going to the doctor's office together or are you meeting me there?" she asked.

"I'll have Denny pick you up first and then stop by the office to get me; we'll go together. Are you sure you want to find out the sex of the baby?" I asked her.

"I thought we talked about this, Connor, and you said you wanted to find out, didn't you?"

"I do, babe. I just want to make sure that you really want to find out," I said as I took a bite of banana bread. It was delicious, just like Claire's. "This is excellent, Elle; I love it."

"You're not just saying that, are you?" she asked tilting her head to the side.

"No, I swear; I love it."

I finished my bread and coffee and looked at my watch. "Shit, I'm going to be late for my meeting," I said just as Denny stepped into the kitchen. "Perfect timing, Denny; we have to roll or I'm going to be late."

I walked over to Ellery and kissed her goodbye, making sure to bend down and kiss her growing belly. "I'll see both of you in a few hours."

"Bye, babe, I'll see you later," she smiled.

***

We sat in the room and waited for Dr. Keller to come in. Ellery sat on the table, and I sat in the chair beside her. I held her hand and looked around at the pictures on the wall of the development stages of a baby, growing inside a mother's womb. It was a miracle to me. It was something that I've never thought of before, not even when Cassidy was pregnant with Camden. Dr. Keller walked into the room and told Ellery to lay herself down on the table. She pulled up her shirt to expose her baby belly as he squeezed some gel from a bottle onto her stomach. He turned the monitor on and started moving the wand around her stomach. I gasped when I saw our baby for the first time. Ellery looked at me, and a single tear fell from her eye. I squeezed her hand gently as I wiped her tear with my other hand. The doctor pointed out the baby's heartbeat, fingers, and toes as he took measurements.

"Would you like to know the sex of your baby?" Dr. Keller asked.

"Yes, we would, doctor," Ellery smiled.

"Congratulations, Mr. and Mrs. Black; you're having a girl."

Ellery looked at me and smiled. "We're having a girl, Connor!" she said excitedly.

"I couldn't be happier," I said as I kissed her.

Dr. Keller handed Ellery a towel to wipe off the gel, congratulated us, and left the room. I helped her up off the table and hugged her.

"I can't believe that I'm going to have a daughter," I whispered.

We left the doctor's office and walked down the street to a local deli for a late lunch. We sat the table and looked at the menus.

"I can't decide what I want," Ellery said.

"You love their chicken sandwiches."

"I know, but I want something to go with it. I'm starving."

The waitress came by to take our orders. Ellery told me to order first as she was still deciding. I ordered the turkey sandwich on wheat bread. The waitress looked over at Ellery.

"I'll have the chicken sandwich, a bowl of French onion soup, and the chef's salad with Italian dressing. Oh, and throw in an order of French fries," she smiled.

I looked at her in horror. "Are you seriously going to eat all that?" I asked when the waitress walked away.

"Yes, I sure am. Why? Do you have a problem with what I ordered?" she asked with an attitude.

"No, I don't have a problem with anything. It's just..."

"Just what, Connor?!" she snapped.

"I just don't want you to get sick from eating too much," I whispered across the table.

She was sensitive these days, and I really needed to watch what I say. Cassidy already warned me about the hormones that come with the pregnancy. She wouldn't look at me. I pissed her off with a simple question. I reached over the table and grabbed her hand.

"Baby, look at me," I said. She was looking off to the side and refused to turn her head. "Ellery, I'm sorry. I didn't mean anything by my question."

"Bullshit, Connor! You were implying that I'm fat because of what I ordered," she snapped as she stared at me.

"No, I wasn't. I just don't want you to overeat and get sick," I said trying to diffuse the situation. The waitress brought our food and set the feast in front of Ellery. I couldn't look at her because I would've started laughing. I thanked the waitress and reached over to take a French fry from Ellery's plate; she smacked my hand. She ate everything in front of her and then took a three hour nap when we got home.

***

I walked up the steps and stopped in the doorway of the

bedroom that we were converting into a nursery. The room was empty as all the furniture had already been moved out. Ellery stood in the middle of the room, staring at the walls. "What are you doing, babe?" I asked.

"I'm deciding what mural to paint on the wall."

I walked into the room and wrapped my arms around her waist. "Anything you paint will be beautiful."

"I've given a lot of thought to this, and I want our daughter to have angels watching over her, like they've watched over me. I'm going to paint a mural on the ceiling of clouds and angels. That way she'll be protected while she sleeps."

"That sounds beautiful, Ellery. Are you sure you're going to be able to paint the ceiling? Do you want me to hire someone to help you?"

"No, silly, you're going to help me," she said.

"Me? I don't know the first thing about painting," I told her.

"I'll teach you. Think of how fun it'll be; just the two of us painting our daughter's bedroom together."

She was so excited to have me help her that I couldn't tell her otherwise. I smiled and told her that I couldn't wait. She put her hands on my arms and started stroking them softly. "I'm horny," she blurted out.

"What?" I laughed. I thought she was joking until she turned around and started unbuttoning my pants.

"Let's have sex and then we have to go to the paint store," she said.

"Ok, if that's what you want to do, here in this room, where our baby is going to sleep."

"Oh, stop it, Connor. Live a little, and make love to me," she said as she pulled me to the floor.

After we made love, we got dressed and we drove to look at paint colors. I really didn't know much about it because I always hired people to do the painting for me. Being that Ellery is an artist, she knows all about paint. It was fun watching her looking at the different colors and trying to decide which ones were better. She was so serious about it. She would ask me my input about the colors, and when I told her what I thought, she'd tell me to be quiet because I didn't know what I was talking about. I rolled my eyes and walked away. She finally made a decision on what colors she wanted. I kissed her and told her they were beautiful. I asked the store to deliver the paint to the penthouse the next day.

Ellery was in bed, reading a book when I came from my office downstairs. I stood in the doorway and stared at her. All you saw was her huge belly and her book that was resting upon it. She looked up and smiled. "What are you doing just standing there?" she asked.

"I'm just admiring the most beautiful woman in the world," I said as I took off my clothes and climbed in next to her. I leaned over and kissed her belly. "Hi, little one, it's your daddy. I wanted to tell you that you're one lucky girl to have the most beautiful mommy in the world."

"Connor, stop; you're making me cry," she said as she ran her fingers through my hair.

"I'm only telling her the truth."

"I can't wait to see what she looks like," Ellery said.

"I already know," I said as I sat up and faced her. I ran one finger by her eye. "She'll have your ice blue eyes and your cute little nose," I said as I ran my finger down to her lips. "She'll have your lips and your smile. I'll have to keep her locked up in the house because all the boys will melt when she smiles at them."

Ellery flinched and put both hands on her belly. "Ellery, what's wrong?" I said, panicking.

"The baby kicked. Here," she said as she took my hand and placed it on the side of her stomach. She smiled at me and bit her bottom lip as I felt the baby kicking. She laid herself down on her side, and I did the same, facing her. I kept my hand on her stomach as she stroked my fingers with hers. I leaned closer and kissed her good night.

***

It was Saturday morning, and I awoke to the birds chirping outside my window. I got out of bed and headed to the kitchen for some coffee. Claire was making breakfast, Ellery was at the table, drinking juice, and Denny was reading the paper.

"Morning everyone," I smiled.

"Good morning, babe. Don't forget that after breakfast we're going to start painting the nursery," she said.

I heard Denny chuckle. I walked over and gave Ellery as kiss. "What's so funny, Denny?" I asked as I sat down next to him.

"I just can't imagine you painting. Do you even know how to hold a paint brush?" he asked.

"That's very funny, Denny," I snarled.

"He'll be fine. I'll teach him," Ellery smiled.

"Ellery, I know how to hold a paint brush," I growled.

"I'm sure you do, babe."

We finished breakfast, and I went upstairs to change into some old clothes. I walked into the nursery, and Ellery was up on the ladder. I almost had a heart attack.

"Ellery Rose Black, get off that ladder, right now!" I commanded.

"How do you expect me to paint the mural on the ceiling if I'm on the floor?"

"What if you fall and hurt yourself or the baby."

"I'm not going to fall, Connor. I've painted many ceilings."

"God, Elle, you make me nervous."

"Stop it, and go start painting that wall over there," she said.

I took the roller, rolled it in the pan filled with paint, and started rolling the wall with it. It wasn't too long before Ellery came over and took it from me.

"Connor, let me show you the proper way to paint a wall," she said as she took the roller from my hand. There was nothing sexier than watching the mother of my child paint a wall. She held out her hand to me, and I took it. "We can do this, babe; you and me," she smiled. I nodded my head as I took the paint roller from her.

We painted all day, and when we stopped, we stood in the middle of the room and looked around. The mint green walls were painted to perfection, and the part of the ceiling that Ellery painted looked phenomenal. She kissed me on the cheek. "You're a wonderful painter, Mr. Black."

A few days later, Ellery finished the nursery just in time for the furniture to be delivered. I got home from the office and headed upstairs to see the finished room. I walked in as Ellery was sitting in the rocking chair with her hands on her belly. I walked over and kissed her as I helped her up from the rocking chair. She had everything in its place. People have been sending us gifts every day, not to mention everything we got from the baby shower. I looked around at the furniture and all the items on the shelves. "This is going to be one spoiled baby," I said.

"Of course she'll be spoiled because you'll be the one spoiling her," Ellery smiled.

I looked up at the ceiling. The mural Ellery painted was perfect, and nobody could've painted it better. I walked over to the crib and stared down at it.

"I can't believe that in a couple of weeks, our daughter will be sleeping in here," I smiled.

"It went by so fast," she said as she put her arm around me.

"Are you still up to going out for dinner with Peyton and Henry tonight?" I asked her.

"Of course I am; why would you ask?"

"I'm just making sure you're feeling ok, and that you're not too tired," I said as I kissed her head.

"Actually, I feel great. Better than I have in a long time," she smiled. "Would you like to join me in the shower before we leave?" she winked.

"I'd love to join you." I took her hand and led her to our bathroom.

***

Denny drove us to the restaurant where we met Peyton and Henry for dinner. They were already sitting down in a booth when we arrived. The waitress showed us to our seats, and Ellery stood there looking at the booth.

"What's wrong?" I asked.

"There's no way I'm going to fit in there," she frowned.

Ellery was big, and she looked like she was going to give birth any day.

"Elle, I'm sorry, I should have requested a table. I don't want you squishing my goddaughter," Peyton laughed.

I called the waitress over and told her we needed a table. She accommodated us immediately. We sat down, and I asked Ellery if she was ok. She looked at me as we both started laughing about her not being able to fit in the booth.

"I better lose all this weight," she said.

"We'll go to the gym together, and I'll hire you a personal trainer," I said.

Peyton grabbed Henry's hand and told us they had an announcement. She held out her left hand and showed off her exquisite engagement ring. Ellery wanted to jump up and hug her, but she couldn't.

"Peyton, it's gorgeous! Congratulations!" she exclaimed.

I got up from my seat, kissed Peyton on the cheek, and shook Henry's hand. "Congratulations to both of you, and may you have a wonderful life together," I toasted as we all held up our glasses of wine, with the exception of Ellery; she had water. Ellery turned to me and gave me a look as if she was trying to figure something out.

"You knew, didn't you?" she asked.

"Knew what?"

"You knew Henry was going to ask Peyton to marry him, and you didn't tell me," she glared.

I smiled and that was enough to let her know that I knew. "Of course I knew. Who do you think went with him to pick out the ring?" I laughed.

"Wow, Connor, how could you not tell me?"

"Maybe because it was a surprise, and I know you and that you would've called Peyton and told her about the ring."

"No, I wouldn't have," she said.

"Yes, you would've, and then you would've told her to act surprised," I said as I kissed her cheek.

Peyton looked at Ellery. "He's right; you probably would've," she said.

"I know, I would've," she said as she rolled her eyes.

The waitress brought our meals to the table. I looked over at Ellery, but she wasn't eating like she normally does. She was picking at her chicken. "You ok, baby?" I asked.

"I'm fine, honey, I'm just not very hungry," she smiled as she turned to me.

Henry and I talked about sports as Peyton and Ellery threw

around some ideas for the wedding. We had a nice dinner, and we were in the company of great friends. I couldn't ask for a better evening. I ordered us another round of drinks and dessert for everyone. The waitress had been flirting with me and Henry all night. She brought the desserts to the table and brushed up against me with her breasts.

"Excuse me," Peyton said. "I saw what you just did, and don't think I haven't noticed what you've been doing all night. That man right there, that you just boob-brushed is married with a baby on the way, and this man right here is my fiancé. If his wife wasn't about to give birth, she would have kicked your ass by now. So back off our men, and go find someone who isn't already taken." The waitress glared at her and then looked at Ellery. "Yeah, what she said," Ellery spat.

The waitress turned and walked away in a huff. Henry took Peyton's hand and started laughing. Ellery put her hand on my leg under the table and squeezed it. I looked over at her as she stared at me.

"Connor, my water just broke; it's time," she said.

To be continued…

Forever Us

The story of Connor and Ellery Black continues in the last installment of the Forever Black Trilogy, Forever Us.

You took Connor and Ellery's journey of love, courage, and strength as Ellery's illness threatened their future in Forever Black. You continued their journey through the eyes of Connor Black in Forever You as you watched them get their happily ever after through marriage and planning for their first child.

Join Connor and Ellery once again as they face the challenges of parenthood. Take their journey in Forever Us as they learn to cope with the demands of a new baby, a demanding career, and the onset of a new challenge in which Ellery must confront on her own for the sake of her family.

To My Readers

I want to thank you for reading Forever You. I hope you enjoyed reading the story from Connor Black's Point Of View. This book wouldn't have been possible without the support of each and every one of you who took the time to send me beautiful and heartfelt messages after you read Forever Black. I cherish every message, tweet, and comment you send! Thank you from the bottom of my heart for your love and support.

Please don't ever hesitate to contact me as I love to connect with you all.

www.facebook.com/Sandi.Lynn.Author

www.twitter.com/SandilynnWriter

www.authorsandilynn.com

You may also connect with me on Goodreads, and Pinterest

http://www.goodreads.com/author/show/6089757.Sandi_Lynn

http://pinterest.com/sandilynnWriter/

Forever You Playlist

Carry On – Fun

Everything'll Be Alright – Joshua Radin

Come Home – One Republic, Sara Bareilles

Feel Again – One Republic

Changed – Rascal Flatts

Wanted – Hunter Hayes

Chasing Cars – Snow Patrol

Ever The Same – Rob Thomas

November Rain – Guns N' Roses

Become – The Goo Goo Dolls

You Had Me From Hello – Kenny Chesney

From This Moment On – Shania Twain

When You're Gone – Avril Lavigne

Fix You – Cold Play

Collide – Howie Day

Your Call – Secondhand Serenade

We Run The Night - Havana Brown, Pitbull

Brighter Than Sunshine – Aqualung

Follow Through – Gavin DeGra

Calling You – Blue October

Made in the USA
San Bernardino, CA
06 January 2014